THE OWL, THE SWORD, & THE EFIL STONE

The Chronicles of Eldershire - Book One

PAM B. NEWBERRY

Publishing, LLC

J. K. Brooks Publishing, LLC
177 Stone Meadow Lane
Wytheville, VA 24382

Publisher's Note: This is a work of fiction. Names, characters, places, and incidents are a product of the author's imagination. Locales and public names are sometimes used for atmospheric purposes. Any resemblance to actual people, living or dead, or to businesses, companies, events, institutions, or locales is completely coincidental.

Book Cover Design ©2018 Julie Kay Newberry
Book Layout Design ©2018 Vellum
Map of Eldershire ©2018 Pam B. Newberry

The Owl, the Sword, & the Efil Stone/ Pam B. Newberry. -- 1st ed.

ISBN-13: **978-1-941061-07-7**

❀ Created with Vellum

For my family, I love you.

"Everyone needs a touch of magic."
~ Kay 'KC' Carson

"War is an evil thing. Only those who survive know its carnage. The dead escape its results."
~ Mr Scruffy, KC's companion

CONTENTS

WHERE IS THE LAND OF
ELDERSHIRE?

THE FICTIONAL LAND OF ELDERSHIRE is a mystical world, unaffected by time. Most only get to visit Eldershire in their dreams, but is readily available within the blink of an eye, if one believes. If a traveler were to visit Eldershire, it would be found beyond the rainbow and reaches further away than the Polar Express can travel. The best method to reach Eldershire is through the assorted and multiple portals that are easily found within the realm of possibilities but most often are only stumbled upon through luck, magic, or mysticism.

Eldershire is vast and flourishes and vanishes depending on the need of the inhabitants, the Elderians, much like Brigadoon. Elderians represent many beings that reside in multiple shapes, forms, and species—tree spirits, nymphs, elves, and talking animals—to name a few. The forests of Eldershire make up the spirit of the land, interwoven with mountains, hills, rivers, lakes, oceans, flora, and fauna. The main forest, the Wild Woods, is in the heart of Eldershire and is ruled by King Elder and Queen Esmé. Together they oversee the rulers of each province or country within Eldershire and rely on the mystic guidance of Mother Elder and Yggdrasil, the Tree of Life.

The Chronicles of Eldershire document the lives and times of the Elderians, their encounters with evil beings, and the story of a delightful human, Kay 'KC' Carson, who portents a series of quests to bring peace to the land.

To view a Map of Eldershire, visit https://pambnewberry.com, and click on Books—The Chronicles of Eldershire.

Elderdhire

Scorched
lands to
Island

Bay of Styks

1. King Elder's Camp
2. The Wild Woods
3. Stone's River
4. Grave's Mountains
5. Emerald Mountain
6. Eskar's Bluff
7. Water Patch
8. Aveenon Hills
9. Lady Lake
10. Wonderous Alley
11. Mist's Lake
12. Fields of Sheep Jour
13. Brook
14. Red Bluffe Divide
15. Falling Water Falls
16. Snow Valley
17. Reed Creek

CHAPTER 1
THE HAT

K ay "KC" Carson, sixty-five, was not what some would call beautiful; she had an impish look that many called cute. Her smile would win many over—all, that is, except for her second husband, Jay-H. Today, KC was on a mission; one of which she knew he would disapprove. She didn't care. It was time she did something for herself—something that made her feel good. She liked helping others. At this moment, KC decided she would help herself. At least that was her plan.

She woke with the sun's rays crossing her face. Dressed, and went to the kitchen to prepare some coffee and get her things together. "Life always seems to stop me just when I'm getting started," she mused to herself. She thought back on her life with her first husband, Jack. Their marriage ended suddenly when his plane went down over the Baltic Seas while on a training mission; his body never found. He never got to meet their son, Bill.

The last thirty-six years living with Jay-H hadn't always been a struggle. Their marriage started off well enough. He'd adopted Bill. Five months ago things went from not so good living with Jay-H to bad. That was when Bill married Marie. Jay-H became more irritable than usual, and less welcoming. He berated KC for little things. It was hard on her at first as KC tried to make her marriage work. Then, she began to develop a dislike for his constant anger. Last night, another argument began when she told him about her plans for Saturday.

"Jay-H, I did tell you I would be going to Bill and Marie's tomorrow." KC struck her fist on the dining room table and walked toward her bedroom. She turned and said, "What's gotten into you? You've been angry with me for along time now. Why?"

"I'm not angry at you. I want us to stay here together today. Why can't you stay here with me and we enjoy our day. Why do you always have to go help others? Why can't you stay here and take care of me?"

KC stared at him in disbelief. "Are you serious? I'll only be gone a few hours. It's their new home for heaven's sake. Come with me. We can stop at the Blue Ridge Mill for a late afternoon lunch. We can enjoy the mountain views and maybe swing by Chateau Duplin for some wine."

"You don't get it. I don't want to go. I don't want you to go. You should stay here. Period!"

"No. I won't!" KC slammed the door to her bedroom. They had slept separately for the last two years. It seemed more was separating them now than just bedrooms.

With the constant bickering and fighting the last few months, she was starting to loathe her life with Jay-H.

KC reached over the kitchen sink to lower the window. It looked like rain. Dark, purplish clouds were forming over the mountaintops. If only time travel were possible. Traveling back and knowing what she knew now, she would sure live her life differently. *I might have had more fun.* Her thoughts were interrupted by the sound of his voice.

"Why do you have to go? I finally have a Saturday off. Can't Bill and his new wife come get this stuff?" Jay-H said as he motioned to the boxes she was closing up to prepare to load in the back of her Jeep.

"Sure, they could come get it. And, her name is Marie. It gives me a chance to help. Why can't you come, too? You know how much we'd enjoy the ride. It's beautiful over the mountain pass. Bill would love seeing his step-dad, too. He loves you, you know."

"I told you, no. I want to stay here and watch some TV. Why can't you stay here and help me? You help everyone else."

KC moved around Jay-H and walked out to the Jeep. Her anger grew thinking about the fact he didn't offer to help carry any boxes. There he was standing in the doorway barely moving when she walked passed. He could be such a jerk; yet, she wanted to let it roll off her back. He was making it hard.

"You know it's not true that I help everyone but you," she said picking up a heavy box. "What about all the times I've helped you with your community work and your Sports' Club projects? I mean, really. I've cooked, made favors, decorated, stood out in the snow and rang the bells for donations."

"That's work. Call Bill to come get the boxes."

She shook her head in disgust, walked out to her Jeep, and then maneuvered the heavy box into the rear. KC walked back into the house. "The Jeep is loaded. Thanks for the help."

Jay-H used to be helpful. One month earlier, he had helped Bill find the four-bedroom cabin on the lake. Bill and Marie fell in love with the cabin on first sight. It had a two-acre fenced in backyard that butted up to the lake, which was perfect for their dog, Boomer, to run, chase squirrels, and take cool sitz baths. KC was happy for them, but she wasn't sure how living alone with Jay-H was going to work out.

He stood at the door not speaking or offering any help. KC opened a kitchen cabinet door. She turned to him and said, "Come with me. I've got some new snacks and toys for Boomer. This move is hard on him not having us around all the time."

"What did you have in all those boxes, anyway?"

"Hand-me downs for Marie's kitchen—dishes, pots, kitchen towels, pot holders, and a collection of old cooking and gardening gadgets that are hard to find." She didn't dare tell Jay-H about her mother's things being in one of the boxes. KC hoped Marie would like getting the things her mother had used to teach her how to read the signs.

She walked out to the Jeep carrying Boomer's box. She remembered back when she married Jay-H. Her first husband had been presumed dead six months prior. She had traveled to try to get the loss of her first love out of her mind. Then, when she came home, Jay-H was there and she was two months away from giving birth to Bill.

A longtime friend of the family, Jay-H was always there to help, give her guidance and support. Bill was born and he was by her side. KC's mother didn't see eye-to-eye with him on many things. She told KC to stand strong; she didn't need to marry so soon. She reminded KC that she had taught her how to take care of herself, to read the signs on when to do things, and to avoid being too dependent on anyone. But, KC's heart was torn between what her mother told her and what she felt Jay-H would provide for her baby —a good father. And so, when he proposed, KC accepted. Her mother had been there for her in so many ways. It felt good to pass on something her mother gave her. She smiled and thought how exciting it will be to see Marie receive the items.

Jay-H walked up, "Here, you left your purse."

"Thanks. I wish you'd go."

"No. I want you here."

KC thought he'd become such a whiner. "You do realize I've taken care of you for thirty-six years. Why do we always have to fight? I'm going to Bill's. I would like for you to join me. I don't want to part angry."

"Why do you have to be so independent?" He turned and walked back toward the house.

KC closed the tailgate. Thankfully, the Jeep's top was on this time; she remembered the many times she'd have to put it on after Jay-H used it. She gave a pensive look at the house. Maybe he understood more than she thought. KC dialed Bill's cellphone.

"Hey, son? Good, my phone is still working…Yes, I'm getting on the road now…No, he can't come this time…Yeah, I know I'm two hours late starting. It'll be fine. You need me to bring you anything?" KC positioned her purse in the seat beside her. "Okay, see ya in about an hour or so."

"Are you going to say goodbye?" Jay-H said stopping KC from closing the driver's side door.

"You seemed angry. I left a note earlier on the kitchen counter because I thought you'd sleep in. I should be home by ten tonight." KC looked into Jay-H's eyes. "Are you sure you won't come?"

He shut the door just missing her hand. "No. You have fun." His tone of sarcasm was enhanced with each stomp he took up the steps to the back deck.

KC backed the Jeep out of their driveway, and turned her sights to her visit with Bill and Marie. She thought about Jay-H while driving toward Bill's. Their relationship was not what she wanted, but she found herself hating where they were. And now, it seemed he was despising her as much as she was starting to despise him. *I'll just have to work at trying harder to make it work.*

KC DROVE PASSED the sign signaling the entrance to the Jefferson National Forest; she did a double take because she thought she saw an owl and an eagle together, perched on the sign. She started to stop and turn around, but figured by the time she did, they would have flown away. She drove through the forest, tall trees lining both sides of the road.

Her love of trees brought her peace. When she visited the John Muir woods on the West coast not long after Jack died, she remembered how she felt when she first walked amongst the majestic Redwoods. Every time since then, when she went into a forest, she felt her stress disappear. She lowered her car window, took in a deep breath, and relaxation enveloped her. She was going to need that kind of mood before she reached Bill's cabin.

The road wound in and around the mountain; with each turn the trees seemed closer to the road's edge. She turned up the radio, *Love is All Around*, the Mary Tyler Moore theme song was playing. The words came out without hesitation. KC sang along, and then said, "That's rich—you are girl! You are going to make it."

Adjusting her radio to sixties music on her favorite channel, she reflected about her short, but fun times with Jack. It was times like this that she missed him most. He loved the woods. Looking out at the landscape, she decided she wouldn't think about his death.

Before long, she was pulling onto Bill's drive. It was lined with large oak, alder, and elder trees. They had an arborist explain to them the value of the trees on their twenty-acre property, which had covered most of the land for almost seventy years. KC wondered since the trees were as old as she was, if they had seen life as she had—hard and uncertain. She thought more about Jack. She'd been doing that a lot lately. Where was he now? It would be nice to think he was by a stream, fishing or just enjoying nature.

KC parked her car. Bill, Marie, and Boomer came down the steps to her Jeep. She greeted her son and daughter-in-law while Boomer, their Brittany spaniel, sat at KC's feet pawing her leg.

"Mom, you take care of Boomer. We'll carry in your boxes," Bill said as he lifted one box out of the Jeep. "Whew! This is heavy. What do you have in here?"

"You'll see," KC smiled and turned to the dog anxiously waiting. "Boomer, you've got your new plaid collar on. It looks great." KC bent down and hugged him. "That other one was worn out. Everyone needs a touch of magic. Come on, let's play fetch!" She threw a toy out into the yard. Boomer ran after it. Marie walked up to where KC stood.

"From the number of boxes, it looks like you've given me your entire kitchen."

"No, just the important stuff. Let me grab a box, too." KC picked up one and together they walked to the cabin. "Don't you love it here?"

"We do. I can't wait to show you what we've got planned for fixing up the place." Marie held open the door.

Bill stood at the kitchen counter, "What is this contraption?" He held up a round, metal cylinder with two handles on either side and a screen on the inside. Bill grabbed the handle with a red knob and rotated it. "I don't remember you using one of these." Bill held it out so KC could see him rotating the arm across the screen.

"That's a sifter." KC took it out of Bill's hands and demonstrated its use.

"I've heard about this, but I hadn't seen one used before," Marie took it and began playing with it.

"You'll find a lot of things in these boxes are not commonly found in today's kitchen. They were my Mom's. She taught me to cook and to keep a well-stocked pantry."

"This is wonderful, but don't you need them still?" Marie asked as she pulled more gadgets out of a box.

"You are starting out in this wonderful cabin in the woods. Grandma would be pleased to see you using her things in this blessed place." KC walked over to the bay window and sat on the window seat propping her legs up under her as she gazed out. She looked back at her son and daughter-in-law. "I'd rather give them to you now." KC turned back to the forest view. She felt warmth embrace her. She thought of how much her mother had loved the woods. A love she had come to have as well. "Does this window open?"

"No, but this side window here does," Marie said opening it, and then sat down beside KC. "This is becoming my favorite spot to sit too."

"You two sit there and enjoy your time. I'll go get the other boxes." Bill closed the kitchen door behind him.

"KC?"

"Hmmmm."

"Can I ask you something?"

"Sure."

"Bill and I were talking the other night and he was telling me more about your mother, Catherine. He said her nickname was Kitty. I love that. I wish I could have met her. Do you mind if I call her Kitty?"

"Of course, you can. She had such a lovely smile when you called her Kitty. Sometimes, as a child, I'd sneak and call her Kitty when Dad wasn't around. When I was older, she said she liked it more than me calling her Mom because she felt we were closer, like school girl friends. She was fun like that. Bill was her special joy in life since she couldn't have other children after I was born. She would have loved meeting you."

"Bill said that she had taught you about forest life. He said that Kitty used to tell him stories about how the ancients worshipped trees. It sounds fascinating. Will you be able to tell me about the life of trees and the plants of the woods?" KC nodded. "I have always been enchanted by the forest. I'd love to learn all about it."

"I'd be honored. My mom taught me to respect all trees." KC

looked with fondness at her daughter-in-law. She had wished to pass her knowledge to Bill, but he was never interested.

"Oh, really? What did she say about helping out your son?" Bill called from the porch. "Could one of you help me out here? I'm afraid I'm going to drop this box if I try to open the door."

"It's true. Grandma shared lots of things about trees with me, like how the ancient people believed that trees had souls and were used in many symbols about religious and governmental practices."

Marie walked over to the door. "Can you imagine ancient people gathered around a tree?" Marie asked holding the kitchen door open. Bill walked passed blowing a kiss.

"It's funny you mention that. It's where 'dancing around the May pole' got started."

"Trees are sacred. Oh, brother." Bill rolled his eyes as he passed by his mother. "Next, you'll be telling us they have souls. I've got one more box to get. Marie, while I'm gone, please do not listen to her."

"Bill, stop teasing. Marie will think you're serious."

"Okay. He's gone." Marie closed the door and walked back over to KC. "Go on. I know he probably doesn't believe in this but I think it's interesting. When did the worship of the trees occur?"

"It existed many years before the building of temples and the erection of statues to the gods. For a long time, the worship of trees flourished side-by-side with other religions that were developing, and in many cases persisted years after some of the religions to gods disappeared. Mom said she learned the worship of the tree was not the earliest form of divine ritual. But, it was the last to disappear before the spread of Christianity."

"This is amazing. I'd love to hear more, but without Bill around, he would just scoff."

"There is so much to tell and teach you. Some of it, I still have a hard time believing, but the woods speak to me. We need to plan to spend a day walking in the woods. Would you like that?"

"Oh, yes. Can we meet next Saturday?"

"Sure. And maybe we can go to dinner with Jay-H and Bill after."

"Love that idea." Marie said opening the kitchen door for Bill who was carrying in another box.

"Thanks," Bill said. "I wasn't sure you would be here to open it. You and Mom could have gone to the forest." Bill grinned and set the box on the counter. "How many rolling pins does a girl need, Mom?" Bill held up three. "There are at least six more in this box."

KC giggled. "Marie will need all of those to keep you in line. Now, let's get these boxes unpacked."

MARIE WALKED INTO THE KITCHEN. "Bill said he wouldn't be home before two this afternoon. There's some kind of meeting at the firehouse, on a Saturday, of all things. So, you've got me until then." Marie put on her sun cap, wiped her arms and legs with sunscreen, and picked up her freshly filled water bottle. "I'm ready."

"Great! Jay-H had to work today too. But, he said to let him know what we would be doing for dinner. We'll check in on him later. Let's go. I think you'll love this walk. The first time my Mom took me on one of these foraging walks, I didn't know what to expect." They walked out onto the porch; Marie pulled the door, reached for Boomer's leash, and began to fasten it on his collar.

"Do you think Boomer needs that leash? We're going to be on your property. Why don't you let him roam free?"

"I guess it will be okay." Marie placed the leash on the porch railing. "Besides, he could use a run. I feel like I'm going on safari. Want to spray your arms too?" Marie held out the bug spray. KC took it.

"Ok, I've sprayed my arms, got on my special hiking shoes, and here's my walking stick."

KC laughed. "I put some munchies in my backpack. And, we've got water, so we'll be good for a few hours. The tree canopy will help knock off the sun's rays as we climb to the top of the mountain. We'll look for various plants along the way."

"I've got my sketch pad and I'm going to make notes too," Marie said stepping off the porch and onto the path that would lead them through the woods.

"I've always wanted to learn how to draw. The woods are full of such beauty. Look, Boomer is already at the edge of the woods waiting on us."

"I'd love to teach you to draw, Mom." KC smiled. It was the first time Marie called her Mom. Marie continued, "It's as if he knows where we are going."

"He's smart. He'll probably find some of the plants I'll want to show you."

"Let's hope he doesn't find any poison ivy."

"THERE YOU GUYS ARE," Bill said walking out onto the porch. "I've been back a couple of hours. I was starting to get worried about you. When I saw Boomer's leash on the porch, I wasn't sure where you had headed off to with both vehicles still here."

"Oh, Bill, we had so much fun. KC taught me so much that my head is spinning. I can't wait to take you out and show you all about the trees and plants. And, look at my sketches." Marie handed her book to Bill. "Did you know there is a plant called May apple?" Marie was still talking as she walked through the kitchen door.

"Thanks, Mom." Bill grinned. "I guess you really did teach her some of that folk stuff Granny taught you. I'm going to hear it all again and again, aren't I?"

KC giggled while hugging her son. "No. She will get it out of her system, and then she will need another refresher course. In the meantime, you be a good son and don't tease her too much about it. She enjoyed herself, and so did I."

They walked to the kitchen table arm-in-arm. "Did you ladies decide what we're going to do for dinner?"

"As a matter of fact, we did. I called Jay-H and told him we'd meet at the Chinese Restaurant about five. He said he'd get a ride and meet us there. I figured I could drive you all there, we'd bring you back, and I'd show Marie a couple of things about the plants I gathered." KC moved her backpack to the kitchen counter and retrieved a deep vase to place the cuttings in, and then filled it with water.

"That sounds nice. I'll get to see Jay-H after all. You should drive our new car, Mom." Bill said giving his wife a kiss on the cheek. KC watched and wished her husband had allowed Bill to call him Dad. It was one of those things Jay-H was adamant about since Bill was only his stepchild.

"I'll go up and change into some nicer clothes. I slipped and fell on some rocks and my pants are covered in dirt." Marie turned and started upstairs. "KC, thanks for today. I had a good time. And, we need to plan your drawing day."

"You're welcome, honey. I look forward to setting a date for more outings with you. It's good to have a daughter who appreciates me." KC winked at Bill.

"Mom, have I told you how much I love you?"

"Sure. But not as often as I like." KC ruffled Bill's hair. He gave her a hug in response. She held him tightly, cherishing him. Boomer sat beside KC and pawed at her leg. "Oh, Boomer. I'm sorry. I love you too!" KC ruffled Boomer's fur and he leaned up close to her. "Bill, I've been meaning to ask you."

"Yeah?" Bill reached for a glass. "Want something to drink?"

"I'm fine. That collar of Boomer's, where did you get it? It looks familiar to me for some reason."

"I'm not sure. We should ask Marie. I've been meaning to ask her anyway. Here she is now."

"Ask me what?"

"Boomer's collar. Mom wants to know where you found it."

"I didn't. I thought you did."

Bill snickered, "Me? When have I ever bought anything?"

"Well, that's true. You never buy anything for anyone, but you sure buy a lot of fire fighting stuff." They all laughed.

"It's true, Bill. Even when you were little, once you decided you wanted to be a fire fighter, that's all you thought about. Come on, we need to get going. We don't want to keep Jay-H waiting." KC reached down and ruffled Boomer's fur and took another look at the collar. Isn't that strange, she thought.

❧

"I DIDN'T KNOW how hungry I was," Marie said as she pushed her plate back. "I don't think I've eaten a complete meal here in forever. That hike today worked up my appetite."

"Was your Orange Chicken good?" Bill asked, taking a sip of his tea. Marie nodded. "My Kung Pao Beef was awesome, too. Jay-H, how was your meal?"

"It was fine. I've got to be heading back to the office soon. We need to take the kids back to their house, right?"

"Yes. It won't take us long. I want to show Marie a couple of things and we'll get right back on the road."

"You've been with her all day. What else can you possibly need to say?" Jay-H looked at his watch. "If you've got something else to do with her, maybe I should get a cab and you can pick me up at the office when you come back to town."

"Oh, Jay-H. Really? Come on. We'll get to their house in a matter of minutes. I want to show her how to prep the cuttings we took, and then we'll turn right around and get you back to the office." KC looked around the table; everyone had finished eating. Jay-H had barely touched his food. It was a wonder he wasn't losing weight. He didn't seem to eat much around them anymore. "I'll pay the bill and I'll be right out. You guys go ahead and get in the car."

"The car? Where's your Jeep?" Jay-H looked annoyed. The kids walked on out to the parking lot, KC paid the bill and left a tip on the table. "What else do you have to do?"

"Why don't you try and relax? You seem to be in a race with somebody. I'm ready to go. Besides, I thought it easier if we took their car. Marie and Bill said I should drive it."

"Of course; guess you're wanting a new car, now."

Jay-H got in the passenger's side while KC got into the driver's side.

"Bill and Marie, so glad you joined us for dinner. It was a good meal. Its nice to have a dinner together as family."

"Unless you've got to work." Jay-H chimed in.

&.

"IT HAPPENED SO FAST," KC said. "There was nothing, nothing, there was nothing…" Her mind tried to grasp what she had seen.

"Is she going to be all right?" The deputy asked the medic.

"I'm not sure. She's had a horrible shock. Seeing her family killed like that while she was standing nearby. I can only imagine."

"I wonder how the tractor-trailer missed the stopped car. Mrs. Carson said she had stopped to help the motorist just moments before the semi came around the curve. By all rights, the truck should have hit the stranded car, not Mrs. Carson's car. Did you see the dog laying on her lap?"

"Yes. Mrs. Carson kept saying, 'He wasn't supposed to be here,' while she caressed and rubbed his still body. I wonder what that meant?"

"We may never know. Are you ready?"

"Yes. We'll take her on to the hospital for observation. One of the medics moved the dog over with her family. They will be transported to Barnett's Funeral home. Did someone call anyone for her – another family member or a friend?"

"I'm not sure who they called. Evidently, her entire immediate family was in the car. Her son was a fire fighter. Did you know him?"

"No. We worked in different areas of the county. Several of the other guys that worked the scene did. They said it was his dog. I saw his name tag read Boomer."

"This is a hard one. You be safe. See you around."

KC TRAVELED out into the county after she finished her errands in town. She had gone to visit a friend that lived on the other side of the mountain. She hadn't been out passed the site of the wreck since that night, six months earlier. She wasn't sure how she'd feel when she passed it, but it was late and she was going to Bill's cabin. Waving goodbye to her friend, KC got in her Jeep, drove about six miles along a winding farm road, and then entered a stretch of woods that was desolate.

Why on earth did I decide to go this way? Even though it was summer, she had stayed at her friend's too long. It was already past nine and darker in the shade of the forest. She turned her headlights on. She hoped she wouldn't hit a deer. Just then, her car stalled. She looked down at her gas gauge—Empty!

She reached for her cell—no service. "Great!"

It's too far to walk back. *I have no idea how far I'd need to walk to find a house or even get cell reception.* She saw that the windows were down. She turned on the ignition and used the power of the battery to raise them. When they closed, she thought better of it and decided to lower them a little to allow air to circulate. *Don't be stupid and use up the battery.*

Hours passed, no one drove by. About midnight, KC accepted the fact she needed to take a pee break. She got out, walked over to the edge of the woods, and squatted. The sounds of the forest at night were making her nervous. She heard the eerie cry of an animal. Darkness had always scared her. Another howl. Her skin began to crawl. She stopped mid-stream and ran back to the Jeep. Closing the door, something slammed itself against it. She screamed.

"Oh, God. What was that? Oh, God. Oh, God. Oh, God!" She began to pray. Whatever it was, moved on, and she heard the howl again. KC crunched down on the Jeep's floor and began to pray for someone to find her. She reached for her cell. Now, the battery was dead. "Great! Now, what? You blooming idiot."

KC woke up when the sunlight broke through her back window and crossed her face. She was cramped and sore. Bit by bit, she rose and looked out around the area. She didn't see anything. Her bladder was full again.

Slowly, she opened the door, stepped outside, and looked around. She started walking toward the edge of the woods, but thought she saw something move in the leaves.

She stopped, waited, and stared.

Nothing.

She decided to take a chance and made her way to the side of the road. She dropped her pants and did her business. Then, as she stood up, she noticed a funny looking hat—black and round with a daisy hanging off the black ribbon band—lying near a tree. She picked it up.

CHAPTER 2
THE BRIER PATCH

Mother was right, KC thought as she peered through the tangled brambles of what must be a brier patch, keeping still as a mouse, or trying to. The creatures on the other side were calling her name. Mother always said not to wish for things—they might come true — what happened?

She thought back to a few moments earlier wondering why she picked up the old, tattered hat lying on the side of the road. She knew better—or at least, she thought she did.

From the noise coming from the other side of the brier, KC wasn't sure what she was hearing. Someone or something was talking, but it seemed meaningless, more like ramblings. She was thankful she was inside the brier patch and not where they were. She listened to the sounds. The gruffs and grunts caused the hair on KC's chin to quiver.

There was a putrid odor like that of meat left too long in the refrigerator. She could tell she was sitting on something soft and gooey. Her mind began to race with horrible ideas of what it was. Inside the cavern of brambles, KC felt shrouded with gloom. Even so, little specks of light made their way through the tangled brier. It gave her short moments when she could peer through the brambles to see what was happening.

A large mass of flesh moved passed where she was peeking through. KC moved back in fear. It stood inches away. She tried not to move or breathe. *Where could I be?*

"Shebad said she'd be showing up here," the stinky beast said. KC peered through an opening trying to catch a glimpse of the other one. She recoiled in disgust when a large glob of slime fell from his nose landing on her hand. She almost shrieked.

Both creatures moved with laborious steps, causing the brush to vibrate. KC prayed her cover would remain in place.

"Smell dead here. If she in there, she dead, too. Morge, are you sure we at right place? Shebad will hurt us if we don't bring her back."

"Gorge, how many times do I have to tell you? We'll do fine if we follow our noses. Come this way. She ain't around here."

KC watched as the two beasts moved out of sight. She leaned back and began to breathe. The odor had worsened since she last took in a deep breath. Her hand came up to her nose. She knew that smell. From the minimal light, KC saw her comfy seat was made of rotten carcasses.

"Eeeewwww." She tried to hold back, but her stomach reacted violently. She sat still; praying the sound of her retching did not reach the ears of the beasts.

By the time KC knew someone or something had grabbed her ankle, she was jerked out of the brier patch, screaming, and scrambling to her feet. "What the—" A cold, clammy hand wrapped around her mouth. She squirmed.

"Be quiet or you'll bring them back. Do you want to die?" KC shook her head. "Good. I'll let you go, Mossy, as long as you stay quiet."

A young, impish-looking being stood before her. It looked like a young boy with elfish features. KC recoiled in fear.

The boy, if that was what he was, stood there watching her. He said, "You are acting like a frightened fox. What are you doing in there? If you want to go on living, you better get out of here fast."

"Where? What? Who?" KC tried to talk.

"You're a weird looking creature. Are you from around here?"

KC stared in disbelief, "I don't know where I am."

"You are in the heart of the Wild Woods." He moved his hand in a circular motion. "You can't be from around here if you don't know that. Now that I look at you closely, you don't look like an Elderian. Where are you from?"

"I'm from Shiloh." KC said still trying to figure out where she was. "Where is the Wild Woods located, exactly?"

"It is in the heart of Eldershire."

KC felt her stomach get queasy. She was definitely far away from where she last saw her Jeep. "Eldershire?"

"Mossy. You aren't from around here, are you?"

KC shook her head. "Who are you?"

"I'll tell you, but we must move away from here. The Atcenians will be back looking for you, and you don't want to meet them—"

"Who?" KC interrupted him.

"They are the two big, ugly beasts that were just here looking for you in that brier patch. Nukpana Fraener rules them. It's bad enough when I have to fight them. I don't want to have to fight them and try to keep you safe. Let's start moving this way," he said and moved into the thicket of woods behind where they stood.

"I guess I should say thanks for pulling me out of there. How did you find me?" KC walked behind him watching her step.

"I was passing through here on my way to the other side of Eldershire. I'm headed to see King Lug Elder. His camp is not far; it is at the bend of Stone's River, down in the valley in this direction. I'm from Eland and I normally do not speak the Elderian language. How do you know how to speak it? And, why are you dressed like that?"

KC looked down at her clothes. She hadn't paid attention before. She was wearing jeans, sneakers, and a tie-dyed T-shirt, something she would have worn as a sixteen-year-old girl. She brought her hands up to her hair and felt long strands. She moved the strands of hair up to her eyes and saw that her hair was dark and long. No longer was it the short gray style she had worn for a decade. The shock of those changes caused her to stumble backwards, tripping over a log. She landed hard on the ground.

"Mossy! Are you okay?" The young boy walked toward her and offered his hand. At least KC thought it was a hand until she saw it.

"What happened to your hand?"

"Why?"

"You only have three fingers?"

"You have five. Why do you need them all?"

"I was born this way."

"Oh, so you're a mutant. What kind of creature are you anyway?"

"I'm human. What are you?"

"A human! I'm not sure I've heard of one of you in many moons. I won't bite. You can take my hand and I'll help you up. I'm an Eland, a wood sprite. We can't stay here. You've made too much noise. The Atcenians will find us for sure."

"Why are you helping me and calling me, Mossy?"

"As for Mossy, I say it without thinking. When I came upon the brier patch, the Atcenians were hunting for you. I waited until they moved on before I approached to see what they were after. I thought you were some poor rabbit or wolf trapped by them. Those two, I think, answer directly to Nukpana."

KC couldn't believe what was happening. It was too much for her mind to grasp. Looking down, she noticed besides having different hair and clothes that her body was different as well. She looked at her legs and saw that they were skinny again. She wished she had a mirror. Her bones didn't hurt even after she hit the ground. That was a good thing. At her age, a fall like that could cause more problems.

"Mossy. Did you hear me? We've got to get moving."

KC took his hand and stood up. She noticed she was physically feeling pretty good—better than she had in years. "Who is Nukpana? And, what exactly are Ata, Ataians? Why are they after me?"

"Nukpana, I'll let King Elder tell you the full details about her. The Atcenians. They are a pair of ogre-like brothers, grotesque, who prey on helpless beings. I have no idea why they are after you, unless they saw you land here. You said earlier that you were from Shiloh. Is it beyond Mushroom Alley? I haven't heard of it before."

"It's in the United States. What is Eldershire?"

"United States? Never heard of it. Eldershire is Eldershire. It's our world. There are many beings and lands in Eldershire. It is what it is. Pure. Simple."

"You asked me about my clothes, what about yours? Why are you dressed like that? And, what do you mean, 'land here'?"

"My mother made my clothes." Ish looked down at them as though he was admiring them. "I think they look fine. And, as for you landing here, I would have thought you flew here since you are from far away. Not many people land in a brier patch like you did. I bet you haven't been flying long. You're a weird witch."

"Witch? What are you talking about?" KC looked around, trying to figure out in which direction to run.

"Mossy. No worries. Follow me. The Atcenians can't be far now." The young boy began to run. KC watched him for a few seconds, and then began to run after him. She was glad she had on sneakers and not the sandals she was wearing before she landed here, wherever here was.

The ground was covered with deep piles of fallen leaves. The trees were just inches apart. KC ran trying to keep up—she was thankful she was young again. She marveled at the fact she was running and couldn't remember the last time she did so. The boy stayed far enough ahead of her that she was afraid she would lose him if she didn't try to keep up. After a while, she slowed. The boy began to walk, and looked back at her.

"Is it possible for us to rest for a few minutes? I'm getting tired. I'm too old to be running this hard. I haven't run like this since I was a kid."

"We can't. We must get as close to Stone's River as we can before dark. There, we'll be able to rest. Then, after getting water, we can head to King Elder's camp."

KC caught up to him. She noticed a curious look on his face.

He turned toward her. "What do you mean, since you were a kid? What is a kid?" He asked.

"You know. A young person."

"Mossy. A sapling?"

KC started to respond but decided to wait. She walked alongside him for a bit, and then she said, "How far to where we're going?" KC wondered if she was going to survive what was happening to her. *Why did I pick up that hat?*

"It's a ways yet. We must hurry. Something's not right with the Atcenians being after you. We've not had a human here in many lunations." He began to walk faster. "Come. We've got a lot of ground to cover before dark, and we need to put a great distance between us and those Atcenians."

KC stopped in her tracks. "If I'm going to follow you. I'd like to know more about who you are and if I can trust you."

The impish looking creature stopped. "If you must have this conversation now, we will. I'm Isherwood. Most folks call me Ish. I've lived in Eland, my homeland on the other side of Grave's Mountain, my entire life. I traveled this two-sun day to the Wild Woods to meet others at King Elder's camp. My family and I are the last of the wood sprites. We live in the trees of the forest of Eland and we guard those who live in the Wild Woods of Eldershire. Who are you?"

KC stared at him. She couldn't believe her ears. Not one place he named did she recognize; she wasn't home anymore. She was somewhere far from the life she had known. She began to pace as she talked. "Okay. I understand I must be having a dream. I'll play along." She turned and faced Ish. "I'm Kay Carson. Most call me KC, and I don't mean to be a pain, but you've got to realize I don't even understand how I got here, let alone where *here* is."

"That's why we need to get to King Elder's Camp. He will be able to help us. He'll know what to do. I can't answer your questions. I've never talked with a human before; I only saw one of you at a distance when I was a sapling. You sound funny. You look strange to me, too. I wasn't sure what I had caught when I pulled you out of that brier patch. I was ready to cut your throat if I thought you were evil. But I don't think you are, and we have a problem of what to do with you. Enough of this talk. We are wasting precious time. Do you think you can run again? I think I hear the Atcenians behind us. They must have been gaining ground while we stood here talking. I keep getting a whiff of their odor."

"I can run."

While they ran, KC observed her surroundings. The forest was thick with trees. The fallen leaves, debris, and logs where older trees had fallen were decomposing and were as thick as when they first started to run. Everything looked the same. It was hard to tell how much ground they had covered. It seemed they had run for an hour or more, but it probably had only been ten minutes. It had been twenty years since she ran. Her knees weren't giving her trouble, at least not yet. She was running like she remembered doing when she ran track in high school; she didn't have to dodge trees then. The thought made her smile for a moment. It felt good to run, but she was having trouble keeping up with Ish. He was swift of foot.

After a while KC noticed the trees weren't as close together. She was able to run a little faster and was even closing up the distance between her and Ish. Suddenly he came to a halt. KC reached him in a step or two and watched to see what he would do next.

"Shhh," Ish stood still looking out into the forest. KC could hear water flowing over rocks. It was the only sound she could hear. The leaves were still. There was no wind. No sounds of birds or other forest animals. She looked in the same direction as Ish but could not see anything other than more tree trunks. While standing there, more leaves fell around them. She started to take a step, and Ish reached back and touched her hand, signaling that she should remain still. It seemed like they stood there for an eternity before he turned around.

"We will make camp here. We won't have time to make it to King Elder's camp before dark." Ish moved over toward a log lying near a tree. "This will do."

KC wondered how he knew it was getting darker. The forest to her was dark enough. "Where are we?" KC walked over to the log and plopped down. "I didn't realize how tired I am. I guess I've been running on adrenaline."

"We are near to the boundary of the Wild Woods. Stone's River is east of here, through there," Ish pointed to his left. "It is a ways. The brook you hear feeds the river. We'll be fine here for the night."

He moved some leaves away from the log, picked up a stick, and began to draw on the ground. He pointed ahead of them in the direction of the water as he said, "The suns will rise in that direction. It will aid us, as the forest gets thicker just before we emerge from the forest at King Elder's camp. This map I'm drawing will give you an idea of where we are now and where we were when I met you. Here is where we are going."

KC looked at his drawing. Bill had made such a drawing after one of their hikes together. KC let her mind wander and remembered.

"Look, Mom," Bill handed his drawing to KC.

"That's lovely. You paid attention while we walked through the woods. I'm proud of you."

"I drew it for Dad."

"Jay-H?"

"No. My Dad. I thought he'd like to know that we go visit where he lives now."

KC put her arms around Bill and hugged him tight.

The drawing on the ground wasn't as detailed as Bill's, but she wished he and Jack were with her just the same.

Ish pointed to several lines and described them. "We are right here. This line is Stone's River. It circles around this peninsula that is bounded by trees. King Elder's camp is off in this direction, to the West."

"Where was the brier patch in relation to where we are now?"

"It was back here to the South."

"That looks like a fair distance. No wonder I'm tired. I don't know how far that is, but it looks to be quite a way. Can we get water to drink?" KC pointed in the direction of the brook.

"We must wait until morning. The water at night is not safe to drink. We must stay here. I'll take you to water in the morning. We'll go by the brook on our way to Iolair's Bluff." Ish handed her his pouch. "Until then, Mossy, there is a little water left in there. Drink it slowly as the water will sustain you longer than any other water you can drink. Yes. We ran a good way, about a league."

KC took the pouch. She doubted him about the water giving her strength. Her mouth was parched; she took a slow swig just the same. The taste was sweet and refreshing, like tasting a fresh, cold watermelon on a hot summer day.

"Thank you." She handed the pouch back to him. "Can I ask you something?" Ish nodded. "Why do you say Mossy when you talk to me?"

"It's a habit, I guess. It's something my Dad always said to me. I picked it up from him."

"What does it mean?"

"I don't think it has a meaning."

"Oh, I guess, it's like me saying 'oh,'" KC laughed.

Ish shook his head, and then he scratched the earth covering the drawing with dirt and leaves. He walked over to another log that leaned against the other side of a tree and sat down.

KC reached down and removed her shoes. Her feet were hurting. "Thank God, I have these sneakers on. I have no idea how, but my other shoes wouldn't have worked for what we've been doing. Who knew that I'd be in a marathon through a forest following a wood nymph—that is what you are, isn't it?"

"Nymphs are female. I'm a wood sprite knight. We are the leaders of peace for all of Eldershire. As a knight, I am one step from serving as the Prince of Eland. I am an expert archer, master bowman, and a trained swordsman and knife fighter; my people trust me to know when and where we will be safe. You'd be wise to listen to me. Now, since you are new to this land, I think you'd be wise to be quiet and talk less."

KC almost stood up and walked away from him. Talk less. She'd hardly said a word since he'd pulled her out of the brier patch. They'd run for the last hour or so it seemed. He was causing her blood to boil. But, she knew she had nowhere to go. She still wasn't sure where *here* was for that matter. She repositioned herself. For the first time since coming into this world, she felt a need to relieve herself. Since Ish scolded her and told her to be quiet, she wasn't ready to ask him about what she could do to take a bio break. She sat still for a bit. Her kidneys were not going to allow her to wait any longer. She looked over at Ish. He appeared to have fallen asleep.

Quietly, KC put her shoes back on, and looked around their makeshift campsite. She decided the patch of woods to her right might be a good place to go visit nature. She took her time and as best she could, walked quietly away from where Ish was sleeping. A few minutes later, she found a log that she could sit on. Finishing her duties, she prepared to walk back to where she left Ish sleeping.

"Wicked. It's just like a human, such as you, to mark my home." The voice came from behind KC. She froze with fright. She heard a hiss, like the sound a snake makes. "Are you dumb too?" the voice said.

"No. No, no. I'm not dumb. Who are you? Where are you?" KC turned around and tried to determine from where the voice was coming. She hated snakes. She was bitten by one a few years earlier and never wanted to cross the path of a snake again. She prayed the voice wasn't coming from one.

"Your prayer will not be answered this time," the voice hissed. "I am a serpent."

KC tried to determine what to do next. She was so frightened, she forgot from which direction she had walked when she left Ish. She backed up, but was fearful as to how far she should move.

"I can read your mind. There's no need to be scared. I'm not here to kill you now. I'm here to deliver a message to you from Nukpana Fraener."

KC looked around; her fear was grabbing at her nerves. If she stepped on the snake, she'd die of fright.

"Your days are numbered, so if you died of fright, it would not be a loss. You succeeded in getting away from the Atcenians, but you won't be so lucky when next we meet. Nukpana knows why you are here. She wants you to know that you won't succeed."

KC was sure the voice was coming from all around her. She tried to think of what to do, but all she could hear was the hissing sound.

"You are smart to be afraid. Nukpana plans to stop you, and your friends too. Have no doubt. You will lose. You've been warned. Now, go back to Ish, but do not breathe a word of what I have told you. I'll know if you do, and I'll kill you in an instant. Turn around and walk in a straight line. The next time you hear my voice, we will be in the battle of death—your death." The final words came out as a hiss.

KC stood still for a moment. She knew her legs were shaking. She couldn't feel her feet move. Yet, just as quickly as she could, she made her way back toward where she hoped Ish was sleeping. Five minutes or so later, she emerged into the camp site area and saw Ish still asleep, leaning next to the tree. She wasn't sure if what she experienced was real or part of this crazy dream she seemed to be living. She walked over to the log, sat down, and debated what to do next. She started to wake Ish and tell him what had just happened, but stopped. If she thought she could find her way back home, she would get up and walk out of the forest. She reasoned it wouldn't help anything. She had no clear idea of where she was or how to get home, or even if she could.

KC's heart was racing and her mind was jumping from thought to thought. She needed to calm down and think. Looking at Ish, she studied his face and felt herself begin to relax. As she stared at him, she noticed he seemed to have many of the same features she had seen in movies of elves and other such creatures. The differences in Ish's face and those she saw on the big screen were subtle. Ish was tall, lean, and had reddish hair. Earlier, she had noticed his eyes— deep blue. She wished he'd open them now. She wanted to tell him what she heard. Would he believe her? Worse, would the serpent come back and kill her and him, too? She was having trouble believing what was happening. *What have I stumbled into? That blasted hat!*

KC settled back to rest. She knew she needed to get some sleep, but the serpent's words kept coming back to her, grabbing hold of her imagination—'Nukpana knows why you are here. She wants you to know that you won't succeed. She plans to stop you, and your friends, too.'

STARTLED, KC lashed her arms out, then she saw it was Ish nudging her awake. "Oh, sorry. I forgot where I was."

"I let you sleep. You tossed a lot before you finally settled to rest last night. Do you need to have a few minutes before we start?"

KC nodded. She set upright, rubbed her eyes. Ish handed her his pouch. She took a swig. "I need to go—"

"Go over there in that direction. I wouldn't go back where you went last night. You shouldn't have left the site without letting me know."

KC stood up, started to explain, but decided it wouldn't help. She walked away from the area. *How is it possible he knew I was gone? Did he follow me? If he followed me, he would have heard the serpent. Should I tell him? No. No, I can't.* KC walked back about five minutes later. "I'm ready."

"Good. We've got a lot of ground to cover today."

KC sat down to tie her shoe. Just then, an owl swooped down, and plucked a hair from her head.

"Ouch! What's going on?" KC jumped up and swung her arms in the air. The owl landed on a nearby branch.

"If you weren't so mean to my friend, Ish, I wouldn't have done that to you." The owl sat back on its haunches and appeared to smile.

"You're kidding me, right? You have talking animals here too?" KC stood staring at the owl.

Ish laughed and said, "KC, I'd like you to meet Tiger Bubo Virginianus Scruffy. We call him Mr Scruffy; it's easier. He's my best friend. Mr Scruffy, this is KC. Glad you could catch up with us. Did you have a good night?"

"KC. Hmph. Is that even a name? You've got a lot to learn. All animals speak. In your world, animals speak only on Christmas Eve. You humans are too self-involved to understand that we are intelligent. Ish, I had a marvelous night."

"Good, Mr Scruffy. We'll talk more. Right now, we need to get to King Elder's Camp. You fly ahead and keep an eye out for us. You can send me a message when you know the way is clear. Let's run!"

KC watched as Mr Scruffy took flight. The sight of his wings flapping a couple of times, giving off no sound, yet lifting his large body up toward the tree canopy was bewitching. The rays of light glistened off his mottled plumage highlighting the grey and white coloring. He was beautiful. She turned and breathed in the smell of the fresh dew of the morning, and the sweet aroma of rich soil. She wished she could see all of the sky. Craning her neck back, watching Mr Scruffy move through the canopy, she wondered how high he would fly. She looked toward Ish, who had already started to run. She followed, trying to keep up.

CHAPTER 3
ISHERWOOD

"We made progress distancing ourselves from last night's camp. Not far in front of us is the brook that flows into Stone's River. We will stop there and take a short break," Ish said slowing up to a fast walking pace.

KC was breathing hard. The run had been full of short hills. They weren't as hard to climb as trying to dodge between tree trunks, but she noticed her legs were sore. She wasn't used to this kind of travel. She longed for her Jeep.

"What I'd give to have a ride right now," she said, slumping over to rest her hands on her knees.

"When we cross over this knoll to the river, we will want to be quick. We'll move in, get our water, and get back under the cover of the tree canopy where we'll take a short rest" KC nodded. "You don't talk much, do you?"

"That's funny. First, you tell me I talk too much, and now, you say, I don't talk. You're just like Jay-H. He always said that to me. At least he used to." KC looked off into the distance. "I do try to listen when expected and I speak when I think it adds value. You've got to remember, this is a strange land to me. I'm dealing with being here and trying to figure out how to get back home."

Ish nodded to her and motioned for them to move on. KC watched Ish scurry along the open bank near the river in a crouch. She mimicked his actions, joining him. She was leaning forward to gather a drink when she saw the reflection of two suns in the pool of water near the side of the bank. Then, she saw her reflection in the water. She stumbled backwards and landed on her bottom. "Oh, my."

Ish reached down and helped KC to her feet. "Quick, we've got to get back under the canopy."

KC ran after Ish. He was standing under a low covering of tree branches.

"I don't understand. What is going on here? Look at me. I'm young. I'm sixteen or so. And, why can't we stay near the water? I've got to look at myself. I've changed! And, you've got two suns!"

"We were out in the open."

"What? Did you expect something to fly down and get us?"

"Yes."

"Oh. Really? You're not serious?" KC shuddered. "Once and for all, will you please tell me what's going on? My life is in shambles right now. I mean I'm a sixty-five-year-old woman. But, here I look like I'm sixteen. I'm wearing clothes I haven't been able to wear in almost fifty years. I can run like a teenager again. And, you expect me to believe that something will swoop down and grab us in this strange world I find myself in with two suns at that. Gees. Am I crazy or what?"

"It seems you only think of yourself. You're not thinking about what could happen in this world you call strange. You don't understand anything about my world, yet you ignore my warnings and stumble around as though you don't care to whom you will declare your presence."

KC stood there and thought about the times Jay-H had told her she only thought of herself. She despised the idea he might have been right.

Ish continued, "We have evil here—deep, dark evil. The kind that keeps you awake at night and around here, during the day too. An evil that takes great joy in your fear, causing you fear, and reads your thoughts to use them against you. You've seen the Atcenians. There is far worse where they came from. I don't know why you are here either. I wish I hadn't found you. But, I did. What happened at the river?"

KC thought about telling Ish about the snake, but changed her mind. "Okay. I get that I don't know much about where I am. As for me falling backward, I reacted to seeing my reflection."

"Is that bad for you?"

"No. I wouldn't have thought so until I saw myself. But, you're right. I'm not thinking. How much further to King Elder's camp, a half-hour or so?"

"Half-hour? What's that?"

"Don't you have time here?"

"Thyme? No, I don't think so. Is it something you eat?"

KC laughed. "Sorry. Guess I shouldn't laugh when you don't know anything about my world. As you've pointed out, I definitely don't know anything about yours. Time is something we use to help us measure how a day is progressing from early light to mid-day to evening or night."

"Here, we honor our two suns and two moons. Yes, there is two of each. We say two suns, mid-morning, mid-day, two-suns high, later day, early two-moons, half-night and two moons."

"That's why it was so bright out from under the canopy. The two suns. Wish I had a camera with me. I'd love to get a picture of the two suns and the two moons."

"A camera?"

"Oh, I forgot. It's easy to do, isn't it? A camera gives us an image like the map you drew earlier."

"I see. We do that with our minds. What was wrong with your reflection? You look pretty good to me. Of course, I don't know how a human is supposed to look."

KC looked down at her clothes and back up at Ish. She had landed in a different world and was wearing clothes of the 1960s. Except for the fact she was running through a forest with a talking wood sprite and an owl, she looked like a teenager. She didn't know if she was dreaming or not, her life had changed, yet she could remember her life experiences.

"It's not that I look bad. It's that I look different. On Earth, where I'm from, I'm old. Like an old tree here. I still get around okay and have a pretty good life, but I don't look at all like I do now. This is how I looked when I was younger. And, the clothes I'm wearing now are what I would have worn when I was a teenager. The slogan on this shirt—'Make Love - Not War—' is not something I normally wear. It was the shock of seeing it on me—not seeing wrinkles on my face or gray in my hair. Do you understand?"

"I'm not sure I do fully, but I know how I feel when I'm in a strange and unfamiliar place."

"Do you have to leave your family often?"

"During war time, I do. Our country has been at peace for many hundreds of lunations. The last few lunar passings have seen recent wars break out."

"What is a lunation?"

"It is the passing of many two-moons over many two-suns."

"What has caused those wars?"

"We believe it is because of Nukpana." KC tried to hide her reaction at hearing the name again. "You'll learn about Nukpana later. As I said, when I found you, I was on my way to King Elder's Camp for a gathering to see what could be done to bring peace. All beings of Eldershire believe in love and kindness. War is not something we enjoy. I lost my sister and brother to a recent war near the base of Grave's Mountain. We had crossed over Stone's River and pushed The Grey Menace back. We had felt good about our efforts until we were ambushed during the night. There were sixty of us but only ten returned home."

"I won't ask all the questions I have going on in my mind. You have told me King Elder will answer my questions. I will say that I'm sorry for your loss. I know what it's like to lose family."

"Your parents?" Ish asked, motioning her to follow him to the glen beside the river. They walked along the glen's edge still hidden under a canopy of trees.

"Yes, I understand the loss of parents, but I also understand loss that is even closer. I recently lost my husband, son, his wife, and their dog." KC paused. "I'm sorry. It is still raw."

Ish pointed to a few logs lying near a berm, not far from the water. "We are at a point of our journey where we can stop and rest a bit. We'll be protected here. After a break, we will follow this path through the forest up to Iolair's Bluff, and then down to King Elder's Camp. With the water nearby, we can take more breaks. Our scent will be carried downstream as long as we stay near the water. The Atcenians are dangerous, but their body senses are inactive. We have some time now, but we need to try and reach camp before dark. Let's sit here a bit. Tell me, how did you lose your family?"

They sat on rocks that were formed into seats. KC wondered if someone had molded them that way intentionally. It felt good to sit and the rocks fit her body's curves perfectly.

Looking over the area, KC saw the two-suns' rays were breaking through the tree canopy. She could see a quadruple rainbow forming in the mist of the water. She shuddered slightly, allowing her mind to drift back to that night. "It was six months ago. We had stopped to help a stranded motorist. I had gotten out of the car. My husband was on the phone. He wasn't pleased I had stopped to help a stranger. I used to do it all the time. A drunk driver hit our car killing my entire family. I've never felt like helping anyone since that awful night. I don't want to be responsible anymore."

"How horrible for you to see that. It was like me seeing my sister and brother die from the Drakein's breath. What is a car? Is it a weapon like a sword or a spear?"

"It is a machine that helps people in my world move from one place to another quickly."

"We could use something like that here."

"It requires cutting down a lot of trees."

"That's truly murderous."

KC nodded. "I'm afraid it is. When did you lose your sister and brother?"

"When the two-suns aligned with the two-moons. I watched helplessly as Nukpana struck them down. I couldn't go to them. Transformed into the Drakein, she had set the entire glade on fire with one breath."

"How awful for you. Drakein? What is that?"

"A Drakein is a winged serpent that flies and breathes fire. They live long, much longer than many other beings here, and possess supernatural powers. That's how Nukpana came to be." KC looked at Ish tilting her head. "I keep forgetting that you do not understand my world. Nukpana is a 'Blender'—half witch and half Drakein. She can transform between one or the other at will. If she is very angry, you will see both come out of her. It is frightening."

"A witch and a Drakein? This Drakein sounds like what we call a dragon. Man, I've really stepped into something strange, haven't I? Was she always evil and 'Blender,' as you call it?"

"I can't explain now. We must get moving."

KC looked up. The sky looked magical with various hues of blue. The swirls of different shades mingled with whites and touches of yellow gave the appearance it was moving in multiple directions. The most striking feature was the two suns. "The beauty of your two suns. We've been under the canopy for most of the day. Are the sun-rays very hot?"

"Not normally. There are moments when rain is scarce and it is very dry. There are legends about why, but many of my clan believe it has to do with the lack of faith by those from other worlds that are linked to Eldershire."

"You're kidding, right?"

"No. Eldershire is a world mingled with other worlds. Our suns ebb and flow like the tides. Sometimes, we have more than two suns and sometimes we have more than two moons. It is during those times that the growth of trees suffers the most. Our rains do not fall often. We suffer."

"That's much like Earth. I would think with your magic you could prevent those natural events from happening."

"Why would we tamper with natural events? That seems counterproductive."

"I look forward to learning more about Eldershire. But, I interrupted you. You were talking about Nukpana when the beauty of the sky distracted me. What happens when she is both—a witch and a Drakein?" KC asked.

"She flies out over Eldershire bringing terror and destruction to us all. Normally, Drakeins only become fierce when their family is being attacked or if someone tries to capture them. A Drakein will fight to the death to set itself free if it is held captive. The legend also says that a witch is the only being that can remove a scale or two from a Drakein's body to use in their spells. But, if a human were to come to Eldershire, a human has the same powers and control over a Drakein as the witch."

"Seriously? A human? How convenient," KC mused and decided she would never want to face Nukpana. Yet, while listening to Ish's story, she thought back to what the snake had said to her. I wonder if that is why Nukpana is after me. She doesn't want me to control her. KC looked at Ish. She could see the pain on his face. It was pain all too familiar to her. "Do you have any other family?"

"Yes. My father is still living and another sister. My mother died not too many moons ago. Unless I have offspring, I'm the last of my family's clan. When I die, my clan will cease to exist." Ish paused. "Enough. We must get going. Before we do, we should get some water in my pouch, and then we'll be on our way." Ish ran back to the brook in the crouched manner again. When he returned, he moved in the same way.

"Every time you move out to the river, you crouch down and move very quickly. Why?"

"When you are in the woods, you have cover and concealment, which will protect you from danger. When you go out into the open, like when I went to the river's edge, you lose your cover, which makes you vulnerable. You must crouch down to give more concealment in hopes you can hide yourself from something that may be out there. When you were in the brier patch, you really weren't in cover. You were concealed by the smell of the dead carcasses around you. That's why the Atcenians couldn't find you."

"Oh, my. Don't remind me of that awful smell."

Ish smiled and his dark blue eyes sparkled in the light. KC studied his face and wished there was something she could do for him and his family. She felt she should return the favor to him since he had risked his life to save her from the Atcenians.

"Did you hear that?" A crackling noise of trees falling came from the direction they had come out of the forest. "We've got to move. Now!"

KC picked up the water pouch that Ish had finished filling and together they ran by the berm that stretched along the brook and up to the bluff.

ॐ

KC KEPT LOOKING UP, making sure the tree canopy gave her cover. She stumbled a few times. The forest floor was uneven and covered with dead limbs, piles of leaves, and depressions. She knew she needed to be more careful, yet she had to run.

"Ish, can we run out in the open near the water. It is so much smoother there. My ankles are taking a beating," KC said stepping into a large pile of leaves and coming to a halt.

"KC, Mr Scruffy just shared he thinks your legs are skinny like a twig." Ish smiled.

KC rubbed her legs. "I know we have to keep moving. But, you just said Mr Scruffy spoke to you. How's that possible?"

"We talk telepathically. He reads my mind, I read his. That's how I've known the area is clear. He's up above us, looking ahead and telling me how things look for us. Now, come on. We'll have time later to talk more about this. We must move."

"Telepathically? What? A talking animal can speak telepathically too? Now, I've heard everything. How is that possible?"

"I can't take time now. But—"

"I know. King Elder will tell me. Your answer is starting to sound like a broken record."

"A what?"

"Never mind." KC said and started to run again. "I may have skinny legs, but you are short."

Mr. Scruffy flew down and landed on Ish's shoulder. He said, "Ish, the way along the brook to Iolair's Bluff is clear in all directions. You probably could run out in the open. I'll keep watch over you."

"Good. We need to move faster."

Mr Scruffy turned his head toward KC. "And, KC, I'm tall for my species." He flapped his wings and KC watched him soar up through the canopy.

"That is so amazing. A talking owl. Wow."

"Come on, KC. The way is clear and we can run hard in this part of the glade."

KC smiled. Mr Scruffy reminded her of her son, Bill. He always made jokes that caused her to relax and enjoy life. She missed him. Looking up at Mr Scruffy flying ahead, she wondered if they would be friends.

They moved closer to the bank where they ran faster and made better time.

❦

AFTER A WHILE, Ish said, "Let's stop for water. See Mr Scruffy up there? He told me that we could be at Iolair's Bluff before early two-moons. When we reach the waterfall, you will be able to see down into the valley where King Elder's camp is in the heart of the Wild Woods. It's about a league away. Come. We don't have far now." Ish handed her the pouch.

KC took it, and then a swig of water. She looked out along the water. "This Nukpana person. Is she so evil she would kill us first before she finds out who we are?" KC took a second swig and handed Ish the pouch.

"That's right." He took a swig. "There is more you need to know about our world and King Elder will want to be the one to tell you." He took another swig, and offered the pouch to KC again.

"No, I'm fine. That water is good. I know I laughed at you when you told me the water would give me strength. You weren't wrong. It does."

Ish put the pouch away, looked at KC, and placed his arm on her shoulder, "Keep the faith. You will learn that Nukpana is worse than you fear. We've lived with her evil for hundreds of lunations. Now, come. We've got ground to cover, and Mr Scruffy said we should make haste as the sunlight is fast fleeing. We must get to the waterfall and Iolair's Bluff."

AT IOLAIR'S BLUFF, KC surveyed the valley below the ridge. They had arrived too late the night before and the two-moons had not offered enough light for them to continue their journey. The morning's two-suns were rising brightly. She could see the Elder trees that framed the edge of King Elder's camp. The spray from the waterfall to her left caused her to shiver. The two-moons were setting and a cool breeze blew through the area. The sounds of the forest were coming alive and the whole effect caused her to think back to when she and Marie had forged to the top of Lick Mountain and of the last hike she and Jack had taken before he was killed.

A tear formed and gradually rolled down her cheek. She wiped it away and gazed over the valley. From her vantage point, she could see for miles. Each tree appeared to stand tall, strong, and with command, as though keeping watch. The leaves bathed her view in gold, yellow, and light brown with splotches of red and orange. The suns' rising rays pierced through the canopy casting shadows on the ground below. She looked around taking in as much as she could. She found herself feeling comfortable in Eldershire. She needed friends like Ish and Mr Scruffy to come into her life.

"Ish?"

"Yes?" Ish walked up and stood beside KC.

"When will we descend into the valley?"

"Soon. We will wait for more of the dew to burn off to help prevent slippage on the moss-covered rock. Mr Scruffy just asked me why you look so peaceful. He said it was the first time he had seen your face smile," Ish said as he pointed to the sky.

KC looked up and saw Mr Scruffy flying in a small circle above their heads. It looked like he had caught a thermal air current and was floating along. "The beauty. I've never seen such beauty before. The trees speak to me. The sky this morning, a crystal blue, calls to me. My senses are awakened. I had no idea I was smiling."

"You do not have a full smile made by your lips, but your face does have a pleasant appearance to the eye. Eldershire does this to our kind, too. The beauty of Eldershire can even touch those who are evil. You ready to start down?"

"Yes. Any pointers? It looks pretty steep."

"Yes. Mr Scruffy, I know. She does ask a lot of questions. KC, try to step where I step. You'll do fine. Now, let's go down to the valley. Mr Scruffy is right. The two-suns will be directly above before we know it if we don't get moving."

They began to make their way down through the brush and overgrowth of the bank. The briers and burrs of the branches scratched at KC's legs, even through her jeans. She tried to push them away, but the branches sprang back, snagging the fabric.

"Ish, can you wait? It feels like my legs are bleeding."

"Mr Scruffy thinks your legs are too skinny and it is a wonder you have any blood at all." KC showed him the torn fabric of her jeans. "Here, take this salve and place some on your cuts. It will stop the bleeding. We can't tarry much longer. High two-suns will be coming upon us."

KC took the salve that Ish pulled from his pouch. It was wrapped in some kind of skin pelt. The odor was awful, but when she dropped her jeans, she saw that her legs were striped with blood. Long slender streams of blood were beginning to pool in the top of her shoes. She rubbed the salve on her cuts. The feeling of healing came over her suddenly as the sting of the cuts stopped as fast as it began. She noticed the blood stopped flowing too.

"Keep the salve with you. I can get another one when we get to camp. And, no, I can't tell you now what's in it," Ish continued down the slope.

"I know. I'll learn about it from King Elder." KC went to pull her jeans up and looked down at her legs. Except for the crusty blood at the top of her socks, there was no mark on her skin. It was as if she had never cut her legs at all. This world was becoming more amazing to her by the hour. She placed the pouch in her back pocket and continued down the embankment into what was proving to be an unbelievable new world.

CHAPTER 4
KING ELDER'S CAMP

KC walked into the camp. She thought about how her life had changed overnight. It was not long ago—that very morning it seemed—she had wished for the life she had before. She wished to be back even though she had contemplated suicide when her family was killed. She wanted to die with them. It was her fault, after all. Then, when she saw the hat, she picked it up, and she wished—she wished to be somewhere else. "Well, you got what you wished for," she said under her breath.

"What?" Ish said. "Did you say something?"

"Uh, no. What do we do now?"

"You wait right here. I'll go over to King Elder's thípi and let him know you are here. Whatever you do, don't talk to anyone."

"Wait. Where are you going?"

"To King Elder's thípi," Ish said slightly annoyed.

"Teepee? Spell it."

"You should ask King Elder that. I'm not sure I know how to tell you."

She watched Ish walk to the tallest teepee she had ever seen. It looked like a real Native American structure, as she would have seen in her world. Then, she looked around at her surroundings. The clearing where the camp was situated was about as large as a football field. The trees along the edge of the camp weren't Redwood trees like she had seen in the John Muir woods. These were definitely taller. She leaned back as far as she could and she still couldn't see their tops.

As they travelled through the Wild Woods, KC hadn't had time to pay attention to the height of the trees around her. When they stood on Iolair's Bluff, the trees still did not seem so high. Now that she had time to look and think about it, the trunks of the trees were slender like those on Earth. But, the tops of the trees were literally out of sight. She became so lost in the grandeur of the trees; KC forgot where she was standing. A creepy feeling came over her. She could feel eyes watching. She looked around and saw she was being watched.

"Don't be alarmed, you are a curiosity to them," Mr Scruffy said swooping down and landing on KC's shoulder. KC jumped. "Whoa! Hold on. I won't hurt you."

"Sorry. You need to warn me when you do something like that." KC pointed. "How should I approach them, if they come toward me?"

"I would stand still if I were you. Most of the Elderians do not recognize who or what you are. You look strange." Mr Scruffy flew up to a nearby post, where he sat tall and statuesque. His large, heart-shaped facial disk turned to look at her. KC noticed his eyes were covered with tiny velvety feathers in a delicate pattern. The light gray feathers were dappled with black on his head, and then gradually turned a darker gray where his feathers grew longer and were arranged in a speckled pattern. Along his breast were large numbers of downy feathers that were mottled with various shades of grays and white that formed a checkerboard like pattern. Being encircled with snow white feathers made his black eyes loom in size before they closed slowly giving the impression he was winking. *I don't think I've ever seen an owl up close before.* Mr Scruffy was beautiful. She looked at him and noticed his feathers seemed to be flushed under his eyes. It looked like he was blushing. *I wonder, is he reading my mind?*

Looking around to the Elderians, she saw several had moved closer to her. Many looked impish or fairy like, the same as Ish did. But, just as many looked old and rugged. The beings stood far enough from her that she had room to move, but they had now formed a circle around her.

She was starting to become alarmed. She couldn't see the teepee that Ish had entered. She tried to look over the crowd to see if she could find Ish, but the beings were too tall. She thought about walking in the same direction Ish took, but she decided against it since Mr Scruffy said to stand still.

KC turned around in a circle while looking at the trees to take her mind off the gathering Elderians. Her twirl caused her to lose her bearings. She couldn't see the camp area any longer. Looking up at the sky didn't help; there wasn't a sky to see. It was dark. The two-suns had set. Yet, there was light. What was happening? She felt overwhelmed. She was in the heart of a forest, lost, surrounded by more forest beings.

"KC? KC? Can you hear me?"

"Ish, don't worry. She will be fine," Mr Scruffy said. "She is going to fit right in as soon as she can learn how to have her mind read by so many at one time. She has the soul of a hobbit, the heart of a hippie, and the spirit of a wood sprite. She is of good nature and petite in size, yet she has a heart that is large enough to absorb the spiritual vibrations of Eldershire. When she wakes, we will need to give her guidance. She'll be able to handle it better the next time."

"I know you are right, but she's got to meet with King Elder soon. Will we have time to prepare her?" Ish cradled KC's head in his lap.

"She will do fine. It is written we must treat humans with special care the first time."

"You're right. I didn't think about it. She had handled you and me reading her mind. She didn't seem to notice."

"Ish, it was just you and me. She was suddenly hit with fifty minds probing her. It's a wonder she didn't die from the frontal attack." Mr Scruffy took a wing and moved KC's bangs away from her eyes. "You might want to place a cold salve on her forehead. She feels warm."

"I don't have one." Ish looked up to Mr Scruffy, his eyes gave an appearance of fear. "What will we do if we've harmed her? I know she is the one. She's got to be."

"Relax. I'll go get something." Mr Scruffy flew up to a hole in a tree. He returned. "Here, I keep things like this stored around the forest. I like to be prepared."

Ish smiled, smoothed the cold salve on KC's forehead, and whispered a few words.

KC opened her eyes. She rubbed them.

"KC, I'm so sorry. Are you all right?" Ish said.

She suddenly set up. "Ish! Where am I? What happened? It's dark. I can't see!"

"I shouldn't have left you alone. No one knew who you were. They thought you were a Menace being from Nukpana's evil army. They locked into your mind all at once. We're so sorry we didn't prepare you. I didn't think it would hurt you. You didn't seem bothered with Mr Scruffy or me reading your mind. The sudden probing caused you to run from the camp into the forest. I'm so glad you are okay."

"What about my eyes?"

"They will adjust."

"Locked into my mind? What do you mean? I was in the center of the camp where you left me talking with Mr Scruffy. How?" KC stopped talking. "Ish?"

"Yes. It is magic playing a strong force on you, KC. It is one of our defenses. As a group, we can be very powerful. It was a mind meld of a power you had not experienced before. The evil of Nukpana has caused us to form alternative ways to interrogate those we believe to be an enemy of our existence. All of the Elderians in the camp are worried about you. They did not mean to harm you."

"This is so much for me to take in right now." She bowed her head and cradled it in her hands. "My head is throbbing. My eyes ache. Do you have anything for a headache? I feel as though my head might explode."

"Mr Scruffy, do you have anything in your tree hollow?"

"I might. Let me see." Mr Scruffy flew away. Soon he returned. "Here, chew on this. Trust me. It will help."

KC held out her hand. "Where is it? I'm seeing shapes, but I can't make anything out yet."

Mr Scruffy placed the bundle in her hand.

"What is this?"

"Dried black cohosh and white willow bark. It is best to take as a tea, but well, chewing for now will have to do the trick."

KC began to chew the leaves and made a face. Her mind raced to when she was a little girl and had to take a large spoonful of castor oil. "Oh, man. It tastes horrible."

"Don't stop chewing it. Swallow as much of the juice as you can stand. It will work quickly when you get enough juice into your system."

"Mr Scruffy, I sure hope this doesn't work like castor oil did on me when I was a little girl."

"Do we want to know?"

"No. You want to make sure you are far away if your nose is sensitive."

"That sounds ominous," Ish said as he placed a pouch of water in KC's hand. "You might find having some water helpful."

"Thanks. I think I do feel the pressure in my eyes changing. You and Mr Scruffy are starting to come into view."

"Do you feel well enough to go to King Elder's thípi now?"

"Before I check, would someone please spell teepee for me? It sounds like the teepee that a Native American Indian would use for his home. What is it?"

Mr Scruffy said, "In a way, that is exactly what it is. When I was on Earth, I marveled at how beautiful the Indian teepees were decorated. Here, the word is thípi, which just happens to be a Native American Lakota word that means house. To spell it, you would say: T - H - Í, which is the letter 'i' with an acute symbol, followed by - P - I. And is pronounced like teepee."

"That's good to know. Fascinating that you are using a Native American word."

"You'll find lots of our words come from your world. King Elder will—"

"I know. He'll explain everything. Let me see if I can stand up, and then we'll go to him." KC sat up first. She saw she was lying on a cot made of wooden slats and several layers of fabric that appeared to be made from leaves of all types. She felt light headed and a little dizzy. She moved her hand to her forehead. "Wow. I haven't felt this way since I got a little tipsy drinking some moonshine when I was a teenager."

"Do you think you can stand?" Ish asked.

"Yes. Give me a minute. What exactly did your people do to me?"

"The Elderians are not *my* people. I'm a wood sprite. We are related, but not close kin."

"Oh, I get it. You're not 'kissin' cousins'." KC smiled.

"Cousins? What are they?"

"Private joke, no worries. So, what now?"

"Can you stand?"

"Yes. Mr Scruffy. Can I spit this wad of leaves out now? I think my headache is gone."

Mr Scruffy nodded. He turned to Ish. "I included some Elderian dried leaves that will help her with the use of further mind-melds. Hopefully, it won't be so hard on her until we can prepare her for more. I added a few Eland leaves, too." Ish nodded to Mr Scruffy.

KC stood up and remained steady on her feet. She turned to Ish and said, "I think I'm ready."

"Let's go see King Lug Elder and meet the other leaders of the Elderians."

KC stopped. "What happened to his thípi?"

"What do you mean?" Ish said encouraging KC to move forward.

"It's different. Before, when you walked toward it, it looked like, well, a teepee, like I'd seen before. Now, it looks like a building, a full-blown sized building."

Mr Scruffy telepathed to Ish, "It's good to know the dried leaves worked. Her vision is no longer camouflaged. She will see more things as they actually are, but will be strange to her."

"We'll let King Elder explain. It will be easier. Come on. He's waiting on us. We must go," Mr Scruffy said aloud to KC.

"This is such a strange place," KC responded.

Ish telepathed to Mr Scruffy, "This will prove interesting."

KC LOOKED behind her to see from where they had walked. The ground, covered with emerald green grass, stretched to the trees that were now further away than when she noticed them before. It seemed to her that the entire area changed each time she gazed upon it. She was beginning to think she was back in the 1960s having a trip, as they used to say.

Stepping through the doorway of the thípi, KC saw the grass stretched before her to a second doorway that opened into yet another area—a forest room. She could see into the second room where trees were in a line forming walls for what could be a great hall of a castle. The effect was that of a building, from her world, interlaced with tall, stately trees that formed a colonnade. The structure emitted an aura of old worldly beauty similar to what she felt when she visited old castles in Ireland.

At the back of the room was an ornately carved throne upon a staged area with three steps leading up to the main chair. The ornateness of the throne portrayed an air of regality. To the left a flame flickered in a pit with hues of red, green, gold, and bronze. Some of the Elderians, KC thought she recognized from an earlier encounter, were standing along the sides. She and Ish continued to walk up to the empty throne. The throne room was overwhelming. She felt an urge to turn and run, but somehow, she didn't.

Ish stopped and held his hand out to signal to KC to stop as well. She looked at him. He stood with his head bowed. She followed suit.

"Welcome, Friend Isherwood, with whom stand you?"

"May the light of the world shine brightly on your kingdom, King Lug Elder. Greetings to you. This is human, Kay Carson. She goes by the name of KC."

"Why did you bring her here, to our camp?" KC wondered how King Elder suddenly appeared or if he had been there all along.

"I found her being pursued by the Atcenians. They spoke of

Nukpana. I felt it important to bring this information to you. I couldn't leave her to them. Thus, I brought her to speak with you."

"Mr Scruffy, do you have anything to add?"

"No, sir. Ish shared the important aspects. I do find her interesting. I think she has potential. And, I do believe she is the one."

"Thank you, both."

KC was becoming irked. *I'm standing right here.* She switched her weight off one foot to the other. *Why won't he speak to me? I have questions. Doesn't he understand that I want to return home?*

"Human?" King Elder said. KC jumped out of her thoughts. King Elder's throne zoomed closer to her. "I'd like to answer your questions. I'm speaking directly to you now."

KC looked toward Ish, who motioned for her to face the King.

"You're wondering how I know what you thought." KC realized King Elder was no longer speaking aloud. "Yes, my dear, we read human thought. Sometimes it doesn't come through clearly, all muddled you know. But, I can speak to you directly within your mind if you prefer. I understand some humans hear better that way."

KC studied King Elder's face. His lips were no longer moving, yet she could hear his voice inside her head. She froze. King Elder motioned for her to sit beside him. She looked back at Ish, who motioned for her to move forward. She hesitated, but felt compelled to continue.

"There is no need to be fearful. We realize that this is a new experience for you. Come here; sit beside me. Queen Esmé, my wife and the Queen of Eldershire, will share her seat with you. We are a peaceful people. It is interesting that you came to Eldershire dressed in the clothes of the 1960s of Earth time. Our world is 4800 in Earth years. In Eldershire time, there is no equivalent number. We were with you on Earth during the turbulent sixties. Then, we were pleased your people had once again begun to worship our brethren —the wood spirits of the universe."

KC walked up the steps to the royal platform, moved to Queen Esmé's throne, and stood beside her. She noticed King Elder was no larger than a short pre-teen child, maybe four or five feet tall. Still he seemed huge when he first loomed toward her. *Are they playing with my vision while they are in my mind?* The effect was similar to several mind-altering drugs she had experimented with when she was younger. Or was that now? She was beginning to have trouble determining what was real and what was magic.

"KC. May I call you that?" KC nodded. "All of life is magic. You humans have never quite figured that out." King Elder paused. He motioned to two of his servants. The servants walked over to a wall. They pulled back a large curtain revealing a huge, oval basin on top of a stand that was covered with an ornate woodcarving. It looked like a birdbath with a majestic tree forming the pedestal.

King Elder walked over to where it stood. "This is a reflexsor. It will depict images of realistic quality and color. You will feel as though you are immersed into the scenes, very similar to what you think of as a hologram." He moved his hand in a sweeping motion. The reflexsor began to show scenes of a vast mountain area covered in large forests. KC watched in wonder because the aerial views were much like a drone on Earth would capture, yet the colors and three-dimensional results were almost dreamlike to her eyes.

"This is the Land of Eldershire. Certain creatures of our land have a connective power to the reflexsor. They provide us with a visual record of our history. Our history is long. Our trusted friend, Mr Scruffy, provided the scenes you are seeing now. I understand he likes you. That is a high compliment."

KC looked out into the crowd. She could see Mr Scruffy standing next to Ish. She turned and watched in wonder as the scenes displayed before her were beautiful sweeping vistas of each season from spring to the present fall. The forest depicted was of trees at various stages all the way to the end of life. Some young trees were sprouting, others growing ever taller, while others cascaded to the ground due to old age. The allure of the evolution of the forest was made all the more real as each tree's spirit could be seen within the bark or branches. When an older tree died away, its tree spirit would move into a new tree sprout. The splendor of it all brought tears to KC's eyes. Her spirit was moved.

King Elder said, "The Rå is the name of an individual type of tree spirit. In some parts of your world, Sweden for one, the Rå are known as the Lofjerskor while we are also known as the Dryads by the Greeks of old. A folk tale is spoken of the Rå, but I can assure you, we are real. Each tree you see before you in the Land of Eldershire and throughout your world has a tree spirit, its resident Rå. Please sit while I continue."

The seat that KC sat on was comfortable, but while she listened to King Elder, she squirmed. She wanted to share that her Mother had told her all about the spirit of trees. She was enchanted to learn about the Rå. She wished she could speak.

"Do not worry about interrupting me while I share the story of Eldershire. You will learn much that may serve you well. Your mother was wise to pass on the teachings, mores, and beliefs of the trees."

Queen Esmé said, "To humans, we are generally invisible. Our function is to guard each tree and we are most benevolent to humans that respect trees. Because of your Mother's teachings, you are such a human. And thus, when you made your wish upon the magical hat—the hat of The Fairy—you were granted your wish. You were brought here amongst the Elderians for a purpose we will explain when you are ready." She paused, looked around the room, and pointed to the various Elderians listening.

Looking to Ish, KC thought about where she was before she landed in the brier patch. Mr Scruffy telepathed to her, "Pay attention, KC. You are allowing your mind to wander. They are preparing you."

KC startled, looked down at Mr Scruffy. He lifted a wing as though pointing up. She looked back to King Elder and saw that the mirror had stopped on a scene that could only be described as the most enchanting she had seen since her arrival. The mountain vistas seemed to extend beyond the horizon with each mountain peak topped by yet another one. The purple and blue hues were broken by wisps of clouds. The phrase 'purple majesty' came to her mind.

King Elder continued, "Our family is known as the Elders. There are many other tree spirit clans within our world, too numerous to name, but a few are represented here today."

Looking into the gathered Elderians, KC saw distinct characteristics of beings that she could only guess the type of trees they each represented or the clans' names. The beings stood tall, nearly six feet, or taller. Their bodies' emitted power—muscularity with fair skin and their eyes, of those she could see, were blue with many sporting long blond or red-gold hair. They had very little markings on their clothes and what adornment they wore was of neck rings made of gold, silver, or bronze. The cloth of their clothing was colorful, filled with different hues as a forest in the fall.

King Elder walked over to a wall of curtains KC had not noticed before.

"Coming into your view, you see the Wall of Reverence. Here you will see memories of tree spirits that brought great honor to our beings and who gave their life in service." King Elder sat down on his throne. "At our peak when we served on Earth, we were beings who covered most of Earth with underground connections through the roots of all trees. We were the peoples of the pre-Celtic land of Irena, later known as Ireland. During the early formation of the Earth, the continents were joined into the super continent of Pangaea. The tree line of your home, the Appalachian Mountains, was combined with the Caledonides into one long mountain range of the countries of Ireland, Britain, Greenland, and Scandinavia. The histories and myths say the Ancient Ones were wiped out by the Romans."

King Elder paused. KC studied his face and thought of her

mother's father. King Elder reminded her of him. Her grandfather was old, wise, and empathic. When he walked into a room, he commanded respect. And, when he told a story, everyone gathered around. KC noticed the same with King Elder.

"The virgin forest roots were, and still are, interconnected," King Elder continued. "We left what is now called Ireland, many moons before the founding of the Northern Continent, long before the Dryads. Our peoples stayed connected across the waters. We use magic and the art of telepathy to intuitively know and understand the workings and mysteries of the world." He stopped speaking, smiled, and looked to Queen Esmé.

King Elder moved over to another wall where KC could see the reliefs of two different tree forms that rose over fifty feet above their heads. It was as if the room grew in size in proportion to the majestic trees. The feeling reminded KC of watching a movie on an IMAX screen. "We are governed by two very distinct tree beings— Yggdrasil, the Tree of Life, as you call it on Earth, depicted here, and to the side," King Elder pointed, "you see Mother Elder, our dear matriarch."

King Elder then walked over to a column pedestal that stood isolated with a light shining down illuminating a barren top. "The symbol of this unity of tree beings is the Efil Stone—our life stone made of the heart wood from Yggdrasil and Mother Elder. All three of these—Yggdrasil, Mother Elder, and the Efil Stone—together form the Trinity, the protection we need to maintain our life force in Eldershire. When one is harmed, stolen, or missing, the life source begins to weaken. The Efil Stone is missing, and as a direct result, strange things are beginning to happen within Eldershire."

KC raised her hand.

"I've already read your mind. And, yes, I'm sure you'd feel better if you could speak your thoughts. I'll allow it."

"Thank you," KC said. "And, it is an honor to meet you. However, I am not sure why I am here. Ish told me that you'd be able to explain what has happened to me. Who are the Atcenians? And this evil-witch Drakein, Nukpana. Will you?"

Mr Scruffy telepathed to KC, "Patience is not one of your virtues. Be wise. Wait and pay attention."

"Well, it seems I'm expected to be more patient. But, it is hard to wait when I have so many questions. What am I supposed to do? How would you feel suddenly landing in my world and not knowing how or why?" KC paused. "I apologize, King Elder. You said the Efil Stone is missing. When did you discover this?"

King Elder's voice changed in tone ever so slightly. "It was found missing a few two-moons ago. There's a legend that has been passed down for many lunations. A Drakein can understand the spoken word. Their ways are ancient. They prefer to live underground in a lair or cave so that they can be one with their world. The fire they breathe is white hot and the noise they make is hard on your ears."

KC wondered if it was like a train whistle startling you. Mr Scruffy telepathed, "It is. Listen."

"The sound is so sharp that it makes you stop what you are doing and you instinctively grab your ears. That pause can cost you your life. The worst and most dangerous Drakeins are purple. The legend says that in an earlier time, when Nukpana was young, and starting to develop her witch's powers, she persuaded a Purple Drakein to allow her to ride its back. They formed a telepathic bond. Over time, Nukpana used her magic to become one with the Drakein. Since that day, she has terrorized all of Eldershire. When she is merely a witch, she lives in Emerald Mountain. She resides in Grave's Mountain when she is a Drakein."

"She flies across the area changing shapes as she goes?" KC thought the whole idea of a witch-dragon was rather strange. Yet, it was obvious King Elder and his followers were terrified. "Can you not use your magic to take her down?"

"Her powers are great. She has used many spells and harmed many of our fellow Elderians. Ish told you of the death of his sister and brother. Nukpana's evil can be swift and unforgiving. We must prevent her from taking over all of Eldershire. If she is able to harness the positive life force, it will allow her to return to her time and place, and to come and go at will. Now that you are here in Eldershire, you must take on the quest to find the Efil Stone. Yggdrasil and Mother Elder foretold of your arrival. This is your destiny."

KC started to argue against becoming a part of their battles with Nukpana, but her voice would not work. She turned to Ish and Mr Scruffy. Neither spoke to her. She looked back to King Elder.

His telepathic speech was directed to her. "I am not pleased with your reaction. I've silenced you. You are acting like an infant in this world. You will be treated as one until you can listen without arguing. We believe in discussing. But, we believe in doing so in a compassionate manner. All ideas are important. We cherish each one, but we do not allow self-centered action and fear to overtake our thinking. You are scared. That is to be expected. Now, I'll release this grip on your voice, if you will sit patiently and wait. I have much more to explain. Nod your head in agreement if you will comply."

She nodded. The release of his tight grip on her throat allowed her to move freely. She looked at Ish and Mr Scruffy. They did not speak, but looked directly ahead to where King Elder stood. She turned to him, giving her full attention.

"Many of the magic and telepathic rules of our land you will learn over time and you will acquire skill in using them as you prove yourself worthy of learning. I'm placing Ish and Mr Scruffy in charge of educating you in fighting and survival techniques first. At the right moments, magic and telepathic powers will be awarded to you. Nod if you understand."

KC nodded.

"Ish is the best fighter in our land when it comes to sword fighting and using a bow and arrow. Listen and learn with commitment. Mr

Scruffy is wiser than most owls in all things. You should follow his counsel. He has already saved your life. It is good he likes you, otherwise, you would have already died here."

KC raised her hand even though she knew King Elder already knew what she thought. He nodded. "Something has occurred to me I've not thought about before. Actually, I don't want to think about it. What happens to me if I die here?"

"When you die here you cease to exist. And, yes, you will not be able to return to your world. It will be as though you never existed in either world. It means you need to determine what is more valuable to you—giving your life here in servitude to the Land of Eldershire resulting in giving up your life on Earth, or returning to Earth now to the life you had before you picked up the Hat of The Fairy."

KC wasn't sure what to think. She wondered if she died here and never existed in her world, would that mean her husband would still be alive? Her son would not have been born, so his death wouldn't be undone, but her first husband, Jack, what about him? He could have a life. Is that what she wanted? She had a lot to consider before she made her decision.

CHAPTER 5
ATCENIANS AND NUKPANA

S he stood tall, her hand wrapped around her scepter, Blazewing. She surveyed her subjects and her heart grew strong with a surge of anger pulsing through her fingers. Blazewing glowed. It was alive.

Nukpana Fraener turned her head toward her faithful scepter. She wore her power proudly and studied her reflection in its shimmering crystal—flawless in every way—its shape; its brilliance reflected her beauty. She had forged it from a part of her heart mixed with an elixir from a Draco, who died by her hand. The purplish hue emitted the perfect light.

Looking at herself, Nukpana steadied the clasp in her hair. Her reflection showed her face alive with anticipation, beautiful and flawless, except for the scar on her left cheek, hidden by her hair held in place with a dragon hairpin. Her remaining long, black tresses, woven into a complicated braid, were covered with a large, tall, pointed hat made from the hides of a fox and raccoon she once knew. She would make a similar example of Gorge and Morge. The Atcenian twins had failed her. She would deal with them in a public manner. The last time she had two servants who failed her in such a blatant way, she was a child. She wore their hides on her head. She surveyed the room. Her courtroom was full.

Gorge and Morge stood before her. She lifted Blazewing and tapped the end of the scepter's shaft on the marble floor. A vibration rumbled through the room. Silence followed. Nukpana stepped forward. She appeared to grow taller from her height of six feet. Her black leather body suit accentuated her long slender arms and legs, as did the knee high spiked heels. She lowered Blazewing toward the crowd. As she scanned the room, everyone's eyes stared back at her in wide-eyed wonder. She loved the fact she held them in her power. Blazewing glowed brighter strengthened by her surge of emotion.

"Gorge."

"Yes, your great Highness, I mean Treoraí," Gorge said lowering to his knees and bowing his head.

"Morge."

"Yes, your great Treoraí," Morge said and looked over to his brother. "We—"

"Silence!"

The room produced an echo as powerful as Nukpana's voice. Her face, with no flaws that could easily be seen, belied her age. To her subjects, she looked young, strong, in control. Looking over the room, Nukpana saw Gorge and Morge whimpering in fear. The way her pets—the fox and raccoon—had begged for their lives many lunations ago.

> She was young, in the early years of learning magic. The fox and raccoon were a surprise present.
>
> "Mom, Dad, I love them. You do love me." Nukpana held the little fox and raccoon next to her heart. "I'm going to call the fox, Dad, and the raccoon, I'll call Mom. That way, when you are away from me, they will be with me, and so will you."

"That's sweet, Nukpana. Go play with your friends. We must go out and see our subjects," her father said.

She did and enjoyed their company, watching them grow. Then, one day, they proved to be weak and betrayed her.

"Nukpana," Fox said, "You can't do that. You will kill many plants if you spread that liquid on the ground."

"I will if I want. Who are you to tell me I can't?"

"You must think about what you are doing," Raccoon said. "Or else, we'll tell your parents."

"You dare threaten me? Me, who has loved you and cared for you? Who do you think you are?" Nukpana's rage took hold of her and she lashed out at both of them.

"Nukpana, stop!" Fox cried. "We mean you no harm. You need to realize your soul is turning evil."

"Evil? Evil! You haven't seen evil," Nukpana grabbed up the raccoon and threw her body to the ground. "Now, you'll see my hatred for anyone that challenges me." She reached and grabbed the fox before he could move, stripped his hide from his body, and ripped his heart out. Then, she reached for the raccoon, lifted her up, and slit her throat. She then cut away its pelt too. "These pelts will make a nice hat for me to wear."

That evening, when her parents were due home, Nukpana paced back and forth wondering how she would explain the fate of her pets. There was a knock on her door.

"What do you want?" Nukpana said.

"Your Princess. We must give you bad news. Please know we didn't do this." The servant bowed in fear.

"Speak. Stand strong and tell me."

"It is your parents. They were caught in a horrible fire started from the flames of a strange liquid that flowed into the river. The flames lapped up around their carriage when they started across the bridge to come home."

"My parents are gone?" The servant nodded. "What do you mean a strange liquid?"

"Two of the coachmen riding with them said the purple liquid flowed down the stream, and then before anyone knew what was happening, the liquid turned into flames."

"A purple liquid?" Nukpana sat down and grabbed her heart. "Leave me." The servant left, and then she said, "What have I done?"

The purple liquid she'd poured on the ground was powerful. She'd been told to be careful when she used her power. They died. Nukpana's heart ached. She couldn't love any more. The pain was too great. *Everything I love dies. So be it. All things must die when they disobey my desires, my wants, my will.*

The two Atcenians crouched lower to the floor. Nukpana slowly lowered her tall frame into her throne. She flipped the long tail of her gothic-styled coat, just as she came to rest on the leather seat. She looked out to her subjects and said, "My hat is a symbol of my hatred for those who fail me and for those foolish enough to betray me. You, who believe you can escape my anger, who do not stay true to me and my ways, you must pay."

She touched her scar. The pain of the moment when the fox's claw cut across her cheek shuddered through her body. She could feel him wiggling in her hands. When Nukpana lifted up the raccoon as she cut the life from its body, the animal spat at her face. Her saliva landed on the cut of her cheek, healing the cut immediately into a large, coiled mark of evil. Over the last two hundred years, she had tried to use magic to change the scar. All it ever did was lengthen her life. The dragon hairpin with purple inlay was a gift from her mother and was the only thing she could bare touching her face.

"Morge, lower yourself, or else I'll dissolve you right now," Nukpana said and waved her hand in the air. Little bits of light began to dance above Gorge's and Morge's heads. "Follow the dance of my Dangerous Beauties as they move toward the Circle of Water. Watch them carefully, as your ability to follow my every command may prolong your life."

The Dangerous Beauties danced toward the huge pond that was in the center of the room. The water, dark and deep, was lined along the outer edge with ornate carvings of dragon images interwoven with the wings, necks, and bodies of those souls Nukpana had ended during her reign. The surface of the circular pond was laced with water lilies that sparkled and snapped; acid burst forth when something touched the water.

Nukpana stepped down from her throne, walked passed the Atcenian twins, and gracefully touched each Dangerous Beauty slowly descending toward the pond with her Scepter. Each time she said,

FROM ME TO YOU,
SIM SALA BIM
TRANSFORMS YOU, TOO.

The Dangerous Beauties changed into acidic water lilies landing gently in the water. After the last Dangerous Beauty landed, Nukpana held Blazewing at eye level where she could see her reflection. She said softly, "You know my desires. You know my distaste for disloyalty. You know my hate for Elderians. I want my revenge for what they did to me."

Gorge looked over at his brother and motioned to look to the right where two Atcenians stood nearby.

Gorge didn't see Nukpana notice his hand movement. She hit Gorge's hand with Blazewing and cried out, "How dare you ignore me during my most solemn ceremony. You failed me! You failed me, and now you will pay! My Dangerous Beauties, you serve me well.

You'll do the work I need. You'll honor me and serve me. Kill! Kill Gorge!"

At the same speed that Nukpana's anger rose, the Dangerous Beauties transformed into flying spikes and pierced Gorge's body in quick action, blowing him apart. The shards blew out away from where he stood. Morge was covered with some of the debris and began to cry out in pain due to the acid splashing from the Dangerous Beauties.

"Help! Help me, please!" He begged.

Nukpana flicked Blazewing and another group of Dangerous Beauties finished their work. The only evidence left that Gorge and Morge had been alive was a small pile of pieces of flesh. Nukpana motioned the two Atcenians that Gorge had noticed to move closer to her.

"Clean up that mess. You will be my new lieutenants." The two Atcenians began clearing the remains.

Walking to her throne, Nukpana sat, and then spoke to her followers. "You see what happens to those who are disloyal. You know I will not stand for disloyalty of any kind. To my many enemies and to those who will fight me and will lose, as others have lost so badly before, each of them are at a loss of what to do to stop me. It is my love for this land I fight for. I fight for you, my followers!"

Nukpana waited a few seconds, and then continued. "Gorge and Morge were total failures. Total losers. They are lost to me! I took them out as I will take out all my enemies who cross me and prevent me from reaching my goals. I will destroy all Elderians. Those evil tree lovers! I will destroy their land, burn their forests, and drive their spirits out of this world. It does not matter to me or to anyone else in this room. The human they call KC will feel my wrath soon. We will destroy them! We will win!"

The room erupted in cheers, chants, and hollers of great pride for their leader. Nukpana stood up and acknowledged their praise. She held up Blazewing to the crowd. As the cries of joy and support rose in volume, the central crystal stone gave off brilliance and shone like a beacon giving guiding light. Nukpana turned and faced the large carving on the wall that was behind her. The image of the dragon seemed to come to life, as she raised her arms up in servitude.

The cries of support of the spectators continued to grow. The roar of sound caused the floor to rumble. Nukpana's black hair glowed with the shade of purple. The light around her took on a light violet tone. Like an evil power engulfing her body, she began to twitch and transformed.

She screamed out, "As life seeds spring forth life, a bad seed transforms from a life of forgotten into a life of power. Little deaths happen each day with all life, while a bad seed is not thought to have life. From death comes life rising from my soul."

The crowd's chants soften to a low murmur as they saw Nukpana change. Standing before them was the Purple Drakein. Her sharp, keen eyes and intense expression surveyed the crowd. Her head, covered in hornlets, reared back stretching her long neck toward her tail and let out a piercing shrill.

The Purple Drakein's front legs reared up arching her back looking like a tyrannosaurus ready for attack. She flexed her bat shaped wings and flicked her smooth tongue as her barbed tail flipped in the air. Tiny flames danced in her nostrils showing the anger that was just below the surface of her joy for her transformation. She was pleased. Her transformation had not scared away her followers. In contrast, they seemed to be enthralled by it all. Her eyes gleamed with unrestrained greed. She knew she owned them. They would be her minions, her evil army, her Grey Menace. The Purple Drakein walked over to the shelf that held her most prized treasure—the Efil Stone. The smells of smoke and sulfur began to move through the room as she settled down into a seated stance.

An unknown creature stood off to one side, taking note of all that took place, knowing if he lived to share what he had just witnessed, he would be lucky.

CHAPTER 6
WHY ME?

K C looked toward King Elder and Queen Esmé. "Would you explain some of the magical things I've seen—the mind-meld, Nukpana, your thípi turning into a building?"

"My dear," Queen Esmé said. "I advise you to listen to our history. It will enable you to understand our magical world. You will also learn how you can return home."

KC looked at Ish and Mr Scruffy, and then she looked back to Queen Esmé and King Elder. "I'll try to be patient. I want to know about your world, but I need to know how to return to my world, my time, my place."

"Relax, KC. We're here to help you." KC recognized the voice as Ish speaking to her telepathically. She looked over to him. He nodded toward King Elder. With all of the voices bouncing around in her head, King Elder talking, and no one letting her express what she knows or the questions she has, she recognized she was a teenager again—their puppet and no longer a human in charge of her will.

"Just now, Ish spoke telepathically to you. You will find different beings in Eldershire have the power as granted by Yggdrasil." Queen Esmé pointed toward Ish. "He is a great warrior and a loyal subject of the Elans, his clan from Eland, a land Northeast of here beyond the great mountain of Grave's. He has earned the right to be an apprentice in the Elder ways. And through his servitude, he is in line to be Prince of Eland."

"Thank you. Ish proved his abilities when he saved my life," KC said. "Could you explain about my vision with the thípi differences and how telepathy works with others?"

"We won't spend much time on either, but understand that when a visitor comes to our camp that is not one of our clan, his or her vision is skewed. The visitor can see, just not what all those of Eldershire can see. The effect is the same as hiding before your eyes. You might be able to relate it to Shangri-La. No one could find it, no matter how much they searched. Yet, hidden right there in plain sight was the Tibetan utopia." KC nodded. "The leaves from the Elder tree with the other herbs that Mr Scruffy gave you to chew worked their magic and cleared your vision. The herbs helped you to see the camp as we all see it."

"Okay. I understand. But, Shangri-La was only a tale in a novel, wasn't it?"

"Was it?" King Elder said. "As for telepathy, it requires only a wave of my hand. It will give you permanent vision powers and the ability to telepath, but only while in the camp area. You will have the ability to block reception of your thoughts when you choose and by how you think, much as you do with your speech. You can divert your thoughts to one or more as you desire." King Elder waved his hand. "You are now aware."

Queen Esmé moved over to a portrait. "We will continue with Eldershire history. As was said before, The Trinity of Eldershire is made up of Yggdrasil, Mother Elder, and the Efil Stone."

"It is important," King Elder interjected, "that you understand that everything we are about to tell you must stay within the confines of this group." King Elder paused, walked back to his throne, and then continued. "Because you are human without magical capabilities you are not aware of how our magical world is controlled by Yggdrasil and governed with Mother Elder and the Efil Stone. This means that all peoples have different degrees of magical abilities. Only the Elders have telepathic ability unless granted to other beings. No one else may possess them without dire consequences." King Elder looked over to Ish and Mr Scruffy. KC had sat down beside Queen Esmé.

"I'm following you so far," KC thought, and King Elder, Queen Esmé, and Ish each nodded. It gave KC a slight sense of pride. She was communicating telepathically.

"When you first came into camp, our people did not know you were connected with Ish. They received confusing messages from you when they tried to read your mind. They kept hearing things about the Atcenians, and so they reasoned that you were working for Nukpana. Thus, they put a spell on you to put you to sleep, to keep you away from our people, and you out of danger. As the spell was cast, you must have realized something was wrong. You ran into the forest. Once you left the boundaries of our camp, our magic was weakened. Yet, enough of the spell was cast to put you in a confused state." King Elder stopped speaking and looked to KC.

She nodded, shifted her weight in her seat, and then asked, "Where are Yggdrasil, Mother Elder, and the Efil Stone kept?"

"Inside the sacred grove of Mushroom Alley, the Land of Promise."

"Can anyone see them?" KC was intrigued by what she thought of as the magic of the trees. If she was going to be here for a while, she felt she should learn as much about this world as was possible.

King Elder's description made KC's mind drift to her mother and her love of the old ways, Celtic myths, and Green man stories. She couldn't help to think about Kitty's love of trees coupled with her fierce desire to protect her and them.

She was seven, and all she wanted to do was play in the forest. It was her theatre. Each chance she had, she'd run to the woods. One afternoon, her mom left for the store.

"You can play outside, but do not go into the woods. Wait until I'm home."

KC watched her mother leave and ran to the edge of the forest. "I won't go in, I'll stand here," she said. "You tree spirits in there, you must come here to play with me." She peered between the tree trunks, looking for her imaginary friends.

No one came.

She stood there dejected. "Why won't you come and play with me?"

"We can't," a voice came like the sound of strings in harmony. "We were called away by the Creator, until we deliver whom he had made. The Alder trees lead us. We must fight the Battle of the Trees."

KC found herself inside the edge of the forest. She strained to hear the last words. Then, she heard the sound of a car. *Mom will kill me.*

Distressed, KC ran to the back door, stepped onto the back porch, sat on the wicker bench, and heard the screen door from the kitchen open. Mom was home.

She hoped, if given the chance to speak with Yggdrasil and Mother Elder, she would be able to share her Mother's love for trees. She also wished that maybe they would allow her to connect with Jack's spirit.

"Before your arrival we learned that the Efil Stone was missing. We believe Nukpana took it," Queen Esmé said standing up. She walked over to a portion of the wall that was carved ornately and draped with boughs. The carvings looked like coniferous trees. KC wondered if the Elderians used the branches and boughs of all trees or only certain ones in their art and decorations.

King Elder stared out into the open area of the crowd. "KC, we do use the boughs of all trees from Eldershire. We use those of the Wild Woods to protect our hallowed and most sacred artifacts."

I'm not getting used to the mental eavesdropping, KC thought.

"Queen Esmé points to the place where the Efil Stone once rested." King Elder looked to KC. She started to move closer. Ish telepathed to her, "Don't move." KC stopped mid-stride. King Elder continued. "You are seeing an image from our mind's eye. You can only go there when permitted."

Queen Esmé walked back toward King Elder, pausing at a cabinet. It was ornately carved of a material KC could not quite decide whether it was rock or petrified wood. The surface looked solid with markings like tree bark. Queen Esmé retrieved a book from within that was covered in similar carvings as the cabinet—vines, leaves, and serpents.

She brought the book to the side of the throne where King Elder sat and pushed a button on the chair's side. A flat surface swung away from the throne like a table attached to a chair for a laptop. KC giggled thinking how advanced the Elderians seemed to be. Back home, she had recently begun to see furniture with such a convenience. Queen Esmé placed the book on top of the table, laid her hand solemnly on top of the book, and then the book opened to a page marked by a silver chain that dangled down its side. On the end of the chain hung a silver ornament in the shape of a tree. She began to read.

Nukpana Fraener - an offspring of the descendants of Anzû, the Father of the Zû, one portion of Nukpana's family. Anzû was conceived by the pure waters of the Apsu and the wide Earth and was seen as a massive bird that could breathe fire and water.

Anzû coupled with Jezinka, a wicked wood nymph believed to be a descendant of Lilith. The demon Lilith, known to be a beautiful, yet evil, woman could transform into a blue, butterfly-like demon, a witch. She is associated with the power of seduction and passed this skill to Jezinka, who then mated with Anzû. The mating resulted in a form of Drakein. The Drakein is believed to be an ancestor of the Purple Dragon, which then gave way for the birth of Nukpana Fraener.

Queen Esmé solemnly closed the book, lifted it, pushed the button to retract the tabletop, and stood back. She turned her head slowly toward King Elder and waited. He looked to Queen Esmé, nodded, and she returned the book to its place in the ornate cabinet. She shut the cabinet, waved her hand over the door, and the sound of a locking mechanism moving into place echoed across the chamber. The door to the cabinet vanished away and morphed into the side of the rock wall. It was gone. KC noticed no one said a word and each one was impassive.

"As you heard Queen Esmé read from the Sacred Grimoire of Eldershire, this ancient text coupled with what you heard about the legend of how her evil has grown reveals that Nukpana Fraener is a force to be dealt with. You must understand Yggdrasil and Mother Elder foretold of your coming. They warned that Nukpana would terrorize our world until your arrival to save us from her."

"Save you? What do you mean, save you?"

"It means you are supposed to be here. In this time, in this place, it was foretold that a human would come to save us; a human would come to find the Efil Stone. That human is you. Your are the Chosen One. You will need to complete this quest before you can return to your home."

KC stood and walked away from the throne toward Ish, her mind fighting the urge to run. She paced back and forth, moving her arms up and down, arguing with herself.

Stopping her agitated worry, she looked to Ish and said with fear resonating in her voice, "This is impossible. I mean, why me? Why would anyone put their trust in me? They've made a mistake. I don't even know how I got here. Why would I come here? This is maddening." Her impatience was growing as she slumped down on the steps leading down from the throne.

"Regardless of your fear, you are here. You must understand this is *your* quest. You must find the Efil Stone. You must prevent Nukpana from taking over Eldershire. This will enable you to gain the positive life force required for you to return to your time and place. If you decide you cannot do it, then you will be stuck here for all eternity. Once we, the Elderians, have retrieved the Efil Stone, Mother Elder and Yggdrasil will be able to work their magic to transport you home."

KC stood up and walked up to Ish. "When you saved me, did you know?"

"No. I suspected, but I didn't know. The legend of a human saving us from Nukpana has been repeated for centuries. I'd never known a human before you landed in front of me like you did, so I figured you were the one."

"That's why you brought me here?"

"Yes."

Turning back to King Elder, KC asked pensively, "Suppose I were to take on this quest. What do I have to do?"

"You will need to search the Land of Eldershire using our information about Nukpana's powers. Through our scouts, we gathered some leads and clues to help you determine where she has placed the Efil Stone. We also realize that you will probably need to confront Nukpana in order to be able to return the Efil Stone to us intact. Not until you complete this task, will you be able to return home."

KC stood before them and shook her head in disbelief. "Who on Earth did I make so mad that this would happen to me?" She looked up, and then walked around, trying to figure out what to do. "Suppose all you say is true. I track down the Efil Stone. I don't even know how to hold a sword, let alone use one. How will I be able to defend myself against her? Magic?"

"Magic will only help you so far. Nukpana is a witch, too. Remember."

"Oh, this is just great. You expect me—a scared, old woman—to step in and battle Nukpana, the wicked-witch of the land. Really?" She made sure the sarcasm in her voice was evident. KC's trepidation began to mount. "I can't do this. I *won't* do this. Allow me to return home." She said with a strong, stern voice.

Queen Esmé left the throne room, and then came back in with a book. She said, "KC, would you tell me about your life on Earth before you came here? We've shared about our world. What is your world like?"

"I'm not sure how this will help." KC looked around the room and resigned herself to talking. "It is in many ways similar to yours, but of course, we are human where you are tree spirits and other beings. We have animals, some we cherish and raise as our own children, while others we hunt and destroy. There are evil humans and kind ones. Again, like it is here in Eldershire. We have a planet full of forests that we have allowed many to destroy large portions. Our climate is in turmoil and our resources seem to be limited, but we are a proud species and will fight to keep what we believe should be ours, sometimes at the determent of others—human and animal. Is that what you wanted to hear?"

"Yes. And you said something important. You said you would fight to keep what you believe should be yours. Do you think we are not doing the same thing?"

KC noticed Mr Scruffy was no longer in the room. She looked to King Elder and made a quick decision. "I've decided that I must stay neutral. I cannot take on *your* fight. I do not have fight in me."

She paced back and forth. She wrung her hands. She stopped and said, "You don't understand. If you put your faith in me, you might as well pack up and leave, because I'll fail. I always fail. I can't help anyone. And, this you must understand," she paused. "No matter what, I'll be leaving Eldershire tonight."

KC turned and flounced out of the throne room. Passing through the threshold, she noticed her mind was less crowded. She continued on to the thípi she was told would be hers. She sat on the cot and put her head in her hands. *What am I going to do?*

Mr Scruffy walked in through the opening of the thípi. KC looked up and started to speak. He moved his wing up to his beak and telepathed, "I want to take you somewhere with me. Are you willing to go?"

She was startled that Mr Scruffy could still talk with her telepathically. She tried to speak back, but nothing seemed to work. She nodded. He motioned for her to follow. They walked out across the center of the camp, through a patch of trees, and into another clearing.

"Don't be alarmed about what I'm about to do. Stand still and don't be afraid or you'll send signals to everyone and they will know what I'm doing. Okay?"

"Sure. But—" KC suddenly felt a sharp pain in her hand. Mr Scruffy had bitten her. She saw blood. She looked to him questioning his move.

"I've injected you with my special saliva. It will allow you to speak to me telepathically without me having to control your voice. You will hear my voice and we can talk while we're on our journey."

"What journey?"

"Are you willing to trust me again?"

"Yes. But, I'm feeling a little funny right now."

"I know. It is my saliva moving into your veins. The magic of the elixir mixed in my saliva will course through your blood and will be a permanent imprint. You will always be able to hear me no matter how far away we are from each other—even if you return to your world. There is a saying in the land of owls. It goes something like this—as long as the tree is in the ground, and the owl flies, do I pledge to you true friendship. I make that pledge to you now."

"I don't know what to say." KC started to continue. She paused, and then said, "Oh, man. I'm speaking to you through my mind."

"Use it wisely and it will save your life, and if I'm lucky, mine too." Mr Scruffy appeared to smile.

"This is exciting! I'm a friend with an owl and we can talk to each other telepathically. No one back home will ever believe me."

The owl's eyes widened large. "Careful. You can talk too loud telepathically too. Keep the old voice down. Now, stand back. I've got a spell to cast. Don't scream and don't be afraid. This is all natural for me."

KC stood back and waited.

She noticed Mr Scruffy's feathers begin to shake. He stood off to the left and leaned forward. He began to grow. He grew to the size of a large horse, a Shire. She couldn't believe how beautiful he appeared. When he had stopped growing, the top of his left wing was level with her head. He was over eight feet tall.

"Climb on my back. We're going to fly."

KC looked around for a way to climb, when Mr Scruffy moved his wing down. She stepped upon it and he lifted her up. It was natural sitting there. She couldn't see over the treetops, but she could see a far distance.

"Grab a hold of my top feathers. Don't worry, you won't pull them out; I'm going to lift off. Relax."

They soared up into the air making a slow loop, climbing above the treetops. KC, in awe, tried to take it all in and let her fear fly in the wind. It was magical and exhilarating. She had never been so free. They flew out over the treetops. A river was in the distance.

Eldershire looked like a virgin land, undisturbed. There were dark forests on each side of the river that went for miles.

Mr Scruffy telepathed to KC key points while he swooped, dove, and caught the thermal uplift. It was like looking at a map of Eldershire when he pointed out the Wild Woods, Stone's River, Grave's Mountain to the East, and Emerald Mountain to the South. In the valley below Emerald Mountain, he pointed out the Atcenian Hills, Iolair's Bluff, where she had landed in the brier patch. Then, he instructed her to look northwest toward Mushroom Alley and Lady Lake.

They flew over King Elder's camp, which was located in what looked like the north edge of the Wild Woods. It protected the camp from attack with the Red Bluffs Divide to the East. The bluffs ran through Stone's River on two sides, due to the river bending around the outer edges of the Wild Woods in a horseshoe fashion. On the East side, KC saw a waterfall Mr Scruffy called Falling Water Falls. At its base was a series of rapids that made white caps as the water rushed along and drained into Moth Lake. Next, Mr Scruffy pointed out Snow Valley at the base of Grave's Mountain.

They made a sweeping turn on the thermal and headed due west. Mr Scruffy said, "This small river is called Reed Creek, which flows into a large, beautiful lake named Lake Lady. It gives off an air of beauty."

At the apex of the bend of Reed Creek appeared a marking that resembled a pathway lined with tall, majestic-like mushroom trees.

Mr Scruffy telepathed, "It is called Mushroom Alley. It leads to a sacrosanct plateau of our kingdom, The Land of Promise." He turned sharply toward the east.

Following along the river that spanned to the horizon, there was a large mountain in the distance. KC asked, "Is that Grave's Mountain ahead?"

"Yes. We are coming in from a different point of view. See down below, the forest that goes right up to the edge? That is a sacred place for many wild animals of Eldershire."

"From this angle, it looks like Grave's Mountain stands out three times larger than the others." She turned back and looked toward the south where she saw towering above the low-lying hills another majestic mountain. "I think I'm beginning to know Eldershire. That's Emerald Mountain, back there?"

"Yes, it is. They are the two largest mountains in Eldershire."

In the distance, KC could see numberless mountain ranges that rose with intervening heights—some rugged and precipitous, others clothed with trees and other forms of vegetation. "The Land of Eldershire is beautiful," she said telepathically.

"I'm honored you think so. I've always enjoyed visiting your Appalachian Mountains," Mr Scruffy replied.

"What? You've been to my mountains?"

"Of course."

"May I ask why?"

"Yes. One day I'll share. For now, enjoy the ride."

KC looked out over the panoramic view before her. She saw a few smaller waterfalls, springs, and brooks leading into Stone's River. She was enjoying her ride and didn't want to interrupt it with more questions. She wished she could share this moment with Jack and Bill. They would have loved it.

Mr Scruffy turned slowly in a sweeping arc. Below them was a deep valley with a narrow gorge penetrating into the hills. To the West was a prairie extending as far as the eye could see. The prairies seemed to empty into nothing but sky. Every now and then, KC caught a glimpse of a strange looking tree that populated one area of the prairie edge. If she didn't know better, it looked to her as though the tops of the trees were large Portobello mushrooms.

"Are you enjoying this?" Mr Scruffy asked.

"Yes. I can't believe we're flying. Is all of this Eldershire? And what are those trees over there?" KC pointed.

"It is beautiful. The trees you pointed to are mushroom trees. I'll tell you about the Land of Promise later. You can now say you've seen an 'owl's' view of Eldershire." KC laughed at the thought of an owl's view. She heard Mr Scruffy laughing, too. It sounded like he was saying, 'Woot! Woot!' mixed with a giggle. It made her laugh harder.

"We've flown through here before. Do you recognize that mountain there?"

"It is Emerald Mountain, right?"

"Yes. I'm going to turn. Hang on."

As they turned, KC leaned in closer to Mr Scruffy. Her fear of where she was and what she was doing had slipped away. She could get used to traveling this way.

They flew in the direction of Grave's Mountain. "Why is Grave's Mountain so barren?" KC asked.

"It is an evil place. It is where Nukpana lives when she is in Purple Drakein form."

"And, Emerald Mountain, why is it so green?"

"It is where she lives when in witch form. Ish told you the hills at the base of that mountain are called the Atcenian Hills." Mr Scruffy flew out over the mountain range; KC looked out over Eldershire and pondered the last few days. She had learned much from Ish, King Elder, Queen Esmé, and now Mr Scruffy. Could she stay here? Would pursuing the Efil Stone be something she could do?

They took a large sweeping turn to the right. "The two-suns are starting to rise. We must return before Ish notices we left. Hold on for our landing."

Mr Scruffy set down gently in the clearing where they lifted off. KC slipped off Mr Scruffy's back. He reduced to his normal size and flew up, landing on KC's shoulder. "Do you mind?"

"Not at all, my friend. What a journey that was! Thank you. The past couple of days, I was under the canopy of the Wild Woods. I had no idea of the beauty."

"While you are here in this clearing, you should take time to watch the simultaneous setting of the two-moons and rise of the two-suns. It is spectacular and very different having two to view compared to your one on Earth."

"Eldershire is an amazing world. I marvel at what I've seen. Thank you for taking me on this journey."

"I'm glad you enjoyed it. We'll have to do it again. You have seen why we are desperate to save Eldershire from Nukpana. She wants to destroy it."

"Why? It is her home also."

"A good question. Why does anyone want to destroy where they live? But, creatures do. I fear it is because she is hedonistic—cold, calculating, and half-mad coupled with being unpredictable. Why is she like that? From what I've observed, she was born that way. A bad seed, many before me have said. She must be stopped before she destroys Eldershire."

"I do not know that I can. My fear is my fear of failure. What then?"

"How can you fail at something if you don't try? Why fear the unknown? Each day of life is a new chance, a new beginning, a new unknown. Life with Nukpana is certain—it is death. May I ask you something?" KC nodded. "Did you have monsters you feared when you were a little girl?"

"Yes. Especially at night."

"When I was an owlet, me too. And, keep in mind I'm nocturnal.

But, dark shadows cast large fears. Facing fear, facing monsters is what we must do."

"That's not me."

"Not now. But, with me, and Ish at your side, and others helping, you'll become what you need to be. You are indispensable if Eldershire is to survive. We need your help right now. No one else can be you. No one else can save Eldershire."

KC bowed her head.

"It's true. You are the Chosen One. You were brought here for a purpose."

"By whom?"

"That, I can't say. I don't know. Powers far greater than me are at work. Allow the magic to be. It is hoped you will be able to make your decision." Mr Scruffy flew off her shoulder.

KC turned and saw Ish standing along the edge of the trees. "I think Ish knows. He is over there."

CHAPTER 7
MOTHER ELDER

I sh moved up beside KC. She looked at him. He smiled. "Did you have a good flight?"

"Yes. Yes, I did. It was miraculous. I've never done anything like that before. It was so exhilarating. I would love to be able to do that all the time."

Mr Scruffy walked over to them. "Remember, I do fly all the time. Let me tell you, it is not always fun. You are a target for many creatures in the sky."

"Oh, my. I didn't think about that. How were we safe this time?"

"I put a spell on us."

"The magic that evidently abounds in this place is wondrous. I'll never learn about it all. Eldershire gives me a deep appreciation for nature in its glory." KC looked toward Ish. He was silent. "Ish? You're not saying much. Aren't you happy for me? I had a wonderful flight with Mr Scruffy."

"I know you did. Did you know that King Elder also knows you took flight? He's not happy. He wants you to join him in his thípi. We should go. It seems Mr Scruffy has taken you under his wing." Ish turned and walked toward the camp area.

Mr Scruffy spoke telepathically to KC, "He is a wee bit put out with me, I fear. You behave now. Don't mention about me giving you the gift."

KC looked down at her hand and noticed where Mr Scruffy had bitten her that there now was an outlined image of an owl—a tattoo of sorts. "What happened here?"

"A gift of our unity." Mr Scruffy winked; at least that's what KC thought he did.

❧

KC WALKED into King Elder's thípi. When she stepped through the threshold, the room transformed into the Throne Room.

"My new eyesight keeps surprising me. I am in awe at how your rooms just materialize out of what appears to be nothing."

Ish stood off to one side. KC smiled. He did not return the gesture. She looked toward King Elder. He gave her a look of reproach.

"Okay. I get it. What have I done that is so wrong?" she asked telepathically.

"Don't you realize Nukpana is at the ready to destroy you? You taking flight only did one thing. It let her know exactly where you are. And, in so doing, you let her know where we are," King Elder said.

"How is that my fault? You entrusted me with Mr Scruffy. What did you expect an owl to do? Besides, you have magic. Why don't you cast a spell so she can't find you?" KC said aloud, not trying to hide her frustration whilst she paced the floor.

"If you must insist on speaking aloud, fine. And, for what it is worth, we have protected our lands. Which, by the way, is beside the point.

We gave you time to think over what we had to offer to help you return home."

"Mr Scruffy did you a monumental favor taking me on that flight. Don't you realize how close to walking away from the quest I was? Do you not know what a millstone you placed on me? Why are you so angry with me for doing exactly what you needed me to do? I had to learn about Eldershire. I had to know for what I was fighting and why I should fight for you. Mr Scruffy made that possible. He didn't just talk; he showed me. You are supposed to be such wise beings. You clearly don't understand how a human thinks or what one needs to make a decision."

"Are you ready to make your decision? Are you going to go on the quest to return the Efil Stone?"

Ish left the room. KC turned to King Elder. "Is there no other way for me to return home?"

"The only recourse is for you to see Mother Elder. You will learn what you need from her." King Elder got up and walked out.

KC WAS LYING on her cot when Ish and Mr Scruffy came in.

"Well, you found out how to have a leisurely day after all," Ish said as he slumped down on the floor.

KC swung her legs around to the edge of her cot. "Gees, Ish, what's wrong with you?"

Ish got up. "Mr Scruffy. I can't do this. I'll be outside." He stormed out leaving KC confused.

"If I didn't know any better, I swear I would think he was Jay-H reincarnated. Gees. I can't make a decision yet. King Elder said I had to visit Mother Elder."

"We know. He put Ish and me in charge of your well-being. Ish is perturbed because he is having to spend time with you and he's not able to be with Princess Derryth."

"Princess Derryth?"

"You've not met her yet. She's seen you. Several times. She is the daughter of King Elder and Queen Esmé. There are times she wears her royalty too proudly. Ish is in love with her. And, to add insult to injury, as your people like to say, Princess Derryth thinks Ish has fallen for you. Isn't that funny?" Mr Scruffy laughs with an owl hoot.

KC winked at Mr Scruffy. "As I learn, as I read, as I watch the world around me, I am forever changing. Interesting. I think I'll need to talk with Princess Derryth at some point. Ish is but a mere boy." KC said.

"You're kidding, right?"

"Why do you ask?"

"Ish is probably six hundred years old in your Earth time. And, you speaking to Princess Derryth may not happen before the end of time. She chooses whom she speaks with, not the other way around."

"What? Ish is six hundred years old? Really? He doesn't look a day over sixteen." KC shook her head. "The water here in Eldershire must be really good. This Princess is something to contend with it sounds like. Should I be worried?"

"No, but I wouldn't expect her to be overtly kind to you. I'd expect the opposite."

Noticing a feather lying on her cot, KC reached for it, and then said, "Where did this come from?"

"It was mine. I thought it might give you comfort for me to be near. You can leave it here. It will be here when you return."

KC placed it at the head of her cot. "I guess I'm delaying the inevitable. Are you ready to take me to see Mother Elder?"

"Yes."

"Will Ish go with us?"

"I think so. He said he would do his duty."

"He is a loyal soldier. I respect that."

"Let's go see Mother Elder. Ish will be happy as long as we get back before dark."

MR SCRUFFY TOUCHED down lightly to the land. Ish and KC slid off of his back.

"That is the only way to travel," KC said as she patted Mr Scruffy. He reduced in size. "Where do we go from here?"

"Aren't you just the happy hero?" Ish said. He started walking up the path in front of them.

KC grabbed him by the shoulder and spun him around. "That's it." She stomped her foot. "I've had enough. You were all happy to help me get to King Elder's camp. But, now that I need *your* help, you act as though I'm causing you great pain. What about me? I don't know what I'm doing here or even why. At least you live here."

"Look. You are the Chosen One. I get that. I don't like it. You don't even know how to use a bow or a sword. How are you going to face Nukpana?"

"You don't think I've thought about that? I'm scared to death. I don't want this. Can you get me home?"

"Ish, what are you doing?" Mr Scruffy said. He stepped in between KC and Ish.

Ish looked down at Mr Scruffy.

KC said, "He's a fool. You wait here. I don't need you with me. Come on, Mr Scruffy. Where do we go?"

"Follow me." Mr Scruffy led the way up the path to Mother Elder's.

❧

REACHING the top of the summit, KC looked around. The top of the mountain was vast. It appeared to KC to be at least the size of four football fields stretching out before her level with the outer edges trimmed with trees. When KC looked behind her, all she could see was blue sky. She saw that the stairs they had just climbed dropped steeply and were hidden from view.

Looking back to the plateau, in the very center stood one large, majestic elder tree that was as tall as it was wide. KC stared up at it in reverence. Mr Scruffy's wing touched her hand.

"Oh, sorry. This is amazing. I don't remember seeing this mountain from our flight."

"That's because you didn't."

"Why?"

"It is hidden. You've heard of Brigadoon, right?"

KC nodded. "It's a mysterious town that only comes into view every one hundred years."

"The Land of Promise is sort of like that, but more magical, if you can imagine. You can only find it when Mother Elder or Yggdrasil allow it."

"The Land of Promise?"

"Yes. This is their home. Come. Mother Elder awaits."

KC stepped forward and just as her back foot came forward, the scene before her changed. She was standing in a great hall, more majestic and stunning than anything she had seen or imagined before. At the far end of the hall, KC saw a stunning woman walking toward her. She was tall, with long flowing hair, and she wore an elegant gown that shimmered in the rays of sunlight that entwined her with each step. KC watched her walk and knew she was in the presence of greatness, yet she felt love and compassion enveloping her.

"Show respect, KC. Bow," Mr Scruffy telepathed.

"Oh, my. Yes." KC bent at her waist and held her face so she could watch the lady walking toward her. KC couldn't take her eyes off the woman's eyes. They were mesmerizing. The woman's beauty paralyzed her.

"Thank you, Mr Scruffy," the lady said. "You may rise."

"Mother Elder, may I present to you—"

"Kay Carson. So very pleased to meet you. Come. Let's go sit near one of my saplings." Mother Elder pointed to an area with small trees in a line along a long bench with an ornately carved table. KC wondered why the furniture would be made of wood. It was after all her kin.

"That's an excellent question." KC was startled and embarrassed. "No matter, I can read your thoughts. The wood used in these pieces was donated by my forefathers, years before we lived as we do now. You will find they are still a life form living here. You learned from King Elder and Queen Esmé, my children, how we carry forward our spirits from form to form. I must explain how Yggdrasil and I are joined. But, before I do, let me offer you some Elder wine." Mother Elder motioned her hand and a young tree maiden brought a tray with cups.

"Allow me to share with you some of the finest wine you will ever enjoy." Mother Elder handed a cup to KC and Mr Scruffy.

KC did not know she was thirsty. She eagerly took the cup to take a sip. Mother Elder touched her hand and gently pushed her hand down.

"You should wait," Mr Scruffy said.

KC blushed. "I'm sorry."

Mother Elder smiled. "Open your mind to *beauty* of thought...the face in front of the mind will reflect that beauty." She held up her cup, and then they sipped.

The mood of the room was warmed with hues of blue dancing in KC's mind. She noticed she was swaying to a soft tune playing in her mind. "What is that tune? I know it."

"It's Cat Steven's, *Wild World*." Mother Elder said. She leaned toward KC and whispered, "I will tell you more about my love of Earth music later."

"That would be nice to hear." KC sipped more of the wine. It had a semi-dry taste with an aroma that included herbs and flowers and a touch of chocolate. The complexities made KC think of the forest. She wanted to ask where she could find such a wine, but thought better of it.

Mother Elder set her cup down and said, "I do need to speak with you regarding several things, but first, let me share more about my connection with Yggdrasil. King Elder told you that Yggdrasil is called The Tree of Life. This holiest of beings is an ash tree, the central force that connects and holds the life of Eldershire. It bounds as well as connects all other forms of the cosmos, including Earth and other planets. The branches of Yggdrasil extend far into the heavens and its three main roots extend far away connecting to many sacred trees and groves. Do you grasp the power of our connection?"

"I believe so. How are the two of you connected?"

"Yggdrasil and I are connected through the Efil Stone. We are two different species of wood—elder and ash—yet we are joined. Our joining forms a third kind of wood with great power. This power is in the Efil Stone."

"Power. I'm not sure I understand."

"You were in the brier patch when the Atcenians were seeking you, yes?" KC nodded. "The brier patch was made of elder. It protected you from them and any other evil lurking around. When elder and ash are joined, the magic is far greater. It reaches into the cosmos."

Mother Elder lifted a flap on her gown above where a heart is generally located in a human. KC saw a huge scar, similar to what is seen on the bark of a tree when it has been damaged. It was large, irregular in shape, and bumpy.

KC winced, "Does it hurt?"

"It does now—now that the Efil Stone is missing. As you've been told, part of the Efil Stone was made from my essence. You would call it your heart. The same with Yggdrasil. This throbs now since I know it is in the hands of Nukpana." At the mention of her name, a deep red glow emerged from the center of the scar. Mother Elder lowered the flap. "It hurts worse when her name is spoken."

Mother Elder's words made KC think about a book series she'd read a few years ago where an evil character brought fear each time the character's name was spoken. Jay-H always got mad whenever she read, never more so than when she was reading that book series.

"Why are you so mad at me Jay-H? I'm only reading a novel."

"You are right. You're reading again and not tending to my needs. When will dinner be prepared?"

"We've got several frozen dinners in the freezer. Why don't you fix something for the two of us?"

"I'm not your work horse."

"That's rich coming from you. And, by default, that means I am to be your servant, at your beck and call. Is that what you're saying?" Jay-H shrugged his shoulders. "I can't believe I fell in love and married you. It seems you only care for yourself. You don't even seem to care for Bill. You won't let him call you 'Dad.'"

"He's growing up. He needs to know how to stand on his two feet. He doesn't need me as his dad."

"He is your son."

"No. He's Jack's son. I just happen to pay all the bills."

"Jay-H, why are you so cruel sometimes? There are times you make me laugh and you are fun to be with, but not now."

"You get what you pay for."

KC's mind left that memory as she looked at Mother Elder, and then down at her hand—her wedding band was not on it. She hadn't worn it since the night Jay-H died. She didn't cry for him. She thought about how evil he was and how evil she felt in not missing him after he died.

"I won't call the evil-witch's name in your presence again."

"Evil? I'm not sure you've encountered evil yet in your young life."

"Young life? You do realize I'm really older at home than here?"

"Yes. But, you need to understand that I'm several thousand years old. I've seen a lot of evil in my life."

KC looked into Mother Elder's eyes. Wisdom emitted from her soul. She knew Mother Elder was aware of all things. The realization brought tears to her eyes.

"You know my true thoughts, don't you?"

"Yes, my dear. Your desire to return home to Bill, Marie, and your first husband, Jack, even though they have passed, is a noble one. Your desire to change the past is a goal many never see to completion. You will, my dear. You will if you rely on your life's experiences, your instincts, and listen to Mr Scruffy and Ish when you accept this quest to find the Efil Stone. Yggdrasil and I will aid you. The road is not easy. Nukpana will see to your death before she relinquishes her new power."

KC deliberated about what to do. She couldn't fight such a powerful being. How could they possibly think she could? She didn't know how to wield a sword, let alone how to kill someone out right. Sure, she'd killed her family, but it was an accident. She stood up, walked to a nearby sapling, and looked out over Eldershire.

"Mother Elder, I can't. I don't have it in me. You can't possibly believe I'll be able to do this. How can I? I'm not a warrior. I'm an accidental killer. No great feat there."

"Come here, child. Sit here before me. I'm going to show you what you need to know. You must believe."

KC sat on a cushion before Mother Elder with her legs in a lotus like fashion. She had sat that way often in high school; it seemed natural to do so now.

Mother Elder began to chant. KC settled into a meditative state. She opened one eye and saw Mother Elder in deep thought. She settled back into the moment and tried to relax.

While Mother Elder helped KC deepen her meditation, KC thought about the decision to stay or leave. She saw herself wielding a sword, fighting off Atcenians with Mr Scruffy and Ish at her side. Just as she came to grips with the idea of retrieving the Efil Stone, Nukpana appeared.

Speaking softly and directly to KC, Nukpana said, *I will destroy Eldershire and your companions—Ish and Mr Scruffy. Make no mistake. I will rule over you here as I have before.*

KC angered and troubled by Nukpana's ability to enter her mind, jerked herself out of the meditative state.

"Mother Elder!"

"I'm here. You felt the evil power of Nukpana. She doesn't want you to remain. She hopes you will leave and not pursue the Efil

Stone. She knows the foretelling of your arrival and she fears you. Don't let her chase you away. Your magic is part of your soul. You must, however, make the choice to return the Efil Stone to its rightful place. You must choose wisely—if you stay, you might be able to change your past. By coming into your meditative state, Nukpana confirms she has the Efil Stone. By your staying, your past may change and in the process, you *will* save Eldershire. If you don't stay, Eldershire will perish. It is not fully understood what you would find when you return home."

KC stared into the vastness of the plateau. Mr Scruffy flew into the room, landing not far from her. He walked over to where Mother Elder and KC sat in the circle. He sat down beside KC. Touched by his loyalty, KC wondered what he knew or even heard during her talk with Mother Elder.

"Nothing." He telepathed. "You're scared. You're struggling with your choice. Neither choice is appealing."

Mr Scruffy spoke matter-of-factly aloud, "If you die here, you know you will be dying while trying to help someone other than yourself. Something, even though you were doing it, you felt you did not do when your family died. If given the chance, would you change your mind about stopping to help that stranded driver if it meant your family would be saved?" Mr Scruffy doesn't give KC a chance to answer. "Yes, you would make the choice to change the outcome. You would do something that would help the driver and save your family. You must think of your choice to stay here and take on the quest to find the Efil Stone in the same way. When you choose to stay, you choose to help save Eldershire—your new family. The bonus is you will be able to return to your home world. If all goes well, your Earth family will be saved too. What have you got to lose?"

KC stretched her legs, stood up, and walked back to the sapling and leaned upon it. She looked out over the land of Eldershire. In the distance she saw Grave's Mountain, in the opposite direction Emerald Mountain cast its shadow over Stone's River. A cold chill ran down her back. Her decision made, she turned back to Mother Elder.

"Now what?"

"Bring them in," Mother Elder said without turning her head. "Over the next few weeks, you will be involved in learning how to fight with a sword. You will be instructed in more magical skills that you will need when you face Nukpana."

The red glow seemed to grow stronger as it shown through Mother Elder's gown. Mr Scruffy flew upon KC's shoulder. "When the four Snowquidians arrive, don't be uneasy, and try not to reveal your surprise. They are sensitive about their differences—looking like snowmen."

CHAPTER 8
THE FOUR SNOWMEN

The four Snowquidians appeared one at a time, popping into view, reminding KC of the magical fairies in a Disney movie. She giggled. Seeing the look on Mother Elder's face, KC moved her hand up to her lips and said, "I'm sorry."

"Open your mind to the *beauty* of thought...the face in front of the mind will reflect that beauty," Mother Elder said. "Don't let the fact they are Snowquidians, which look like snowmen from your world, fool you. This group is formidable. They live in the land of Snowboro, farther North of here. It is important for you to know that the Four Snowmen is one of the most exalted fighting units in the whole of Snowboro—dare, I say, all of Eldershire. The first I present to you is Seif."

Seif bowed.

"Glad to meet you, Seif," KC curtsied. She noticed he had a round bottom, a narrower bodice, and a perfectly round head. He wore a black top hat. In his mouth he held a corncob pipe, a red scarf was wrapped around his neck, and he wore a tight-fitting patchwork vest. Seif's right arm stuck out to the side, and he held a lantern in his hand. His left hand rested on his hip as though he was in charge.

"This is Foursure," Mother Elder said, as Foursure stepped forward. It appeared his body wiggled together as though he were clicking his heels, which he did not have. Foursure was markedly different from Seif. His top hat had a broader rim, draped in snow with specks of sparkle dust. His mouth was made of five coals shaped in a smile; his eyes black and shiny, gave an air of inquisitiveness. Both arms were out stretched as though in welcome, and large blue mittens on his hands sparkled with blue dust. A red plaid scarf wrapped around his neck and draped down his slender Snowquid body. At his feet were packages, a football, and another lone mitten. KC wished she could talk to him. He looked jolly.

Next, KC saw a striking Snowquid that reminded her of her grandmother. "This is Mylo," Mother Elder said. Mylo nodded her head as she held her stick arms out as though she could grab KC and hug her close. She wore a blue bonnet tied snugly around her beaming face marked with a broad and happy smile. Her nose was a large orange carrot bent upwards. She had on a red flowing shirt that seemed to have a life of its own as it bellowed and moved. At her feet were hollies with red berries and a bucket of something KC couldn't quite make out. Mylo's overall appearance was one that caused KC to want to know more about her.

"And, last, but not least, this is Sam Slavetomé. For ease of discussion, we just call him Sam. I'll leave it to Sam to share the meaning of his name at a later time." Mother Elder stepped back to reveal Sam.

He had been standing slightly behind the others. The second KC saw him she knew he was special. He had that special kind of look. Like Mylo, his nose was made of a carrot that was longer than the others and bent upward. His mouth was made of seven pieces of coal that were formed into a large smile. He wore two scarfs — one a green plaid that wrapped around his neck cozily and one that was a blue, white, and yellow woven scarf that draped around him like a shawl. His hat was large, battered, and brown, more like an old farmer's hat. And, like Mylo, he had stick arms, but Sam's were in the form of tree branches. He also had four distinct shapes to his

Snowquid body with four large black coal buttons making their way down the front.

"Before the Four Snowmen begin your training, you need to know their value to us. Each represents the spirit of four of our ancestors from the six kingdoms of beings in the cosmos—plants, animals, protists, & fungi. The other two—bacteria of Arche and Eu ancestors are The Twins, which are only called upon in dire straits. We leave The Twins alone to thrive and multiply as necessary for the completion of life here in Eldershire." Mother Elder walked over to the Four Snowmen and pointed to each as she spoke. "Each will explain their relationship with faith, hope, love, and luck woven with their understanding of righteousness, justice, war, and death. They will instruct you in the art of war, sword fighting, and other magical skills that you will need to fight Nukpana and the Grey Menace, her odious army."

"Glad to meet each of you," KC said as she offered her hand. In turn, each of the Four Snowmen instantly appeared before her, shook her hand, and stepped back in line. KC looked them over and speculated about what she would be able to do after their training.

"You'll learn a great deal, dearie," Seif said. "I may be a Snowquid, I may be old, but I have strong mind power. My connections are in having faith, the reality of death, and the kingdom of Fungi. If you learn from me how to control your thoughts, have faith, not fear death, and recognize the capacity of fungi, overcoming the dark, you will have power over Nukpana that no one can fathom."

"Oh, I didn't realize…"

"That we could read your mind too," Mylo said stepping next to KC. "While Seif has the power of mind, I control the power of sense, share the value of hope and need for righteousness with the keen sense of animals. From me, you will learn how to use your senses to their full potential. A strength you will need against the Grey Menace and to fool Nukpana."

Sam stepped forward next and pulled a feather from his pocket, handed it to KC, and said, "Opinion is important on many levels when you battle an evil, such as Nukpana. And, you need luck and justice to help you in your quest. The kingdom of Protists is at my soul; having strength when least expected. But being green with envy can also cause your opinion to sway. You must believe in what you think is right for Eldershire in order to rule over Eldershire. We trust our opinion over blatant lies. We fight the lies of those who do not know what is best for us. This is a necessary skill in order to fight tyranny and the unjust."

KC looked at the feather, recognizing it as the feather Mr Scruffy had given her. She started to speak when Foursure walked over and took the feather from her hand. He turned around and looked at the other three. "We all know the value of our mind, our senses, and our opinion, but we must include science coupled with love to help us know when one of them go astray. The science we know and understand of this feather I hold here tells us how animals, such as Mr Scruffy, fly. Flight for you in your world is only possible through mechanical means, but it follows the same science as we must follow here. Plants, the kingdom I embody, also have the power of flight through the movement of their leaves and their seeds. Yet, war is also part of the cosmos. There is a time for war that we must be mindful. All four of us will give you what you need to help you know how to use the magic we teach you with good effect."

"Are we ready to begin?" Mr Scruffy said stepping forward. "We don't have much time left."

"By all means. I'll leave you to your work, Mr Scruffy. The Four Snowmen are ready when you are. You might explain to KC what she will be doing." Mother Elder was gone with her last word echoing in the air.

KC placed Mr Scruffy on her shoulder.

"Thank you, KC. This helps me see the Four Snowmen easier while I point out what we will do. Ah, Ish, there you are." KC turned to see Ish walking toward them.

"So, we ready to do this?" Ish said putting down two quivers filled with arrows and two bows.

AFTER MUCH TIME and even more effort, KC was worn out. They had worked her hard. She stopped in the middle of wielding a sword with Seif, wiped her brow, and looked at the others.

"Is there any way we can stop? I've jumped around, dodged, and twirled to the point that I'm starting to think I see myself charging at me. I'm not sure how much longer I can continue."

Seif said, "You've learned well. We've covered a lot of ground in a short time. Most swordsmen and bowmen learn their craft over years. You've had to learn how to hold a sword and how to pull a bow, use your feet properly, and how to maneuver without hurting yourself. You've done well." KC smiled.

"You were quick to pick up your footwork so well," Foursure said. "You are light on your feet and that is important when wielding a sword in the heat of battle. How did you learn to move your feet so quickly?"

"I was a dancer when I was young. I guess I never lost my feel for the quick step." KC held up the sword she was working with. "Will this be my sword to use?"

Seif said, "For now. There will be the proper time when the right sword will join with your hand. A sword carries its own special magic. With the right sword in your hand, you can inflict multiple, fatal wounds. The sword will always return to its rightful owner. That is the law of the art of the sword."

"I had no idea that swords were magical."

"Magic plays a role in many aspects of life. You are familiar with the legends of Merlin and Excalibur?" Sam said.

"Yes. I've read and heard many stories about Merlin. And, who could forget the many movies and stories about King Arthur, the round table, and Excalibur?" KC mused.

"This is more serious in the sense that Merlin and Excalibur are real. Most people of your world consider the sword a symbol of war —death, destruction, and victory. The sword is actually a power of the user, as Excalibur was the manifestation of Merlin. When you receive your sword, and you will know when it happens, it too will be a manifestation of you." Foursure said and stood next to Mr Scruffy.

Mr Scruffy said, "You've been going strong for about three weeks' worth of your Earth time. You've learned a lot about the sword, bow and arrow, and how to use them against a single foe or a group of them. The basics of magic are slowly being revealed to you, as you need to know them. But, you haven't practiced the maneuvers in flight."

"Three weeks? You mean three hours, don't you? And, flight? Of course, I've not done flight." KC giggled. "Mr Scruffy, you can be so funny."

"No, I mean three weeks. We cast a spell to enhance your learning time. We didn't have time to tarry here. You've learned in three hours what would take most humans three weeks. You've still got a lot to learn, but you'll have to learn it on the job. What we need to do now is take you to the air where you can practice your sword work and archery while in flight."

"Oh, I see. So, just out of curiosity, what magic did I learn? How to be hit with it and not know it? Am I going to crash and burn when this spell wears off? A lot of good that will do me." KC walked over to Mylo and retrieved a pouch of water. She gulped it down, and then splashed it on her face.

"KC, you must be reasonable," Ish said taking the pouch from her hands. "Besides, if you keep drinking from this pouch, you will extend the power of the spell." He sat the pouch down beside Sam who had a large smile on his face. "You do understand; we had to do something to speed up the process of your learning. Nukpana could strike at any moment through any means, through anyone. We don't know whom she has won over. We don't know when she'll strike."

"I understand. Do you mind if I sit here for a bit? I'd like to just be quiet for a bit."

"Not at all," Foursure said. "While you relax, we'll clean up the weapons. Mylo, why don't you visit with KC and see she doesn't fall off her seat from falling to sleep. She is starting to come down out of the spell."

Mylo walked over to where KC stood. "Here, let's go sit over there on those benches." Mylo lead the way and KC followed.

"Do you mind if I ask you some questions, Mylo?"

"No. I'm not sure I can answer, but I'll try my best."

"As my Mother always said, 'that is the best you can do.' So, here's the first one. I wanted to ask Mother Elder this, but I didn't feel it my place. What is her connection with humans and Earth? She seemed so knowledgeable about everything, even our music."

"Now that is a hard question. I don't know everything, but I can tell you many have talked about the fact she is old enough to have been one of the ancients that lived on Earth. If she was, she still has a connection there through the tree root network. I imagine that is how she knows about life as it is on Earth now."

KC contemplated what she heard. "That does make sense. More than what I was thinking. Now, how about only being able to drink water from Stone's River during the day. What gives with that?"

"Oh, that's simple. It is so you won't get killed or stolen away."

"What?"

"Yes. Many Elderians have up and disappeared when they went to

Stone's River to get water. It is something you never do at night and you most certainly don't do it alone."

"Well, I'll be. I wonder why no one ever told me about that?"

"Maybe they figured it might worry you. You are an independent little cuss, you know." Mylo laughed.

KC said, "I guess so," and she joined in laughing.

"Got any more? So far, it seems I'm doing pretty good."

"Yes. You are. I don't want to be rude, but I'm enjoying speaking with a Snowquid. I've never done that before."

"You do realize, I'm actually female, don't you?"

"To be honest, I didn't know. Your name is a male name in my part of the universe."

"Yes, but it is my nickname. My real name is Myloanna. Sam calls me Mylo. He has for years."

"We're all finished cleaning up here. You didn't have to worry about helping us," Sam called.

"You got me. I'm tired. I'm more tired, evidently than I realized. I want to go back home. But, I'll have to settle for going to my thípi. When can we do that?"

"Here in a bit," Mr Scruffy said joining Mylo, Sam, and KC. "I'll fly you home. And, along the way, you'll continue with some training."

Just then a bald eagle flew down along with several companions. The companions stayed back as the largest bald eagle took a step forward from his convocation. Mr Scruffy flew over to meet him.

KC had the uncanny feeling that they were conversing. Ish and the Four Snowmen stood by. She felt like she should be doing or saying something. About the time she started to speak, Mr Scruffy turned to her and gave her a look most children receive from their mothers in church. KC leaned on her sword and waited.

Mr Scruffy and the bald eagle flew over to where KC stood with Ish and the Four Snowmen.

"The time is upon us. KC, this is Iolair, the Eagle King. He and his convocation have come to fly back with us to King Elder's camp. Nukpana has begun her strikes. She is flying down through the Atcenian Hills moving the Grey Menace, and what other armies she can bring together, towards King Elder's camp. We must make haste."

"But, what about my training?" KC asked. The Four Snowmen popped out of sight. "What do I do now?"

"You'll be learning as you go," Ish said climbing onto Iolair's back, which had grown in size as Mr Scruffy had done.

"Wait, I never got to greet Iolair."

"That can wait. Come on, girl. Get on my back," Mr Scruffy said. "We're off."

IT HAPPENED QUICKLY, too quick for KC's liking. They had just lifted off when out of the sky they were barnstormed by grey, shadowy beings.

"What was that?" KC asked Mr Scruffy telepathically while he flew.

"Hold on. Nukpana's Grey Menace is coming at us from all directions. They must have been laying in wait."

KC looked around in the directions she could while tightening her grip on Mr Scruffy's feathers. "I hope we make it through this."

"We will. Lean in with me as I make a dive. Don't panic when I do a roll. You won't fall off. I won't lose you."

Mr Scruffy swooped up and to the left, and then took a dive as fast as he had gone up. KC was afraid she'd upchuck right there. Somehow, she managed to hold on. She caught a glimpse of Ish and Iolair. Ish was laying waste to the grey beings while Iolair reflexively swooped down and around. Each of Ish's arrows found its target, mortally wounding a beast, puffing it out of existence.

When a beast transformed, KC could see the remnants of a being that once walked Eldershire—a rabbit, a bear, or an occasional tree spirit. Ish's quiver held a few remaining arrows. The Grey Menace kept coming. KC pulled out the sword she'd practiced with, and began swinging. She tried to remember the moves the Four Snowmen had shown her, but she kept missing her mark.

Then, just as suddenly as it began, the Grey Menace was gone.

"What happened just now?" KC asked.

"Somehow they got what they came for."

"What could they have come after? Ish and Iolair look to be okay. I'm okay, not because of anything I did. You aren't hurt, are you?"

"We're fine," Ish said telepathically. KC looked for him and suddenly Iolair was flying beside Mr Scruffy. Ish continued, "Make no mistake. They got something or we'd be still fighting them."

"Mr Scruffy? Are you okay?" KC asked.

"Yes. I'm fine. We must get to King Elder's camp quick."

As they flew onward, in the distance large clouds of smoke bellowed up from where Nukpana in Purple Drakein form was leading her army towards the camp.

Mr Scruffy walked into KC's thípi. "We need to talk. Things are going to change quickly in the next few hours."

"Yes. I know."

"Are you ready?"

"To die? No, I'm not ready. If I could pop out of here like the Four Snowmen, I would. What are you and Mother Elder thinking? I can't do this. I'm not any good at it. You saw how I did. Ish was slaying the flying beasties left and right. I never made the first connection. I might be sixty-five in my world, but I'm too young to die, even for here. I'm scared."

"As you should be. We all are. Don't underestimate your power. The Grey Menace left for a reason. They saw something in your fighting that we can't see yet."

KC looked at Mr Scruffy and realized their entire world was about to be attacked. If she could go back home she would in a heartbeat. Where would they go? What would they do?

"I'm sorry. I'm just an old woman wanting her life changed. Oh, why did I ever make that wish?"

"As Mother Elder told you, you came to us because it was your destiny. Your wish would have happened no matter what initiated your thought. You do realize that, don't you?"

"I wanted my family back. That's all I wanted. I'm not worthy of this challenge. I can't kill. Sure, I spent three hours—Ha!—three weeks learning how to wield a sword, shoot a bow and arrow, and somehow cast a spell or two, but I'm not a Viking fighter. You realize I'm just me. You know yourself the worst warrior has trained for years to be a fighter. I never slew the first Grey Menace; not that I wanted to do so."

"We all have a purpose, a goal to reach. Your goal is to retrieve the Efil Stone. My goal is to help you do that. Each of us must work toward our goal if we are to beat Nukpana. I'll be your companion, I'll be there for you along the way, but you must take the step forward. You must accept your fate."

"I know."

"You can believe that Nukpana sent the Grey Menace to check you out. She wanted to see your abilities, your strengths, and your weaknesses. You showed you weren't afraid to fight."

"You can't be serious. I was scared to death. I could hardly brandish that sword. She's probably thinking this will be a piece of cake. I know I'd be thinking that if I were her."

"You are selling yourself short. Maybe the sword you carry is not the right weapon for you. You do realize that a sword must be forged to fit the hand. This sword you were given to use may not be the one you are meant to use. Have faith."

"Faith? With what? I'm in a strange world. Do you even believe in a being, a higher power?"

"KC. After meeting Mother Elder and hearing about Yggdrasil, and how they form the triad, you have to ask that?"

"I get your point. I'm just so lost here. I feel so helpless. So inadequate. I'm not a fighter. I don't like being mean. I don't want conflict. How can you have any faith in me when I don't have an ounce of it myself?"

"You've got to believe. Mother Elder would not put her faith in you if she didn't have faith that it would work out as intended. You are here for a reason. You will find your way. You will find your strength. You will become what you need to be when you need to be it, if you only believe."

"Believing is hard, especially when it requires a miracle."

"You came here because of a wish to change events in your own time. Suppose those events are changed when you go home. What will you do? How will you react? You need to think about what you want, and things will evolve to where you will receive what you need. They go hand-in-hand. That's the secret."

"Mr Scruffy, you are pretty profound for an owl. Now, what do I need to do?"

"We need to get you geared up. You can't fight in those clothes. Ish said he was going to gather some other equipment for you. You will need your own bow and arrows, and a hand knife. Nukpana will be coming this way, but she won't be able to come directly to the camp. King Elder has cast a spell that has placed a protective dome over the area. It is our last holdout. We've been preparing for this for some time."

"How will we fight her from inside the dome?"

"We won't. We'll have to go out into the Wild Woods. We'll have to face her head-on."

"What will protect us?"

"Our wits. Our skills. Our cunning. And, a little magic sprinkled here and there. We will be at the mercy of our abilities."

"Oh, lovely."

"Remember, you will be with me. I am your companion, but I'm also your protector."

"You do realize that is a big job. I wish I had the ability to do more. To protect you in return."

"Remember, your wishes tend to have great power. Don't underestimate them. But, first you must believe."

"You keep telling me to believe. I know I should, but this is so strange to me. I've never really believed in anything my whole life. I've always done what I've needed to do with a gut instinct. It's hard to let go. I think I'm more scared of letting go then of dying."

"The first step to a cure is recognition. I think you just made that first step. The rest is easy. Allow it to be. Let it go and have faith. That's all that is ever asked of any of us. Believe in who you are, your destiny, your time. I wouldn't put my life in your hands if I didn't believe. Trust that you are only given those troubles you can handle. And, I happen to know you can handle more than you realize."

KC looked at Mr Scruffy with a newfound compassion. She watched him walk over to her cot. He picked up something she had not noticed before.

"Oh, my. Where in Eldershire did that come from?"

Mr Scruffy held out the Hat of The Fairy for KC to take. It was the very same one that had transported her to Eldershire in the first place.

"Good things come to you when you least expect it. That's the secret to life in Eldershire," Mr Scruffy said handing her the hat.

CHAPTER 9
EVIL LURKS

Nukpana, as the Purple Drakein, made her way through the Atcenian Hills and along the edges of the Wild Woods, flying high like a vulture scanning for prey. She had laid waste to the land on both sides of Stone's River. Many were killed; most were homeless. She watched as the few survivors of Red Bluffs Divide reacted to her plunder. *I'm sure they think that making their way to King Elder's Camp will protect them.* KC now has something to worry about, she mused as she laughed, and turned her sights toward Grave's Mountain.

THE TREES of the area had been scorched; tree spirits that were able escaped into sanctuaries, and then made their way to camp. Hundreds were lost. Mr Scruffy flew over the scorched land and could see the path Nukpana took letting her fiery breath do its worst. KC felt a tear fall on her cheek; she leaned forward and patted Mr Scruffy.

"Do you feel it?" Mr Scruffy asked telepathically.

"Yes. It's like nothing I've felt before, not even when my family was killed. My heart is breaking. How can we help?" KC responded.

"We can't."

KC laid her head down along Mr Scruffy's back. She wrapped her arms around his neck; he turned back toward King Elder's camp. The sorrow was mounting and she was helpless.

"What caused her to stop attacking?" KC looked down over the area near the edge of the Wild Woods, not far from the brier patch where Ish had found her. "Was it only a few days ago?"

"No. It's been about twenty or twenty-five days now in your Earth time since you arrived. We may never know what caused her to suddenly stop her destruction. But, she has left for now. We must return to King Elder's camp and report. Hold on."

KC looked back over her right shoulder, and then to her left. She hadn't gotten over the Grey Menace showing up unexpectedly. She craned backward to see overhead. Nothing. The sky was as open and blue and cloudless as any beautiful sky she had seen on Earth. Yet, below her were death, despair, and fear.

Mr Scruffy glided to the ground in a graceful landing that gave KC assurance that he was in control. His grace never seemed to wane, even in stress. The calm exploded into a wail of voices. KC placed her hands over her ears trying to crush out the sounds hammering her head.

"Stop!" King Elder called out. "KC, are you all right?"

She slid off the back of Mr Scruffy, and collapsed to the ground. King Elder walked over to her, bent down, and placed his hand on her forehead. KC opened her eyes. Startled by the closeness of the King, she rubbed her head.

"Are you okay?"

"I think so. What happened?"

"The newly arrived tree spirits were wailing in sorrow. When Mr Scruffy arrived, they came in search of answers. They had hoped to learn of those who had perished and how many had made it to a sanctuary. Their voices all speaking at once knocked you out as you stepped to the ground. We must help you overcome this part of learning telepathy as it is affecting you more than the rest of us. After you rest, Mr Scruffy and Ish will bring you to my thípi. Can you join us there?"

"I should be able to. I'm weak, but I should be fine." King Elder walked away. KC turned to Mr Scruffy, "Wow. That did a job on me."

"Yes. The energy required to take in all of those voices zapped you. As good as you're becoming with telepathic powers, it takes time to adjust to so many voices. The mind tea that you'll receive will settle that for future encounters."

"I don't want future encounters. I felt like my head was going to explode."

"It may have been about to, but you fainted and shut out the voices," Ish handed his pouch to KC. "Drink some of this—"

KC grabbed it and took a big gulp. "I feel stronger already. What's in that stuff anyhow? It can't just be water?"

"Actually, it is." Seif popped into view. "Stone's River flows through the Hills of the Atcenians, passing along the edges of the Fields of MaryJane, where the runoff is filtered into Stone's River giving it a little touch of the light fantastic. Then, it goes right passed the entrance to Mushroom Alley, and then on down the valley to here— a perfect spot to gather the liquid of Eldershire," Seif replied holding out a stick arm to help KC up. "Come on, we need to take you to King Elder's thípi."

QUEEN ESMÉ CARRIED a tray with an elixir over to the table near where KC laid. She had collapsed on her way into the room; Seif had picked her up and placed her on the ornate chaise. Her head rested on a pillow. King Elder sat beside her, and held her hand, tiny in his palm, worried about recent events.

"What will we do if she doesn't come out of this trance?" King Elder said helping with the tray. "Nukpana can't know what has happened, can she?"

"She most likely does," Seif said. "She has eyes everywhere. You need to be worried about who is serving as her ears and eyes. It could be someone close to you. It could even be me."

"Seif, why do you say such things? You've not only helped to save hundreds of tree spirits this day, you carried KC here knowing that it would harm you. Your laws prevent you from touching any living soul, let alone a human, and now you are beginning to suffer the consequences. You are melting." Queen Esmé handed him a cup. "Drink this quickly. It won't change the inevitable, but, it will stave off the effects until we can get you back to your land."

Seif nodded. "Has she taken any of the elixir?"

"We're administering it now. Since she is still unconscious, I'm dripping it over her lips. Enough will seep through that it will begin to work its affect." Queen Esmé sat back in the chair she'd pulled up beside KC's bed. "For now, we must wait."

WHERE AM I? KC walked along a path leading passed a series of trees in full bloom. The last time trees were in bloom like this was six months ago, before her family died. It looked like the edge of Stone's River where Ish stopped to get water for his pouch. The rock seat to the right was where they rested while running away from the Atcenians. *I don't remember seeing trees here then. Something's not—.*

"You're right, KC. Relax. It won't take me long now. I've got those who are helping me in the heart of King Elder's camp. You will be in my grips soon, and all of Eldershire will die like the blooms on these trees." Nukpana breathed heavily.

KC saw the blooms slowly wilt, dry up, and then crumble off the branches.

⁊⚬

"KC! Calm down. KC?" Seif said holding her down on the chaise. "You are here in King Elder's thípi. Mr Scruffy is here along with Ish, King Elder, and Queen Esmé. You are safe."

KC rose up on one arm, looked around, and was scared at first, not recognizing anyone.

Mr Scruffy placed his wing on her hand and spoke to her telepathically, "You are safe. Can you tell me what you saw?"

"No, not yet. I must think about what just happened," KC replied to him, and then said to everyone, "I'm fine. I didn't mean to give you a scare." KC rose up, swung her legs over the side of the chaise, and steadied herself to rise. "I think I should be getting back to helping you save Eldershire."

"KC, you can't go out there and begin fighting without more rest and training. Nukpana is strong. She'll take you down," Seif said. "You all agree with me that she should wait, don't you? She should wait."

"It probably isn't a bad idea, KC," Ish said handing her his water pouch. KC took the pouch. She started to raise it to her lips, and Ish stopped her. "No. Hang on to the pouch for now. You may need more water later."

"I think what I need to do is go back to my thípi. I need to prepare for what may come." KC turned to Queen Esmé, "Thank you. I know you worked magic with your elixir. I feel stronger and will not forget what you've done for me."

"Wait. Is that all? You're just going to leave. You were clearly upset while you were knocked out. Can we do anything for you?" Seif implored.

"You can get Nukpana out of my mind. She entered it while I was out cold. How is that possible? Where is your magic protecting me?"

King Elder shook his head. "She has somehow gotten someone to serve as a go-between for her. That's the only explanation."

"Is it really? Are you kidding me? You want me to be your savior and you can't even protect me where you say you have all the means to be protected."

"We can help, if you will let us," Seif said.

"Seriously, I think you all need to determine if life under Nukpana isn't so bad. 'Cause let me tell you, life with you right now is the pits. So far, the only beings here that have attacked me have been Elderians. What about that?"

Mr Scruffy flew back into the thípi. "KC what is happening?"

"I'm learning that the Elderians aren't as strong and together as they claim to be."

"You shouldn't think that. You can't believe that we'd harm you or turn you over to Nukpana," Seif said.

"No. No, I don't think so. I'm only human, after all. I don't know anything. I won't put the blame on you." KC walked out.

THE WALK along Stone's River gave KC time to think. She had a lot to consider, her life for one. She was about to reach a decision when a few droplets fell on her head. *I didn't realize it would rain here.* She looked up. The two-moons were shining through the droplets that fell in a steady stream casting double moonbows in front of her. She'd always heard that if you saw the end of a rainbow, you would find a treasure. *I wonder if the same is true when you see double moonbows.* It was good to feel light-hearted during such uncertain times.

"Legend says it is so." Mr Scruffy fluttered down and sat on a branch and telepathed to KC. "You ready to talk with me now?"

"Is it safe?"

"Yes. What happened? I know you spoke with her. What did she say?"

"She told me I'd be hers soon. She also said she had helpers in King Elder's camp."

Suddenly, there was a burst of flames nearby. Mr Scruffy quickly grew in size, KC jumped upon his back. "I don't have my sword."

"A sword won't help us now. We must make haste. Hold on!"

Mr Scruffy swooped up and out as the flames darted around them. KC craned her neck looking behind them and saw that it wasn't Nukpana throwing flames. "I don't think we need to worry. It's only the Grey Menace."

"We must move quick. We're outside the protection waves of King Elder's magic. Hold on, I'm going to— "

KC landed hard in the bush. She scrambled to her feet, and looked up to see what happened to Mr Scruffy.

"Mr Scruffy! Mr Scruffy, where did you go?" she screamed.

"He's not here." KC turned around quickly. "Here, you're going to need this." Seif handed her the sword she'd left on her bunk. "Come with me. We haven't much time." Seif moved toward the cliffs in front of them. "We'll hide in there. It's a cave at Iolair's Bluff."

"Iolair's Bluff? How'd I get here? Isn't it on the other side of Eldershire?"

"Yes. It is."

"I don't understand."

"Do you want me to tell you here while you risk the chance of being hit with fire, or can we get in the cave, where it is safe, and I tell you there?"

"Uh, sure. Yes. Of course. Lead the way."

KC and Seif made their way to the cave. In the darkness, it seemed like it took them a lot longer to maneuver over the rocky plain than it had taken her to run through the Wild Woods. When they reached the cave, KC was starting to feel the effects of her fall. She reached for her pouch Ish had given her. The swig of water hit the spot. She felt stronger. She was glad to have the water with her.

"Are you going to stand out there or are you going to come in? You don't want to be seen," Seif had moved on inside the cave. "I'd start a fire, but we don't need to give anyone a way to see us."

"Of course not. Besides, wouldn't a fire cause you to melt?"

"Yes. It doesn't help me. But, you may not realize I'm melting at any rate."

"You are? Why?"

"I need to return to my land. Queen Esmé was going to send me back. But, I learned something while carrying you to King Elder's thípi. I had never touched a human before."

"We're even. I've never met a talking snowman before."

"Yes. I'd wager that talking to me wouldn't kill you like me touching you. Well, now. Come to think of it. That's not exactly true."

"What do you mean?"

"You don't get it, do you? You really had no idea?"

"What? What's going on?"

"I am a double agent. I work for King Elder, but I also work for the people of my land. We're tired of being forced to fight war after war. Knowledge is good and enables choices to be made while living true to self and the effects of change. I am the one with knowledge of death. Through knowledge, I've come to discern the negative value of death; the results of war. I told King Elder he should avoid war with Nukpana. He wouldn't listen to me. So, I've decided to take things into my own hands."

"But, Seif, King Elder isn't the reason we're at war with Nukpana. You realize that, don't you?"

"He could stop her."

"How? She's a Drakein. She's also a very powerful witch. While I was under, she came—"

The rumbling sound grew quickly, and suddenly the entrance to the cave was gone. The darkness made it impossible to see.

"Seif? Seif, are you okay?" KC reached down and felt around. She could not feel him. She took her sword and used it to help her stand up. Then, using the sword, she began to feel the way in front of her, hitting the sword and scraping along the cave floor to find out where Seif may be laying.

After ten minutes of searching in the dark, she could not find him. She reached down for her pouch, and took another swig of water. The air wasn't hot, but it wasn't being refreshed quickly. The lack of moving air added to her worry about what she could do in the dark to get them out. They hadn't been in the cave long when the landslide happened. She never had a chance to look around and figure out if there was another way out.

As she carefully continued her search for Seif, she wished that she had received more training on the use of magic. In the dark, she looked down at the sword she still held in her hand and thought, I can't even begin to use this on anyone, let alone use it to help me dig out of a cave. KC slumped down against a wall. If Seif was still alive, he must be knocked out. She could understand taking advantage of a good sleep.

"Are you comfortable?" KC jumped at hearing the voice. She had fallen asleep.

"Who's there?"

"I'm hurt. You don't recognize my voice?"

"It's different. You sound near, Seif. Keep talking and I'll try to find you."

"I'm more aware, as they say."

"I looked for you. I figured you must have made it out of the cave before it caved in. I had hoped so. You could have gone for help."

"You're stronger than I thought. I'm pleased to see that in you," Seif said. He lit the lantern in his left hand. "This light should help you. My powers are weak. I'd pop us out of here, but we'd die during transport. I can't let that happen now."

"Did you cause the cave in?"

"No. It was Nukpana. I told her I'd bring you here. I wanted you to talk. I saw her up near Stone's River when I was looking for you. It was me that popped you off of Mr Scruffy's back, landing you here. I wanted to save my land and Eldershire. I thought if I gave you to Nukpana, it would change things. I realize now, I was wrong."

"Are you crazy? You thought you could parlay with Nukpana? Seriously? I'm not even from this world and I know better than to mess with her. She is evil personified. Gees, she's been trying to kill me ever since I arrived."

"Before."

"What? What are you saying?"

"Nukpana knew about you before you arrived."

"How do you know?"

"We all did. You were our savior. You were foretold."

"By who?"

"Mother Elder and Yggdrasil. Who else?"

"Oh, Them. Great. I guess I got this coming to me for being gullible. You see how well that's working out. Now, what?"

"Now, I'm dying."

"Can I do anything for you?"

"I have little time left. I am dying because I carried you. The act of me touching a human began my death spiral. I will use my light to help you dig your way out; I have little strength for much else. You better start digging now. I'm not sure how long I'll last."

KC turned to him and said, "Thank you for that." She picked up her sword and started to dig where she thought the entrance to the cave might have been. Seif's light helped her figure out that much. KC thought she was making progress when suddenly, her sword snapped in two.

"Seif, my sword broke too close to the hilt to make it an effective digging tool. What now?" KC held up the end of her sword and looked to him. "A lot of good this has done me."

"Keep digging," Seif's head fell forward. His light was still burning, but KC could tell the glow was growing weak.

I'm not going to die here, not like this. She turned back and continued to dig with her bare hands.

CHAPTER 10
THE CAVE & THE WITCH

K C didn't know how long she had been digging, but her hands were hurting. Her heart felt another pain. Seif's light went out long ago. He had died without the slightest sound. She hadn't tried to find out if he had melted away. Tears stained her face as she struggled with removing the dirt and rock. She was tired, scared, and wished for home.

She sat back against the wall to take a breath. Reaching down for her pouch of water, she wondered how much was left. The darkness had grown on her. Her ability to hear sounds had improved and she was starting to rely more on her ears and touch and less on her eyes. And then, a quiet eeriness came over her. She felt a cold tingle down her spine, as if she was no longer alone.

"Someone there?" KC asked a little above a whisper.

A light began to glow not far from where she last saw Seif's light. An image was materializing before her and it caused KC to lean back toward the rock wall. I wish I could melt into the wall, she thought.

"I can make that happen, if you wish."

Standing before KC in a glowing iridescent light was a most

strikingly, beautiful being. A tall, slender woman stood before her giving off a presence of power and strength. Dressed in a fitted black body suit with leather knee-hi boots, at her waist was a long flowing skirt that sparkled in various shades of black. In her left hand, she held a long staff that at the end held a bright jewel; its light gave a glow to the cave wall. As KC looked up to the woman's face, she gasped at her beauty.

Her lips were as rosy red as the darkest rose, and her hair was ebony and complimented her porcelain skin. Her eyes caught KC by surprise as she looked into them—they glowed with power. Their power grabbed at KC's heart; she longed to be with this woman. The tall black hat that spiraled up into the most perfect looking witch's hat was complemented by some of her hair pinned into place by a hairpin in the shape of a dragon with purple inlay. The power that emitted from her eyes convinced KC she was looking at Nukpana.

"You are right, My Pitiful One. It's me."

"What do you want?"

"To make your life miserable before I kill you."

"Why? Why do you want to kill me? I've done nothing to you. I didn't ask to come to Eldershire. Why don't you just send me home?"

"You're a threat to me. You can't live here or in any other world. As long as you live, I can be destroyed."

KC let out a laugh. Her fear and tension had built to a crescendo. "Me? You think I'm a threat? You've got to be kidding me. Here, I am stuck in this cave. You can do whatever you wish. I don't even have a sword that I can use to protect myself." KC picked up what was left of her broken sword. "And, you think I can harm you?" She giggled nervously shaking her head.

"Don't be impertinent, little girl. You know you have power. You have a great power that I want."

"Well, why don't you take it then? I don't know what you could be talking about. All I'm interested in is getting out of this place. And, to do that, you know I need the Efil Stone." KC could feel her anger growing. She was tired of the charade. "Go ahead. Give me all you got. If I'm going to die here, so be it." KC turned around and continued to dig with the hilt of her sword.

"You dare turn your back on me, you insolent little swine," Nukpana pointed Blazewing, her scepter, toward a spot off to the side of where KC was digging. A light beam struck the rocks, blasting them into pulverized stone. The flying rocks pelted her, causing KC to fling her sword and cower. The sound rippled through the cave, as KC let out a scream of fear.

"That'll teach you to insult me. I knew when I saw you in the woods running from those stupid Atcenians, Gorge and Morge, I might be wrong about you. Why did I think you'd be a challenge to me? I must have had a weak moment. You are just a scared, little human being. You have no power."

"You are right. I have no power. But, what would you expect from a human?" With her back against the pile of pulverized rock, KC looked around the cave. She hoped to find something she could use to protect herself. "I don't understand why you haven't killed me already. What's the point?"

"It is fun, My Pitiful One. I enjoy watching weak things squirm. Look at you. You're lying in a pile of dirt. Dirt that I created with Blazewing. I can take out all of Eldershire now that I have the Efil Stone. Not you, not King Elder, no one can stop me."

KC watched as Nukpana seemed to change. Her beauty began to exude ugliness. It occurred to KC that Nukpana's evil was overtaking her power. Her willful pride, cruelty, and wickedness were causing Nukpana to transform before her eyes.

"You may be right. I don't know. I don't know how I can possibly defeat you," KC's left hand searched behind her. "I only know that I'm here for a purpose, a purpose greater than my own desires and wishes. A purpose that somehow I must fulfill in order to return home." KC's hand stopped on something. It felt like the hilt of her broken sword. "As Mr Scruffy has told me, I must have faith."

KC pulled what she thought was the hilt to take her last stand while standing up to face her nemesis. A weak effort at best, but an effort nonetheless to help her feel less powerless. As she pulled the handle from behind her, she realized that what she held in her hand was different. It was a complete sword, and it glowed.

Nukpana recoiled like a serpent. "Where did you get that?" She used her arm to protect her eyes. "This isn't over." Before KC could blink, Nukpana was gone.

KC slid down the wall of the cave in shock and relief. Looking at the sword, she saw its glow was less powerful; still it put off a light that enabled KC to see where Seif laid, still and quiet. She got up and walked over to him.

Placing his broken hand on his chest, she noticed his lantern began to glow.

KC said, "Seif? Seif, are you still alive? I wished you could have seen me. You would have been proud. But, now I have no idea how to get out of this place."

Seif's voice came to KC in her mind. "Have no fear. I will be with you. You will have my knowledge. I pass to you the words of our teachings. Listen and keep these words in your heart—

Do not build your happiness on the present.
Time passes on even as it returns; what you see will be gone one day, then may
come back.
Everything is subject to change; life is unsettling.
Change is good if you learn and take heed; do not let change hurt you.
When it does hurt, the rebellion you feel is meant to give you strength of courage
to go forward; to reach your goals, and to remind you that you should not allow
desires to rule you.

These words I give to you to empower you with mindfulness, which gives you strength, hope, and love."

KC looked down at Seif, his life force faded from view. He was gone, but his lantern stayed behind giving off a faint light. KC remained there for a bit and pondered all that had happened. She got up and resolved to get out of that cave. So, she began to dig.

§.

IT SEEMED like hours had passed since Nukpana made her appearance and Seif faded away. KC made some headway into digging. One good thing about Blazewing zapping the rocks, the boulders were gone and most of what KC was digging were piles of dirt.

I wish Mr Scruffy and Ish would appear. I sure could use some help.

"Your wish is our command!"

"Is that you, Ish?"

"Yes, it is. We're outside the cave digging on this end. Are you okay?"

"I am. Can't you just pop me out of here?"

"Only Snowquidians can do that. We don't know where the Four Snowmen are. Our magic is limited here at Iolair's Bluff."

"Seif was with me. He melted away. His lantern remained, and the light it gave off is almost out. He used the last of his energy so I could see to dig. I'd broken my old sword, so I've been using my hands."

"We'll work as fast as we can. We have several here helping us."

"Is Mr Scruffy with you?"

"I am. You seem different. Are you okay?" Mr Scruffy asked directing his telepath to KC.

"I have so much to tell you. I don't know where to start."

"Sit still. Let us do the digging. Be calm and I'll visit your memories. It will tell me all."

"KC, can you see us? I'll just move this rock. How about that?"

As the last rock was moved, an opening appeared, and KC could see out to her friends. Quickly, they removed the remaining rocks that were blocking an easy exit. By the time they cleared the way out, KC was eager to greet her friends. Mr Scruffy jumped over to KC and knowingly looked up to her. KC reached down and placed him on her shoulder.

"If I can survive this, I can survive anything." KC turned to Ish. "Let's go. I want to get back to camp. We've got work to do. I've got to find the Efil Stone."

❦

THE JOURNEY back to King Elder's camp was long, and made more miserable by a sudden down pour. Drenched to the bone, KC's head was protected by the outstretched wing of Mr Scruffy acting like an umbrella.

"It is kind of you to protect me. Is your wing getting tired?" KC telepathed only to Mr Scruffy.

"I'm fine. It's Ish that I'm worried about."

"Ish? Why?"

"He and Princess Derryth had an argument before he came to help us find you."

"Is there something we can do?"

"Not now."

KC pondered Mr Scruffy's latest thoughts about Ish and his princess love. The walk back to camp was long and hard. They climbed up and down over the high-hills into the valley toward the Wild Woods.

"I wish we had a Snowquid around to help pop us out of here and into our warm tents. I'm starting to get cold," KC shared as she folded her arms up against her chest. "At least the winds aren't blowing strong." No one replied, which was just as well. KC knew that in her own world, a cold, bitter rain could make anyone miserable. She shivered and wondered if Seif had made it to his home world. She wondered if his fellow Snowmen knew of his demise.

"They do." Mr Scruffy lifted off of KC's shoulder. "I'm going to fly out and see if I can tell who might be out in front of us. We should be getting close to the edge of the Wild Woods."

"Be careful." KC thought about the fact her senses were stronger since she had acquired telepathic powers. She looked down to her hand where the owl tattoo looked like a natural birthmark. She couldn't help thinking back to when she was home, in her house that fateful night her family died. She was angry and sad then, and she was alone. Walking toward camp, if she chose, she could allow many to hear her thoughts. She was thankful for Mr Scruffy—his friendship and compassion, and his integrity at keeping her innermost thoughts protected.

"Thank you." Mr Scruffy landed gently on a branch. KC walked over to him. "The rain has stopped, the clouds have moved on, and the moons are shining bright. We can see our way to the forest."

Ish walked up to them. "The way is clear, then? We should move faster. We will need to stay under cover since the sky is opening. The moons will show our location to those in the sky. We should be able to reach camp in a little over an hour from here. It's time to run."

"The night's sky is beautiful above the trees. If it weren't for the chance of running into Nukpana, I'd take you for a night ride. One day this war will be over. We'll fly together then."

"I'm holding you to that promise," KC said as she reached for Mr

Scruffy. He walked up her arm and rested on her shoulder. "Let's run."

"Wait. Let the others go. I'll fly ahead in a minute. I wanted to let you know that the way is clear for now. Be mindful that the Grey Menace is always nearby. Call to me, if you find you need me."

"I will Mr Scruffy. Thank you. Now, if I don't start running, the others will be out of sight soon. Take off and fly under the radar."

"Ha! Under the radar. That's cute." Mr Scruffy was soaring above.

"I heard that all the time when I listened to my favorite radio DJ, Dusty. See you at camp." KC telepathed to Mr Scruffy.

THE RUN through the Wild Woods was uneventful. KC caught up to the group at the same time that they entered the larger forest. The moons' light suddenly came to a halt. KC almost ran into something or somebody standing just inside the forest canopy where darkness took over.

"Whom have I run into?" KC said.

"It's me, Ish. I wondered where you had gotten. It is good you didn't get lost again. You best stay nearby. We don't have light to share with you to see. I have this scarf I use to hold my quiver to my back. You hang onto it, and it should help you make it through the forest."

"I'll do my best. At least, this time I can talk to you if we get separated."

"Yes, but only if we're a little ways apart. Stay close. Let's go."

The first twenty or so minutes of running were not too difficult. KC remembered enough of her last run through the forest to know she needed to step quick, and keep up with Ish. Then suddenly, without warning, the scarf came loose in her hand.

"Ish? Ish? Where are you?"

No answer. KC had slowed to a trot. Fearful of hitting a tree, she paused and listened. No sounds.

"Mr Scruffy?" KC telepathed.

No answer. KC looked up. The canopy was solid and no light penetrated it. She reached out with her hands; she could not feel any trees. Her eyes had adjusted earlier enough that she could make out a shape of a tree occasionally. As she looked out in front of her and turned ever so slowly, she could see nothing. She was alone.

"Hello?" She stopped moving, stood still, and waited.

No answer. No sounds.

"Come on, guys. Where are you?"

No answer.

"Okay. This isn't funny. Mr Scruffy, you said you'd answer me." KC was scared. She hated the dark. And, then she held her breath. She heard the hiss of a snake. *Oh, God.*

"No," the voice hissed. "He's not here. I am."

"Nukpana?"

"Yes."

"Why are you doing this?"

"I'm not done tormenting you."

"Are you really here or have you tricked my mind into hearing something that is not real?"

"Aren't you the sly one? I'm not with you right now. I'm in your mind's eye. No one can hear you or me."

KC pulled out her sword. It was glowing. "What is the sword telling me?"

"Can't you guess? I might as well tell you. I lied."

"I'm no longer in the Wild Woods, am I?"

"No."

"Where am I now?"

"What is the fun in telling you that piece of information? It is so much more fun watching you squirm."

"I don't see myself squirming," KC increased her grip on her sword. She turned slowly around; the glow grew stronger and faded as she moved in a circle. She turned back to where the sword grew its brightness, but could not see anything distinctly in the dark.

"Clever. I'm glad to see you using your powers. I may find out what all you can do, if I just watch you."

"What do you mean you may find out what I can do? Don't you know already? I'm only human, after all."

"Oh, My Pitiful One, you are so much more with that sword in your hand. You don't know everything do you?"

"You know I don't. Why don't you enlighten me? Better yet, why don't you let me see you?"

"That I can't do, KC. Besides, from my vantage point, I am able to see everything I need to see."

"Will you allow me to reach for my pouch and get a drink of water? It's hot in here and I'd could use some water."

"Sure, go ahead. I'll be glad to hold your sword for you."

"Nukpana, I'm surprised at you. Did you really think I'd fall for that one?"

"I wasn't sure. You are human after all."

KC started to laugh; suddenly she felt a cold, wet liquid on her face.

"KC?"

"KC?"

"KC, wake up!"

KC's eyes began to open; slowly Ish's face came into view. She looked passed him and saw Mr Scruffy sitting on his shoulder. She turned her head and saw several of the other tree spirits that had been traveling with them. She groped for her sword. It was hanging on her belt. Her hands moved along where she was laying, she heard leaves crackle.

"What happened?" She tried to sit up.

"We don't know. You let go of the scarf. When I turned back around, we couldn't see you. Mr Scruffy was able to find you using magic. Once we found you, we lit a fire, moved you closer to it, and have been trying to wake you. Do you know how long you've been knocked out?"

"Knocked Out? I wasn't knocked out. Nukpana pulled one of her tricks again. I was with her."

"Nukpana? As far as we could tell, you never left here." Ish looked to the others.

"Then, I was there in my mind. I called for you both. Mr Scruffy, you never answered. I was so scared."

"I'm sorry. I tried. I could tell you were trying to reach me. Can you tell us any more?"

"I don't think Nukpana realized I would be able to return to you. She was telling me how she planned to play with my mind a while before she would destroy me. You saved my life. Again."

CHAPTER 11
PRINCESS DERRYTH

P rincess Derryth paced back and forth across her thípi. She hadn't heard from Ish in over two days. She was worried. She stopped in front of her mirror, looked at her hair, making sure her long brown tresses were perfectly coifed. Her eyes and porcelain face were perfectly painted, her lips rosy red. She checked her gown. There weren't any wrinkles. She hadn't sat down on it since she put it on earlier that morning.

She stood back and looked over her view in the full-length mirror. She wanted to look perfect for Ish when he arrived. She loved him almost more than her own life. Even though she knew in her heart she was the one that was the most important in their pending life together, she would share her love with him when they joined by giving him a sapling. As the future Queen of Eldershire, she had a duty to perform. No one or nothing was going to stop her from being Queen. It was her destiny. She loved her parents, but she hoped they wouldn't rule as long as her grandparents had ruled. She watched her parents stay loyal and true while waiting to be rulers. *I told them I wouldn't be as patient as they were.*

Queen Esmé walked in.

"My dear. You look like you were all wrapped up with yourself just now. You might want to freshen up and put on a smile. Ish will be here soon." Queen Esmé walked over to her daughter and touched her shoulder. Princess Derryth shrugged away from her touch. "You have no reason to think ill of KC. She's done nothing to you. She didn't ask for this quest. She only wants to go back to her home and have her family with her again. Why are you acting this way?"

Princess Derryth slouched down into a seat. Queen Esmé continued, "You are beautiful when you are not sullen and acting like a princess. You should hold your head high with pride and not act as though you are entitled. Yes, you are the Princess of Eldershire. But sometimes, I'm not sure you understand what that means to those around you. Ish is in love with you. He only helps KC because Mother Elder and your father have instructed him to do so." Queen Esmé reached out to touch her daughter again.

"Stop! You don't understand," Princess Derryth moved away from her mother. She turned and tears began to flow down her cheeks. "I can't compete with her. She's human. She's beautiful. How can I even try to overcome those two things? Then, to top it off, she has to be the Savior!" Princess Derryth dropped to the floor, covered her face with her hands, and sobbed.

Her mother walked over to her and stood beside her. "Can we talk? You always get mad and lash out." Queen Esmé pulled up a chair and sat beside her daughter. "You know your father and I love you. And, what I'm about to say is not to make you mad, but to try and get you to understand how you are coming across to us and to others in the kingdom." She lifted her daughter's chin up. "Will you at least look at me while we talk?"

Princess Derryth pushed her mother's hand away, got up from the floor, and turned back to her. "Look what you made me do! I had not sat on this dress all day. You made me so mad that I sat on it without thinking. Now, the dress is ruined. Leave. I must change."

Queen Esmé looked at her daughter, shrugged her shoulders, and left the room. The Princess took the tiara off her head and threw it after her mother. "I want to die. I want to die right now!"

"My sweet, Princess," hissed the voice. "No need to do that now. Why don't you help me and I'll help you?"

Princess Derryth looked up from where she stood and could not see anyone. "Who's there? Why do you mock me?"

"Mock you?" hissed the voice. "I'm not mocking you. I'm here to help you if you want me to do so. I have much power. I can help you get back at KC and win your love, your Isherwood."

"What?" Princess Derryth looked around the room, but could not see to whom she was speaking. "Show yourself to me. I demand it, now."

"Oh, you demand it," the voice giggled with the hissing sound. "Are you sure you can stand seeing me? Not many can. I am powerful."

"You dare speak of power to me. Do you know to whom you speak? I am the Princess of Eldershire. I rule over all."

"You rule over all? Really? I stand corrected. I thought it was your father and mother. Well, excuse me. I bow to you."

Princess Derryth pivoted looking for the voice. "I don't see you. Where are you bowing?"

"How might I help you in your hour of need?" The voice had grown stronger, yet continued to have the faint hiss sound of a serpent. "I'm at your service and will gladly help you."

Princess Derryth smiled. Satisfaction eased its way into her heart. The last words caused her to ponder. "What if I asked you to take her away from here? Could you do that? Could you rid Eldershire of KC?"

"Well, of course, I can. But, you must do something to help me help you. Are you willing to do that?"

"If I must. I'll do anything to get rid of the likes of her. I do not care what happens to her. I must have her gone from here."

"My, you are jealous of her, aren't you? I like that in your voice. You are sure that you are willing to take this step?"

"Yes. But, I haven't seen you yet. Who are you?" She was becoming a little fearful of what she was plotting to do to KC. Maybe her mother was right. She thought on her mother's words that KC didn't ask to come to Eldershire.

"True. KC didn't ask to come here. I brought her here."

Princess Derryth stopped dead. "How did you…? Who are you?"

"Do you want my help, or don't you? I don't have all day to wait for you to make up your mind. Either you want KC gone or you don't. Which is it?"

"You'll only take her away from here, right? I don't want her harmed; I just need her gone." Princess Derryth walked around the room as she wrung her hands. She was talking more to herself when she said, "But she must be gone so that I may have Ish all to myself."

"You are talking like a weak princess. I thought you'd do anything to rid Eldershire of KC. Are you a weakling after all?"

"No! I am not! Show yourself. I'll prove to you I'm not."

Hearing the sounds of water flowing, Princess Derryth had the sensation of dreaming come over her. Ish was walking toward her, his hand outstretched. She ran to him. They embraced. Off in the distance, she saw the outline of a tall, slender woman standing with the view of Eldershire behind her, holding a scepter.

"Before I show myself, hold out your hand. I must seal our deal." Princess Derryth defiantly held out her hand. Nukpana cut off her right forefinger.

Princess Derryth screamed out in pain, "What have you done?"

"Wait. Our deal is not complete. I will do as you command. You are the princess, after all. Now, you must agree to my request or you forfeit your life, if you fail."

Princess Derryth held her hand tight. "What must I do?"

"While buried in the cave, KC found a sword. Ish and his companions are at the cave rescuing her now; they will bring her back to camp shortly. When she is back, you must steal the sword. When you do, I'll replace your finger. Until you retrieve the sword, no one else—your mother, father, or even Ish—will know your finger is gone. I placed an illusion spell on your injury. But, you will continue to feel the throb of pain until you place the sword in my hand. Do you understand?"

Princess Derryth looked up with tears streaming down her face. "I do. I will do as you ask. Remember, you promised you would not hurt KC."

The image of Nukpana came into Princess Derryth's full view, "You poor, Princess. I always keep my promises when I deem it necessary. Just like you."

"What have I done?" Princess Derryth drew back in fear as she realized to whom she had made a promise.

"You have lived up to your potential, my Princess. You owe me the sword, else I own your life." Nukpana faded away at the time that Queen Esmé walked back into the thípi.

"Princess, come quick. Ish and the party are returning and its great news. KC is with them. Come, your Father wants us there as they bring her to us."

Princess Derryth looked at herself in the mirror. "You go ahead, Mother. I'll be there shortly. I must freshen myself up for Ish." Queen Esmé stepped out. Princess Derryth looked down at her hand, *what have I done?*

KING ELDER and Queen Esmé stood by while Ish and a couple of the other tree spirits laid KC down on the cot in her thípi. They arranged her head and propped her up with covers made of cloths woven from fine wood and sacred plants.

"These coverings will help to protect her while she sleeps. She needs much rest. Nukpana reached her while she was in the cave, and then evidently again while we were making our way here. But, I think we got her here in time," Ish said as he stepped back.

"King Elder, there is nothing we can do for her right now. She must rest," Mr Scruffy said. "It is best that she not be left alone. While we traveled here, I prepared an elixir and she will need to lay undisturbed so it can work its magic."

Princess Derryth walked into the thípi. "I can sit with her, if you like?"

"That is—" Mr Scruffy said.

"My dear, how kind of you?" Queen Esmé interrupted. "Yes, you take the first watch. That will give Ish and the others time to rest. I'll relieve you in about an hour. How will that work for you, Mr Scruffy?"

"I believe it will be fine. I'll check in on her in a little while."

"Shouldn't you rest too?" Princess Derryth asked moving next to KC's cot. "I mean I can watch her. There is no need for you to worry. If I need something, I can always call you. Or, I can call Ish." She looked up to him and smiled her most provocative smile. Princess Derryth thought Ish might have blushed when he smiled back at her.

"Let's all clear out of here now," Ish said. "We need to give KC some air and time to recoup. Princess, if you need me, summon me. I'll not be far away." Ish turned to the King and Queen. "It means you both must go. And you too, Mr Scruffy. Come on. Let's give KC time to rest."

Mr Scruffy looked over at KC, "Princess Derryth, you know you can call me anytime. I'll be up above in the treetops. I'm seconds away if she comes to and needs me."

"I know. Both of you go on. I'm fine. I've sat with sick folks before. I mean, after all, this is KC. She's strong. She's our Savior; remember. I won't let anything happen to her."

Mr Scruffy walked over to KC, picked up his feather from above her head, and placed it under her arm. "She is still resting. I won't be far away." He looked at Princess Derryth. She eyed him back. He nodded and flew out of the thípi.

IT SEEMED like everyone had left KC's thípi several lunations ago, but it had only been a few clicks. Princess Derryth went over to the doorway and checked to see if anyone was standing nearby. She dropped the flap, and then walked over to the cot. She looked down at KC and worried about what to do next.

After waiting a brief time, she sat down beside KC's cot. She listened to see if anyone was near. Sensing no one, she got back up and began to search the thípi for the sword. Moving around, she didn't have a lot of items to move. *It's obvious KC came to Eldershire with nothing,* she thought. After searching awhile, the sword was nowhere to be found. Standing at the far end of the thípi, Princess Derryth looked around as she thought where the sword could have been placed when Ish and the other tree spirits laid KC on the cot. It dawned on her that the sword must have been lying with KC, since it was the only place left to search.

She stood off to one side of the room trying to figure out how to approach KC. Just then, KC moaned and moved. Princess Derryth's finger began to throb, as though Nukpana was sending her a signal. She moved over to KC and looked the cot over to decide how to search without arousing KC. About the time she started to move her hand up under the cot at KC's feet, she stirred.

Princess Derryth jumped back in fear she had awakened KC. But, KC only rolled over onto her side. A glimmer of light caught her eyes. She saw a slither of light coming into the thípi was reflecting off a part of the sword that was now exposed beside KC's back.

The stub, at the end of where her finger had been, sent a sharp pain up her arm. She covered her mouth to keep from crying out. Princess Derryth decided she needed to act, and to do so quickly. If she reached for the sword, and turned fast enough, she could be outside the thípi before KC was awake and knew what was happening.

Right when Princess Derryth reached down to take the sword, KC's arm came around and caught her hand.

"Oh!"

"What are you doing?" KC asked sitting up on the cot.

"It looked like this metal thing was in your way. Let me move it so you can lie back down. You need your rest. I didn't mean to wake you. I so want to help you."

"How nice of you." KC took the sword away from Princess Derryth. "But, there is no need for you to worry. This sword wasn't hurting me, and I need to keep it at my side."

"No! You can't! I must have it. You don't understand." Princess Derryth tried to take the sword away from KC.

"Why do you need my sword?" KC wrenched it away. "You don't need it to fight. You don't know how to wield a sword do you?"

Princess Derryth looked at KC and realized she was caught. She began to cry and fell down on her knees. "Oh, forgive me. Forgive me." She wept.

KC moved over to her, put her arm on her shoulder, "What is this? What's got you so upset? Why do you need my sword?"

In between sobs, Princess Derryth explained her pack with

Nukpana. "You have no right to Ish. I love him. I love him more than you. I've failed, and now, I'm to die. You can now have Ish all to yourself. I suppose you have won."

"Listen to me, silly girl. I don't want Ish. Where did you get the idea that I did? I never wanted him. He saved my life. That is all. You have put you and all of Eldershire in great peril because of your jealousy." KC got up and walked around the room. Princess Derryth watched her and tried to figure out what to do next.

KC said, "Nukpana must know you've failed her."

"I know she knows. The throbbing in my hand has intensified. She will come for me." Princess Derryth continued to cry. "Oh, what have I done?"

"Let me call Mr Scruffy. He'll know what to do."

"No! No, you can't. He'll tell my father. It will kill him."

"Yes. But, if you don't, and Nukpana strikes the camp, what will you do then?"

"I don't know."

"You don't think very far ahead, do you? You do realize that Nukpana played you? We've got to get you help."

"What? Why do you want to help me?"

"Nukpana saw your weakness—your jealousy. She used it to get you to do what she wanted. You fell for the oldest trick. We've got to get Ish and Mr Scruffy in here. We've got to tell them. I failed to tell my loved ones, and it cost me. You don't want to end up the way I did losing everything."

"You? You're the Savior. How can you know what it means to lose someone?"

"You are innocent. I'm not the Savior, as you call me. I'm an old woman, from another time, another world, who made a wish on a magical hat because I had done something foolish. Something so foolish that it cost me my entire family—my husband, my son, his wife, and my son's dog. They all died because I *had* to stop and help a stranded traveler. I watched helplessly as they were killed. I was so wrapped up in my desire to help someone, to be the savior, as you called me, to do what one should do that I allowed my family to perish in the zeal to help someone else. Do you not see the irony?"

"I don't know what you mean by 'irony,' but I think I understand. Here you are *our* savior. But, are you?"

"Time will tell. I do know that if you fail to tell Ish what you've done, if you keep secrets, it will ruin your relationship. You can't keep secrets and expect Ish to love you. You must tell him. You must. I failed to talk with my husband. I failed to share my most inner thoughts. It cost me. Do not start your relationship with Ish in the same way. Do you understand?"

"I think so. But, what should I do now? Nukpana will not let me live. She already has taken my finger. You can't see it is gone, but the throbbing pain is constant. What will I do?"

"There's more to your plan with Nukpana than taking this sword, yes?" KC held up the sword as she walked over to Princess Derryth sitting on the cot. "What else were you to do? You must tell me if we're to have any hope."

"I was supposed to deliver your sword to her at the outskirts of the camp. Then, she was going to take me away with her to Emerald Mountain where she would bring Ish to me. We would live in the mountains at the edge of Eland. She promised this all to me in a vision."

"And, you believed her?"

"Well," Princess Derryth paused, "I did. I am such a fool."

"You are. Give me a minute to think." KC used her telepathic connection with Mr Scruffy explaining what Princess Derryth was up to in her thípi.

"KC, are you all right? Do I need to come there?" Mr Scruffy replied to her.

"No. But, what can I do about her? We must stop her."

"Use the Charm of Jealousy that Seif taught you. Do you remember it?"

"No. I must talk with her now. She is getting curious about what I'm doing."

"I'm on my way."

"Princess Derryth, let's figure out what we can do. I've told you that you shouldn't keep secrets from Ish. Let's bring in Mr Scruffy and Ish and tell them what has happened. They are bound to have an idea or two."

"I don't know. I don't want—" Princess Derryth stumbled on her words as Ish and Mr Scruffy walked into the thípi.

"Thank, God." KC smiled as she sent her telepathic message to Mr Scruffy. Ish moved over to Princess Derryth and KC walked over to Mr Scruffy. "What now?"

Mr Scruffy telepathed back to KC. "Don't get overly confident. And, you might want to pray to Yggdrasil and Mother Elder, while you are at it."

"KC, what's going on here? Princess Derryth is distraught. What did you do to her?" Ish moved toward KC.

"Me? I was lying on the cot when she roused me while she was trying to take my sword. Princess Derryth, you should tell him everything."

"Tell Ish? There's nothing to tell him," Princess Derryth stood up to leave.

Mr Scruffy stepped in front of her to stop her leaving. He raised one wing, and said,

"As the wind whips through the boughs
Yggdrasil bends and sways
May every ailment, every jealousy, every envy
Be plucked away
With the flow of your soul…"

"What are you doing?" Ish moved over to Princess Derryth and caught her in his arms as she collapsed.

"It had to be done. Nukpana put a spell on her and caused her to be jealous of you and KC. Any movement that the two of you did together, Princess Derryth took as a love touch, even when you were angry with KC," Mr Scruffy wiped a string of hair away from Princess Derryth's face. "Nukpana used her jealousy to get inside the camp. Princess Derryth will sleep for a while and Nukpana's spell will be broken. Place her on KC's cot."

After Ish positioned her on the cot, KC and Mr Scruffy motioned for Ish to join them in the corner of the thípi.

"Nukpana is using all of her tricks to get to us. We've got to be on guard. We must inform King Elder. If we begin to fight each other from within, she will win," Mr Scruffy said looking at Princess Derryth. "She lost a finger?"

"How did you know?" KC asked.

"I can see it missing."

"What? Where?" Ish asked moving toward Princess Derryth.

"Wait, Ish. Don't touch it? Nukpana will know we can see it is missing if you do," Mr Scruffy cautioned. "Her reach is stronger than I suspected. We must take Princess Derryth to King Elder, now."

CHAPTER 12
THE SWORD OF FEA

"Wh at's this?" King Elder said. Ish carried Princess Derryth into the throne room, laid her down on a nearby lounge, and stood before the king.

"KC. You are up and about. How are you?" Queen Esmé asked walking into the room. She noticed her daughter and moved to her side. "What happened?"

"I placed a Jealousy Charm to remove the spell upon her. She should be about ready to come around. Be careful. She has lost a finger," Mr Scruffy pointed to the missing digit on Princess Derryth's hand. "Nukpana took it in payment when she cast the spell on her."

"This is all too much for me. What are you saying? Nukpana had control of our daughter?" King Elder stood in anger.

"Caution, King Elder," KC said. "Nukpana is stretching her powers to inflict pain on us and to cause us to fight within. How better to conquer us then if we are weak from the inside."

King Elder said, "I don't understand." He walked over to his daughter. "The protection spell I cast on the camp. Why did it not hold?"

"I believe it did. But, there was a weakness, and Nukpana found it," Ish said. He stood before his King and Queen. "We have fallen in love. Princess Derryth thought I was chasing after KC. She did not believe I was doing my duty. Her jealousy ate at her until her weakness allowed Nukpana to break through."

King Elder sat down beside his daughter, placed a hand on her forehead, and began to moan. "What have we done?"

A large glow of light brightened the room as when a sun's ray first breaks through the canopy of the forest. Standing before them was Mother Elder. KC looked at the second being and guessed it was that of Yggdrasil.

"You are correct, my child," Yggdrasil said. He held out his hand, which to KC seemed strange coming from a tree, but a hand it was. The light around him, an aura of color radiating out in a flow of color, shown like a rainbow. "Don't be afraid. My touch will not feel strange."

KC took his hand and he helped her step up to where he stood beside Mother Elder.

Yggdrasil turned to the others in the room. "Nukpana has gained great strength. Her ability to put a spell on Princess Derryth is a sign we must heed." Yggdrasil looked to King Elder. "Are you at the ready?"

"We need to be better prepared. We need more time."

"There is none."

❦

"Did you have a good talk with Yggdrasil?" Mr Scruffy said. He wiped KC's forehead. She looked around and realized she was lying, once again, on her cot.

"What happened? I was just with Yggdrasil. How did I get here?"

"When you talk with the majestic, it takes a large amount of energy. Yggdrasil knew you would be zapped from his visit. He brought you here before he left. Mother Elder said to take care of her gift."

"Her gift?"

"Fea, your sword." Mr Scruffy handed it to KC. She noticed a bright, shining crystal embedded at the end of the hilt.

"Oh, my. What happened to it? It looks new."

"Yggdrasil restored it to its brilliance. When you wield this sword, all who are in battle will know it is you."

KC stood up. She griped the hilt of Fea, and then held it up. The light glistened off the metal as brightly as a beacon shining from a lighthouse. As she turned it over, she noticed a pulsating throb radiating up her arm.

"Look." KC pointed to the stone and showed Ish and Mr Scruffy how it pulsed. The stone continued to pulse as KC held Fea out from her body. Suddenly, a spiral of light came out of the stone, wove around the blade, and then wove around KC's arm, moving up to her shoulder, wrapping her arm in a glow of light that emanated a sacred quality.

"What do you think it is?" KC asked in wonder mesmerized by the light. "It's so beautiful."

"It's the Sacred Light. The Seed of Life," replied King Elder walking into KC's thípi with Queen Esmé. "The ancients spoke of the Sacred Light appearing when there is a need to become self-aware. The ancients believed the experience of the Sacred Light was essential to the education of the soul and the flow of knowledge. They knew the Sacred Light was symbolic of the inner realm. It's the subtle structure of awareness of the universe, Eldershire, and Yggdrasil, the Tree of Life."

KC nodded and said, "Yes. I remember now. Yggdrasil said those words to me. Why didn't I remember?"

"His approach is to have you experience it in the Land of Promise. Then, to bring home your teachings, you hear his words again—this time through me. As I was about to say, the *sacred* is necessary to develop the wonder of self-awareness by bringing consciousness and understanding together. The Sacred Light has now bound Fea to you. No one will be able to take it from you. Only death will separate the two of you." King Elder looked into KC's eyes.

She recognized a determination coupled with a sternness she had not seen in him before. "If Princess Derryth had managed to take this sword away before I held it as so, what would have happened then?"

"It could have been used by anyone. Fea will only glow when it is in *your* hands. And, when striking an enemy, it destroys the evil within. It will give you protection when you least expect it."

"The evil within?"

"Even Nukpana will not be safe from its cut. Use this newfound gift carefully. And now, I will leave you to prepare for battle." King Elder turned, took Queen Esmé by the arm, and they walked out into the camp together.

Mr Scruffy walked over to KC, "Are you ready to begin preparations?"

"I guess. I am troubled. Nukpana must know of the power this sword gives me. She won't let me keep Fea to use it against her."

"No. She won't," Ish said standing next to KC and Mr Scruffy. "She will use any and all means at her disposal to stop you and to destroy Eldershire. We cannot think she will do less than that."

"You are right to be concerned," Mr Scruffy replied. "We must gather in the center of camp and begin our work. Come. Time is fleeting."

"How is Princess Derryth? I've not had a chance to ask," KC asked Ish as they walked out into the camp center while Mr Scruffy flew up to a post.

"She is resting in her thípi. When you left with Yggdrasil, Mother Elder gave one of her special elixirs to Princess Derryth. It worked quickly, but she was weak afterward. Queen Esmé told me before we came to see you that Princess Derryth is beside herself with fear because we know what she has done. I went to see her, but she would not speak with me."

"I'm so sorry you are suffering through this."

Mr Scruffy flew down to Ish and KC, landing on her extended arm. "The Three Snowmen are here. It's so sad to see them without Seif."

Ish said, "I'll go get them set up. Maybe you and Mr Scruffy can come up with something we can do to help Princess Derryth?" He walked over to the training area.

As the group gathered in the center of camp, KC telepathed to Mr Scruffy. "There is something I need to share with you after we are done here."

"Can you not tell me now?"

"No. I think it best I wait. I must give her a chance."

"Who? Princess Derryth?"

"I'm not sure she will follow through with keeping her promise to keep us informed. She must. Only then will we have a chance."

"Trust me, she will do what is right in the end. I've known her since she first was a sprout. She will. Have faith."

"Faith is hard." KC bowed her head with solemn concern.

"It is and it is the power of the night. It helps me take flight each time I fly. Faith is my power."

KC nodded. They joined Ish and the three Snowmen—Sam, Mylo, and Foursure—who were already working through various sword-fighting moves.

"Before we start, I want you to know Seif did what he did for you and his homeland. Before he passed on, he shared with me his words of his power of mind. He loved you very much."

"Thank you," Mylo said. "We know. He sent his thoughts to us as he melted away. His heart was well intended. Now, we must prepare for battle."

All stood with bowed heads. KC pulled Fea out and the glow from the firelight falling on the blade gave her a sense of power. They all stopped what they were doing and stepped closer to her.

Sam said, "I don't think I've seen anything so beautiful that was also a weapon," Sam admired the sword. "It is engaging. I feel like I could take on the world with it by my side."

"It is a powerful weapon." Mr Scruffy moved Sam's stick arm down and away from KC. "You will find it also has untold magical powers as well."

"It's a sword that Nukpana would want, I am sure," Mylo spoke as she looked into KC's eyes. "I worry about this burden that has been placed on you." Mylo placed her arm on KC's shoulder.

"Thank you, Mylo. I'm fine. I have all of you. Mr Scruffy gives me good council. Ish is a strong bowman. And, the three of you have shown you care deeply about our quest. Between us, we'll retrieve the Efil Stone. I must have faith."

Mr Scruffy picked up his sword and said, "On guard!"

Princess Derryth paced up and down her thípi. She was still angry that she was not able to get the sword. Nukpana will kill me now she thought as she slumped down in a chair in the corner of her room.

She leaned her arms down on her knees and was about to move her hands up to her forehead when she heard the hissing voice of Nukpana. "Where are you?" Princess Derryth looked around the tent.

"I'm no where you can see me, not yet. My voice is coming to you through my magic. Your heart is not right. That is why you failed. You didn't wish KC harm. You only wanted to save yourself. You weak, foolish imp."

"I did try. You weren't there. You don't know how close I came."

"I was there. I am always with you. Don't you know how powerful I am?" Princess Derryth rubbed her left hand where her missing finger still throbbed. "You see, I am with you always." Nukpana let out a laughing, hissing sound.

"Are you going to kill me?" Princess Derryth began to cry.

"No, My Princess. Not if you want to try one more time for me. You can, you know. Are you willing?"

"I don't know. Ish, Mr Scruffy, and even Father seem to always protect her."

"Ish looks at her with loving eyes. Have you seen? And, KC looks back with the same intensity. While you, Princess Derryth, suffer from the loss of a finger. You can have your Ish and your finger back. You must do one thing for me—one small thing. Will you do it? You'll have your Ish when you are done. It is so simple. So simple. You won't know how simple until it is over."

"Tell me what I must do?"

KC LIFTED Fea and used a shield to block. Sword-shield-sword-shield-bam-bam-bam she followed the cadence that Mr Scruffy called out, continuing until she thought her arms would break. She was wearing out, even so she knew she needed to keep fighting. Her vision of Nukpana coming at her kept her practicing harder.

"You know, KC, you are not going to be fighting Nukpana and the Grey Menace by yourself." Sam said to KC telepathically. He moved in for a sweep and choke with a threatening move.

"Good one, Sam," KC responded. "The armor protection I have on is wearing me out more than brandishing this sword. My back is exhausted."

The hand-to-hand armored combat continued with Mylo, and then Foursure, each stepping up to take on KC when Sam stepped back to observe. "The goal is to wear you down until you no longer represent a threat. That's what the Grey Menace will do. They will advance and advance and advance. There will be hundreds of them and only one of you. You must wear the body armor in training as it will help you to engage your opponents for longer periods when you will not have on the armor while fighting out in the forest."

KC, Ish, and Mr Scruffy continued practicing various sword-fighting moves until KC said, "Enough! I'm tired. I can't lift this sword one more time. I'm going to my thípi, and then I'm going to go down to Stone's River for a dip. You guys want to join me?"

Mr Scruffy coughed, "You do realize, I don't swim."

KC smiled. "Actually, no, I didn't. Ish? What about you? Coming?"

"No. I think I need to take a break from all of you crazy beings." Ish said as he picked up his arrows and quill. "I probably should try and speak with Princess Derryth. She must be feeling rather distressed after what happened."

KC watched him walk over to Princess Derryth's thípi. "What am I to do with her?" KC asked Mr Scruffy. She stopped abruptly, reached down, and put Mr Scruffy on her shoulder. "I'm not sure what I was thinking. Now I can hear you speak while we walk."

"Thank you. I could have spoken telepathically, but you seem to be very tired."

"I am. I think after I get that dip, I'll be ready for some good ole-fashioned sleep."

"What do you mean by 'ole-fashioned'?"

"You know the kind I mean. Where you hunker down in the covers and when you wake you have no idea what day it is, you've slept so hard and so long."

Mr Scruffy hooted. "You do realize I generally do not sleep at night and I don't use covers."

Laughing, KC said, "I forget sometimes that you are not human."

"I know." Mr Scruffy used his wing to pat KC's head. "Princess Derryth isn't your problem, you know."

"I do. It's Nukpana. I'm sure Princess Derryth is a pawn for her. If I try and help the Princess, it will be hard to convince her I'm not doing it for Ish. She is the most jealous female I've ever encountered." KC stopped at the door to her thípi.

"You need to come right out and tell her that her jealousy is getting the best of her." KC took Mr Scruffy off her shoulder and set him down on the ground.

"Mr Scruffy, I would. But, did you know—" KC stopped speaking when she saw Princess Derryth approaching. "Here she comes now."

"I'll go on. You will want to speak in private." Mr Scruffy flew off to the tree canopy.

KC walked on into her thípi and started preparing her things to go to Stone's River. Princess Derryth followed her inside.

"Good Evening," KC said as she laid down her sword on her cot. "What brings you here?"

"I felt I needed to speak with you. Ish came to see me. He explained he didn't really have any feelings for you. I felt bad about my actions toward you when you were not yourself."

"I am glad you came. Did you tell him or King Elder about what Nukpana did to your hand? Did you explain she had broken through the spell?"

"No."

"Princess Derryth, are you insane? You should have told them. Come to think of it. I should have told them."

"Why didn't you?"

"I thought if you were strong enough to tell them, it would break Nukpana's hold on you. No good deed goes unpunished."

"What?"

"It was something my mother would tell me."

Princess Derryth said, "If you love Ish so much, show your might. Do your duty as the Savior, and save us. Fight Nukpana."

"You are a pawn. Do you realize that?" KC wrestled with her anger. She knew she wasn't getting through to Princess Derryth. She walked over to her cot, picked up her sword, and turned back toward her. "You know that I don't love Ish. In your heart, you know. But, you've allowed your jealousy and your unfounded hatred to rule you. You've allowed Nukpana to rule you."

"The almighty KC knows all. So, then, you're going to let us all perish? What's the matter with you?"

"I haven't known you long, but you know in your heart those aren't your words. Nukpana is speaking through you to me. I'll speak to her. Come get me!" KC stormed out of her thípi.

❧

KC MADE her way to Stone's River; she grasped what she'd done. Nukpana will use any method to stop me, she thought while she stepped out of the cover of the canopy and looked up. The sky was a deep mauve color. She was in awe. *I've never seen the sky that color.*

She walked over to a series of rocks that were carved like a seating area. KC climbed upon the highest one, positioned to lie back, and looked at the sky. Lying there, she couldn't help remembering how her family would go on hikes and lie down on large rocks when they reached a summit or a pretty place along the water's edge. She longed to be home with her son and his wife. Bill, Marie, and their dog, Boomer would come over on Sunday afternoons after church. They shared stories while she chopped the veggies for their afternoon lunch. She missed their time together—

"Son, you know how much I love you both, right?"

"Yes, Mom. You have told me that my whole life," Bill said as he put his arm around his wife's shoulder. "Marie loves you too, you know."

KC moved the chopped vegetables into the large bowl that would hold a salad large enough to feed an army, as her Mother would say.

"When is dinner going to be ready," Jay-H said as he walked into the kitchen. "I'm not starving, but a ball game comes on at two. I'd like to be finished in time to see the kick-off." He walked over to the kitchen counter and took a handful of chopped green peppers and popped them into his mouth. KC smacked at his hand.

"You missed." Jay-H smiled and walked back to the TV room.

"Only because I was busy," KC said winking at Bill. She tried to be a good wife to him. He was a hard man at times and made it difficult to like him. She had thought of divorcing him. He wasn't physically abusive, at least not yet. But, he did berate her and deride her accomplishments.

Bill sat down at the bar-side of the counter and Marie joined him on a barstool.

"How does it feel to be married? It's been what, two weeks now?"

"Two weeks, one day, and six hours." Bill smiled and held Marie's hand up kissing her fingertips.

KC smiled at Marie, "Newlyweds. Ah, those were the days."

"How long were you married before you had Bill?" Marie asked.

"Two years. Jack, my first husband, and I had had an earlier pregnancy, but it failed. I wasn't sure if I could handle losing a second child. Jack was so good to me during our first pregnancy. He never let me go a night without my favorite bowl of lemon custard ice cream. And, every Sunday the last two months before we lost our first child, he took me to our local park. There we would have a picnic, and Roxie, our dog romped and played. It was such an innocent time. Unfortunately, he never had the chance to repeat his care during my pregnancy with Bill."

"It sounds like you were so in love," Marie said. "Would you like a glass of water, Bill? I'm getting me one." Bill nodded.

"We were, and then I married Jay-H," KC smiled.

About an hour or so later, the table was set and the food ready. "Jay-H, come have dinner with us. Steak is on!" KC called. She brought two open bottles of wine to the table. Bill and Marie took their seats, and KC poured the wine.

"Well, you did everything in your power to make sure dinner was ready at two. Just like I knew you would," Jay-H said as he grabbed up his plate.

Bill said, "Come on, Jay-H. Sit down and visit with us. This is our first-time home for dinner since the wedding."

Jay-H threw food onto his plate, stuffed his steak knife and fork in his shirt breast pocket, cradled his glass of wine in his hand, and then stormed back to the TV room.

"Gees, Mom. I'm sorry," Bill reached over and squeezed his mother's hand lying on the table.

"He means well. He did ask that I get things done. If he had told me earlier this morning, I would have been able to finish by one. It is what it is. Bill and Marie, let's toast your life in your new home."

It was the last dinner she cooked for her family. KC was a dedicated wife and successful mother. Before she met Jay-H, she was an effective businesswoman. He wanted her to be a housewife. It wasn't something she had a mind to do all the time. Yet, she loved cooking, keeping a home, and taking care of her family. She also wanted to have an independent career.

While she made a good living, she took her job as a mother seriously. Bill had grown up, gone off to college, met Marie, and then they married. Jay-H never understood her; she never understood him. Then, they all died.

A tear started to fall down KC's cheek as she remembered the awful night that ended their life together. She repositioned herself on the rock. The two-suns were setting, and she was starting to feel a slight chill.

CHAPTER 13
FACE-TO-FACE

K C climbed down off of the stone chair, and sauntered over to the bank of Stone's River. The water was smooth as glass. It seemed to be standing still and no longer flowing. She leaned over and looked down into the deep. Her image came into view gradually, as though she was looking through a camera out of focus, and her eyes had to adjust to make the image clear.

It wasn't that she was startled by her reflection. She had adjusted to the fact that in this place she was no longer sixty-five. To see her young face again, after all the years that had past, caused her to think through her life. But, she couldn't get over how young she looked. Jay-H would have laughed and made a joke about me finding an elixir of eternal youth. *Oh, God, why did I stop that night? It is all my fault.* Bill and Marie were gone. KC rubbed her head in her hands.

The loss of family—her parents, first husband, a distant cousin, a high school friend, and a friend-of-a-friend—was something KC had experienced. She had not thought much about her own death. For all of her immediate family to die in a horrific crash all but destroyed her. She tried to grasp the significance of her being in Eldershire where death was seen as a forgone thought while on Earth, death was not discussed until it happened, if then.

During her short time in Eldershire, she had seen the ebb and flow of life. The waters of Stone's River meandered along much like life moved through its phases—sometimes turbulent, sometimes calm. The grasses beside the bank were a mixture of new growth and dying blades, leaves lay on the ground slowly marinating, turning black down the edges where green once shown. Death was part of life; she knew that. What was stark to her was the recognition that she had not had to look her own death in the face. Not until now.

She maneuvered around a small bush, and sat down on the bank, dangling her legs over into the water. The sky above was a muted deep purple laced with blues and grays. The two-suns sent their rays down, weaving as though forming a tapestry. The trees cast shadows that stretched out across the ground toward her like arthritic fingers —bent and twisted. Heavy, sweet, and musky aromas mingled with the smell of trees in bloom. The sky's gloom gave KC a feeling of looming danger that called and tugged at her heart. The pain she still felt from the death of her family was intensified when she watched Seif die. Could it only have been two nights ago? KC thought. Time moved slowly in Eldershire.

Nukpana had taken one life since KC's arrival. How many more would perish before the quest was over and she could return to her home world?

"That blasted hat," KC wailed. "Where are you now? Why can't you take me home?" She kicked her feet in the water. The cool droplets landed on her legs. She leaned back and looked up into the sky. Soaring above was a large bird. *It wasn't Mr Scruffy. He would talk to me*. It was a larger bird. He flew like he owned the sky.

Suddenly, the bird turned and swooped down landing with ease on the bank beside her. It was Iolair.

KC leaned back and studied him. He was a regal bird—a bald

eagle. With closer inspection, she noticed his white markings on his head contrasted sharply with the many patterns of chocolate-brown feathers on his body and wings. She loved to bird watch.

Iolair's beak was level with her face. He was about two feet tall, and wore a hat very similar to the one she had found that had brought her to Eldershire. Shaped like a bowler, it was black with a round dome-shaped crown ending in a large round rim. A plaid band wrapped around the base. A flower hung off the band, out from one side. Could it be the same hat? KC wondered. *I thought I left it in my thipi.* KC stared. Iolair stared back, his eyes intense.

"Hello," KC said.

"Good day to you, KC."

KC wasn't sure if she should ask. "Go ahead. Ask me," Iolair said.

"You read minds, too? I should have known. Does everyone around here?"

"Only the gifted ones."

"Apparently, I only meet the gifted ones. It is becoming normal for me to talk to animals."

"Not normal for your world. This is so, but normal for Eldershire. You know, you've always had that air about you. You think you know everything, but you know so little." Iolair clawed at the ground, as if he were looking for something.

"What do you mean I've 'always had that air' about me?"

"I shouldn't have said that. Are you ready to face her?"

"I'm about as ready as I can be. You?"

"We've been preparing to face the Grey Menace for some time now. They are a force to not take lightly."

"I can't imagine you afraid of fighting anyone."

"If I'm fighting fairly, I'm not afraid. It is evil that causes me concern."

"Nukpana is able to wreak havoc. That is a fact I've come to realize. I think it is because of the ability of the Grey Menace to surprise."

"Yes, it is a trait I admire, as a hunter."

"I imagine you would. Surprises to me, before coming here, were always a thing of fun."

"Even during Halloween in your world?"

"You know about Halloween?"

"I know much about Earth, as do many beings of Eldershire."

"You and Mr Scruffy, you both will have to tell me sometime about your visits to Earth." KC splashed her feet in the water. "May I ask you something?"

"You can ask. Not sure I can answer."

"Where did you get that hat? It looks like—"

"It's not. Things are not always what they seem. This hat has been passed down through my family for centuries. Is that all you want to know?"

"It sure looks the same," KC looked at it with care. "It does have a different colored band and a flower that is different from mine. Are you sure—"

"Positive. Look at it closer still. Go ahead. You can take it and look it over." Iolair leaned over toward her. KC took the hat off of his head. As she touched it, she was transported back to her backyard.

KC observed her family walking around her, yet it was as if she was really there. Her body would not move, but she heard her family talking. She didn't speak, even so, her family continued to talk with her as though she had. KC was confused and not sure what was happening.

She could hear Iolair's voice in her mind. "Be one with your faith. Believe. You will see what you need to know. When you are ready, let go of the hat."

"Well, Bill. Do you have to do that now?" Jay-H said as he moved around the table placing the silverware down for a meal. "Your Mother has made a very nice dinner. We are going to sit out here this evening, eat our meal, and enjoy where we are. You can stop being a pain in the neck. It won't kill you to wait. You can watch TV later."

KC observed Bill pout. He wasn't too much older than thirteen at the time. She remembered how she always loved to serve their dinner on the patio. The family tried to have a family dinner at least twice a week.

Jay-H walked back out onto the patio. He placed a large salad bowl on the table, set out three plates, and turned to Bill. "Do you think you could get up and go inside and help bring out some dishes? Your Mother has worked hard. Show some appreciation."

Bill got up, shrugged his shoulders, and went inside. Then, KC walked out carrying a large platter of steaks with baked potatoes wrapped in foil.

"What did you say to Bill? He isn't eating dinner with us now. Really? Could you not be a little more respectful of him? He is a young boy. He said you bawled him out for wanting to watch his favorite TV show. They moved it to this evening because of some special Presidential event yesterday. Honestly, I sure could use some help from you. I don't need you causing Bill to be upset." KC turned and walked back into the house.

Jay-H walked over to the patio bar, poured himself a drink, and sat down.

KC let go of Iolair's hat and was back sitting on the side of Stone's River with him to her side. "I didn't know that Jay-H tried so hard with Bill. I thought he left it all for me to deal with. I had no idea. He really tried to help."

"Yes. Then, he did try. He soon gave up. In your eyes, Bill could do no wrong. Jay-H saw that once Bill began to have a character all of his own, you fell out of love with him and in love with your son."

"I never stopped trying to love Jay-H. He was my husband. I felt like work became his main focus. He never wanted to come home. He always had to work—to make himself better, to provide more. We had plenty. I wanted to have my own career. He wouldn't let me."

"He thought that if you had your own career, he would no longer be needed. He loved you. The night he died he was on the phone when you got out of the car."

"Yes. He made me so mad that night. He had given me a horrible time about stopping to help that stranded traveler."

"What did he say?"

"He told me that because I felt I had to stop and help people all the time—that one day, I would stop for the wrong reason, thinking I was doing something good for somebody, and I'd find out. He said that I'd find out that what goes around does come around. He used to do that you know?"

"Do what?"

"Use lines from quotes or things he heard to prove a point to me. But, he always twisted them to fit his needs. The line, 'Karma, what goes around comes around,' was something I'd say. He would use it to make me feel guilty about something I was doing. That night I wanted to stop and help someone. He despised me for it."

"Now, you are in Eldershire. You have lost your family. And, you are preparing to go on a quest for the Efil Stone. You have a companion to guide you—Mr Scruffy. You have a magical sword to protect you —The Sword of Fea. What is there left for you to do?"

"I must find the Efil Stone. And, when I do, I must take it from Nukpana."

"Good. You need to know that when you have the Hat of The Fairy on, which is what my hat is called by many of Eldershire, and hold Fea, you will be more powerful. You should keep it with you. You may find it will help you."

"Why?"

"The hat you have is special for you and you alone. Keep it safe. Together with Fea, you have two of the pieces you will need to have the full power for your quest."

"And, all this time I was hating that hat for bringing me here."

"Don't hate something that may bring you your wish. You did wish on it, after all. Are you ready? We should get back." Iolair scratched at the ground again.

"I'm not. I'm scared to death. How can I possibly be ready to fight the likes of Nukpana and her army? I don't even know where to start."

"Sure, you do. Start by doing what you always do. Look for a way to help someone. Remember and let it go. Be one with your faith. Believe. You were brought here for a purpose." Iolair took the hat back from KC and put it on his head. "Jay-H always believed in you even when you didn't believe in yourself. He goaded you to get you to act—to pull up your bootstraps, and to get to work on whichever project you were determined to do. He believed in you. Now, you need to believe in yourself." Iolair's wings flapped up and down as he lifted off for the sky.

KC watched him leave and wondered if she'd see him again. While watching him soar into the treetops, she noticed the sky was beginning to change. The air moved in swirls. It reminded her of the clouds she saw rumbling into the valley when she and her family were in Kansas. A tornado was coming toward them. Jay-H was driving their van; they were on their way to Disneyland.

A strong wind began to blow. KC looked back at the water. White caps were starting to form as the wind continued to pick up in speed. She positioned her hand to stand up when she looked back into the water. Startled, KC sat down. Nukpana stood behind her.

She turned around and no one was there. "You've got to be kidding me. Now, I'm seeing things. Get a grip, KC." The water settled back down into the calm waters it was before and the wind stopped. She reached beside her belt and found Fea still there. *At least, I haven't lost that. Not yet, anyway.*

"What am I thinking?" She said aloud while looking into the water. "I'm going to die. Who am I kidding? This is madness." She pulled Fea out of its sheath, and held it up, and then looked at herself in the water. "Look at you. You're a silly old woman. You're in a strange land, have an owl, and now a bald eagle as your friends. This magical sword is supposed to help protect you. And, you don't even have on decent clothes to fight any battles. A Celtic warrior, you are not."

"You're right. You are doomed," Nukpana said.

Fea began to glow in KC's hand. She couldn't step back as she was on the edge of the river.

"You do realize you are about to die." Nukpana said as she held up Blazewing. The scepter's crystal ball began to glow. "It can be over quickly, if you like."

"Why? Why have it end here so easily? You've gone to a lot of trouble to meet here. Why are you going to end it now?"

"You're right. You are a lot of trouble. Why don't you give me that sword? We will be done with each other and you can go home."

"No, I can't. And, you know it. I must retrieve the Efil Stone."

Nukpana let out a wail of laughter. "No, My Pitiful One, you don't. Mother Elder and King Elder have filled you full of a lot of falsehoods. You only need to give me the sword. That is all you need to do and I can send you home. Quick as when you came."

"Don't come near me. I know that Fea can harm you. All I have to do is use it in the proper way. According to the prophecy, a human will bring you down. I'm that human. I will cause you great harm, unlike the Elderians. That's why you fear me, isn't it?"

"I see you've been talking to that fool of an owl. You're doomed. You're useless. And, you will lose in the end. That's all that matters to me. It doesn't matter what you say. It doesn't matter what you do, or, how you do it. You are weak, useless, and worthless. You are pitiful."

Angered by her words, KC said, "I'm here to take my stand." She held up Fea ready to make a strike. "Here, I will be what I'm supposed to be." She began to make her move. Fea came down on Blazewing and there was a loud sound that reverberated throughout the valley.

KC began to move forward for another strike, Nukpana's hand came up and knocked KC down.

KC looked up in fear. "I can't go down like this. I won't go down in this way." She used her will to get back on her feet, and swung Fea out with all of her effort.

A loud flapping sound was heard, and KC saw the sky filled with the Grey Menace. Within seconds, they had landed around her and some were hovering over the river behind her. At the sight of Nukpana's army, KC started to waver. She gathered her strength and stood her ground. "I will go down fighting."

The Grey Menace enveloped her in their dark forms, beating her down. Two lifted her up and held her bound in front of Nukpana.

"You thought you could beat me? You little insignificant human. You have the audacity to make me think you have the ability to kill me. Me? Nukpana Fraener! It will be a joy to watch you die at the cauldron. Take her away to the dungeon. Be sure you take that thing she calls a sword away from her, too. Once it is away from her, I'll be able to touch it. Until then, keep it safe. You'll know where to put it, won't you Sam?"

"Yes, ma'am. I do." KC looked in horror as Sam Slavetomé walked out of the Grey Menace toward her. He waved his hand in front of her face, and she fell limp in the bounds. Using a protective glove, he picked up the sword. The glow of Fea increased tenfold. "It appears we got to her in time. The full power of the sword has not made its complete connection with her soul. We should be able to break its magic after the second moon, before then could prove dangerous."

"You are a loyal servant. You were wise to come to us. I knew that night when I observed you watching me punish Gorge and Morge that you were of my evil nature. And, as I promised, I will reward you and your people. All Snowquidians will be protected. Seif tried to trick me. I wasn't sure what you would do. I'm glad to see you are loyal to your word. Your people will not be destroyed."

Sam bowed to Nukpana. KC, coming out of her induced sleep, couldn't believe that Sam was party to what was going on. She tried to speak, but her mouth would not work.

He said, "That's right, KC. You can't talk. I put a spell on you so that you could not warn the others through voice or telepathic means. You will be Nukpana's to do as she pleases, now that the sword is out of your hands."

"Be sure when you take her to the dungeon, she is chained. I don't want to risk any chance of her getting the sword back before I'm ready for her. You understand?" Nukpana disappeared in a puff of purple mist.

"It's your turn to travel now, little girl," Sam continued. "The Grey Menace will take you to the dungeon. I'll be by to check on you later. Be aware that I can still read your thoughts. You don't understand why I did this? Of course, you don't. You've thought of nothing at all but yourself since you got here. My people are suffering. Nukpana needed a way to get to you. I saw it as a bargaining chip. I used my ability to get close to you through King Elder's spell. Nukpana will set my people free. It is no worry of mine if others must suffer to save my people."

"You're the fool," KC managed to mouth. "Nukpana will trick you. She will rule over you. She will kill you in the end."

"How did you manage to speak? What goes on here?" Sam moved over to KC where the two Grey Menace held her arms. He opened her mouth and looked inside.

"You think you are the only one who knows some magic?" KC smiled.

"It can't be. There is no way you knew."

"You forgot that Mr Scruffy took me aside and taught me several spells and incantations. The bush that is over there was one he told me that whenever I walked passed it, I should take some leaves from its branches. He said that when I chew on it, the juices from the leaves would enable me to protect myself, if I ever encounter an evil force. When Nukpana called you out, I stuck some in my mouth and chewed."

"No mind. I can shut you up again."

"No. Once you cast that spell while the leaves of juice were in my mouth, the spell will not work again. You get to hear me talk and talk and talk."

"You're wrong." Sam moved his hand and KC felt weak in the knees. Her mind began to race. She wasn't sure if she was getting ill or what was happening. "Take her away," Sam instructed the Grey Menace.

The Grey Menace lifted her off the ground. In a stupor, KC said, "Let it go. Be one with my faith. I will see. I will fly. Here, I stand. Here, I will be what I'm supposed to be."

CHAPTER 14
DESTINY COMES

T he ground was hard and cold. KC took a secret look out of one eye and tried to determine where she was. She listened. The sounds were muffled; she couldn't tell what or who was making them. The taste left in her mouth from chewing the bush leaves was metallic. It sparked a memory. Was it the aftertaste that her Mother called 'pine mouth'? It had a pine flavor and reminded her of the smell a small pine tree gave off.

There was a faint light coming through an opening. KC wasn't sure if the opening was a window in a wall or an opening in a door. She could feel something under her. Is it possible? She reached down and could feel cold steel. It was Fea, her sword. It was still with her. How? She searched her memory and played back the scene. Sam had taken the sword from her, but she remembered something she didn't notice before; he winked at her.

Pulling the sword out of its sheath, KC stood up and held it out in front of her. She tried to concentrate and remember what she did the last time it glowed. Nothing happened.

Slowly, her eyes adjusted to the lack of light. She wondered where Mr Scruffy or Ish might be, and how long she'd been wherever she was. KC decided to move around, and determine in what kind of place she was stuck. She took each step with care, making sure she didn't stumble on something. As she stepped forward, she held her empty hand out in hope that she would feel a wall or some kind of surface before she banged her nose or Fea into it.

"This is frustrating," KC said in a soft whisper. She hoped that hearing the sound of her voice might help her determine the size of the room. Jack had taught her that when they were caving during one of their first dates. She smiled thinking about how much fun they used to have. She wished he were here now. He'd know what to do about seeing in the dark. What did he always tell me? 'That's right,' he'd say. 'Stop talking and listen.'

KC stopped walking and stood as still as she could. She listened.

In the distance, she thought she could hear the sound of someone crying, but she wasn't sure. The dark was too quiet to her liking. Fea started to glow. She wanted to jump for joy, but held herself back. 'Little steps,' she remembered Jack always said. She held up the sword and used the glow of the stone near the top of the handle to shine some light. As she walked around, she began to form a picture of where she was. It was a dungeon—dirt floor, walls, and the door appeared to be made of wood. She walked over to the door where the top had the small opening that the slither of light streamed through. The bottom of the opening began just above her eyes, even when she stood on her tiptoes, she couldn't see out.

From the way the room appeared and the fact she couldn't see anything on the other side of the door, she wasn't sure if Mr Scruffy or Ish would ever be able to find her. It dawned on her she didn't consider trying the door. *How stupid of me?* She walked over to the door, moved Fea up and down searching for a handle. There was none. She turned to walk away, and then she stopped. *Don't be stupid again.*

KC turned back to the door and pushed on it. Nothing. And then something. The door swung out and she could see into another room that was bathed in a little more light. She held Fea ready to strike and walked through the door. Stopping just as she went through the opening, she looked in all directions. From the way the shadows were cast around the room, she couldn't see anyone. She stepped into the room. The door slammed behind her. She jumped. No one was there.

This is bizarre, she thought. Why did they move her in here? Why did they leave Fea with her after she was knocked out? 'Keep your guard up,' Mr Scruffy and Ish would say while they trained. Having more time to train would have helped. 'Stay confident,' she heard Iolair's words echo in her mind.

There was a noise to her right. She stood in silence and wished Fea would stop glowing. It did. The room was darker and less likely for her to be seen, yet she could not see anyone either. She listened. There was the faint cry, again.

"Is there someone in here? I'm KC. I was with King Elder, Mr Scruffy, and Ish. I will not harm you. Where are you?" KC listened. The crying became more pronounced. "Hello?"

The answer came to her through muffled cries, "It's me, KC. Princess Derryth."

KC strained to see where the Princess was, but couldn't make out her shape in the darkness to the right. KC held up her sword. "Princess Derryth? Are you all right? How did you get here?"

"Nukpana brought me when I failed her the second time," Princess Derryth walked out of the shadows toward KC.

Fea began to glow. KC noticed Princess Derryth was dressed in a different garb, more like the way Nukpana dressed. She had on tight fitting leather like pants, a fitted bodice with straps laced up the front as the laces in a pair of shoes. The colors were grey and black, indistinct, like the dark dungeon. KC could tell from the low light that Princess Derryth's hair was gathered up and tied to the back. She had on knee high leather boots with spike heels.

"Did Nukpana make you dress like her?" KC asked taking a

guarded stance. She held Fea tighter against her chest and it glowed brighter.

"No. I decided she looked like she was a strong woman. A woman in control. I wanted to feel what she felt. I wanted to be in charge as she is in charge. I believe in her. She isn't a bad woman."

"You can't be serious. Princess Derryth, what will your father and mother think? You know——"

"My father and mother are weak. They have no idea what Nukpana could do for our kingdom, our world, our universe. She has great expectations for us. She believes and I believe she can make us great. Strong. More powerful than we've ever been. I want that." Princess Derryth walked closer to KC.

KC took a step back. Fea's glow brightened more. The color began to turn a yellow-orange. "I think you have come close enough. Fea doesn't like you getting too close. And, neither do I."

"Why? Are you afraid of me? I don't even have a weapon. You could strike me with your sword and kill me with one blow. Why are you afraid?" Princess Derryth stepped closer.

KC stepped back and her back touched the wall behind her. Hands reached out and held her fast. KC tried to strike out and twist her arms, but even her legs were grabbed. She couldn't move. Fea must have grown brighter because of what was behind her and not because of Princess Derryth. You fool, KC thought. She wished for someone to come to her rescue.

Princess Derryth took a step closer. She reached for Fea, and took it out of KC's hand. As she touched it, she began to cry out in grief. "No! It can't be. What have I done? What have I done? Mother Elder, forgive me."

"Princess Derryth, don't be frightened. Give me back Fea and I can help you. Release me and I'll fight to get us out of here. You don't need to be worried about what you saw when you grabbed Fea. You can come with me and all will be well."

Princess Derryth turned toward KC and glared at her. "You tried to trick me. It was you that made me see Nukpana kill me. She wouldn't do that. You were faking my vision. I should have known. I'll take your sword to her. She will be proud of me. She will reward me and make me Queen of all of Eldershire. Nukpana told me you were a witch like she is. But, Nukpana is a good witch. She will take care of us all."

"No. She won't! You can't believe I would harm you. I've never done anything to cause you pain." KC understood her words fell on deaf ears. Princess Derryth walked out of the room carrying Fea and with her all hope for KC to leave the dungeon. The hands that held her let go. She could move. She turned to look at what was holding her and the wall was plain. Simply dirt. Nothing was there.

MR SCRUFFY WOULD WRING his hands if he had them, he thought as he paced back and forth in KC's thípi. "Why can't we locate her? I don't understand what is blocking us? Have you tried everything?" He looked up to Ish.

"Yes. King Elder is just as confused. Nukpana must have her. That is the only explanation. But, where? Our spy is deep within the Grey Menace. We've not heard anything—good, bad, indifferent."

"This worries me. If KC is in the dungeon, we will need to go in to rescue her. We need to make our move before Nukpana kills her or tortures her beyond our saving."

"You're right, Mr Scruffy. We must act now," King Elder said. "All of Eldershire have been summoned. We are making plans to move soon."

"I appreciate your need to bring your armies together, but KC doesn't have that much time. We were caught off guard when Nukpana took KC. We must act now. I'm going to Grave's Mountain. It must be where Nukpana holds her. Anyone coming with me?"

Ish stepped forward as did Queen Esmé. "You can't be serious," King Elder said to his wife. "What will you do?"

"Our daughter is there, too. I hope to save her, if it is not too late." Queen Esmé raised her hand in a swooping motion. As her hand came down, her regal gown was transformed into a tighter-fitting garment that fit her form and allowed her to move the sword she now held. The effect created a long-waisted appearance and was enhanced with a skirt that trailed to the ground that signified her regal status among the Elderians.

King Elder shrugged his shoulders, maneuvered his hands, and was transformed into battle gear. "I guess we must join my wife."

Mr Scruffy flew through the thípi opening, "It's about time."

THE PACING BACK and forth was beginning to wear on KC. She hadn't seen Princess Derryth since she took Fea. *At least I've got some light to see.* The light came into the room from no apparent source. It was simply there. KC looked the room over and found no way to escape. It wasn't apparent how to leave the outer room. She walked into the inner room, though with not as much light, she determined it, too, did not have an egress.

What am I to do? She wished she had someone to talk with about her situation. "Where are you Mr Scruffy?" she said aloud. No answer. Trying her telepathic skills again seemed futile. They weren't working. *I guess Nukpana has placed a spell on me after all. Or, is it this room?*

KC walked out into the outer, larger room where the hands had held her. She looked in the direction of where Princess Derryth exited. It couldn't be that simple, could it? She walked over to the area where she thought Princess Derryth walked through the wall. KC stood there and pondered the possibilities. 'Think out of the box,' she recalled Mr Scruffy saying during her training. She walked forward and found that as she got to the wall she kept walking through. She was jittery with joy at finding the opening, but fearful that it was another trap.

With caution, she stepped forward. The light grew brighter. There was a long hallway. *This can't be right.* KC worried Nukpana was leading her to more trouble. But, what else could she do? She had to take a chance.

KC decided to try her telepath abilities again. "Oh, Mr Scruffy! I wish you and Ish could hear me. I'm in a passageway, leading away from a dungeon. I'm making my way as best I can." KC walked cautiously, prepared for Nukpana to jump out at her. "It's scary in here without Fea."

The passage was long and mostly straight. A hand reached out and grabbed KC's arm. She stood in a side alcove and faced Princess Derryth.

"Shhh. Don't say a word. Don't think. I haven't much time. You did get to me. When I grabbed Fea, something you said changed me. KC, I'm not sure we'll get out of this, but know you are not alone here. There are others. Not all members of the Grey Menace believe in her. I won't say her name. But, know I have Fea and will keep her safe. I'll return her to you as soon as I can."

KC started to speak and Princess Derryth placed her fingers to KC's mouth. "Here. Take this. When you get to the end of this passage, go left. No matter what you do, do not go right. It will take you straight to her lair. We are in the bowels of Grave's Mountain. You do not want to see her when she is transformed into you know what."

Again, KC started to say something. Princess Derryth held up her hand. "I wish I had time to tell you everything. I can't. I do know my Mother and Father, Ish, and Mr Scruffy are on their way. You must continue to believe. Have faith. You will triumph. And, what ever you do, don't forget me. Remember your visit to my thípi right after I left. Go there again when you return to King Elder's Camp. You will know what to do."

Princess Derryth looked out into the passageway. She stepped back into the alcove. "You don't have much time. You must make haste. Go down the passageway; go left. Follow that passage and there will be someone you know that will greet you. Know that I'm here for you, KC. I'm sorry for all I said to you before. It wasn't truly me, you know." KC smiled. Brought her fingers up to her mouth to signal she would not speak. She gripped Princess Derryth's hands and held them close to her chest. Then, she let go of Princess Derryth's hands, turned, and went down the passage.

🐾

"ARE YOU SURE?" Mr Scruffy said telepathically to Ish. He flew out over Snow Valley at the base of Grave's Mountain.

Ish looked up. "It was her. I'd know her voice anywhere. Princess Derryth said KC had helped her break the spell Nukpana had on her. She said she would do what she could to help. We should go to the West side of the mountain. She said we'd find KC there."

"Forces are mounting and are bringing good to overpower evil this night!" Mr Scruffy flew leading the way.

🐾

THE PASSAGEWAY NARROWED down from being wide enough for four people abreast to walk to that of a single body width. *I wished Princess Derryth had come with me and I had Fea.* KC continued to walk with caution. Her senses on high alert, she was certain Nukpana would appear to stop her.

Without warning, KC got an overwhelming fear and an enclosed feeling. Her heart began to race. *Oh, God. What's happening to me?* She sat down. The need to cry over came her as a panic attack took over.

"Lord, what am I doing? This is too much." KC could feel her fear growing. "It's going to overtake me if I don't keep focused. I can't stand tight places. Mr Scruffy! I wish you were here. I'll continue to talk telepathically whether you or Ish hear me or not. It will give me much needed confidence and courage. You can be my afflatus, a divine intercedent. My fear is working its way into my heart. My faith is wavering. I need to use my instincts. Think, KC. Think!"

"Ish, did you hear her?" Mr Scruffy said as he flew down and landed in a tree. "KC is in a dungeon. Did you hear?"

"I did. Calm down. We are moving toward Grave's Mountain as fast as we can. All we can do is hope that KC can hold on until we can get there. I didn't hear anything about Princess Derryth. Did you?"

"No. I don't understand how we can hear KC, but she can't hear us. It must be Nukpana's doing. She's playing with us. We must keep our wits about us. I'm going to fly ahead." Mr Scruffy took off and as he did so, he grew in size. "I may be able to fly close to the West side. I'll telepath what I find."

"Be careful," Ish replied. "We should reach the West side of Grave's Mountain by dark."

"The rabbit does not laugh at the bear," KC said aloud. Repeating the mantra that Jack taught her while they were hunting many years ago. It helped her to keep focused, and it helped her to remember that she was as strong as she needed to be. *I am strong.*

KC saw something sparkle in front of her down the dirt passageway in the light that came through an opening. Could it be? KC walked cautiously forward to where the gleaming object lay. She couldn't believe her eyes as she came closer to it. "It is Fea!"

She stopped about four feet away from her sword, and then looked behind her, and then in front of her. The light cast only enough for her to see about twenty or so feet in either direction. She stepped closer, bent down, and reached out to pick up her sword. As her hand reached the hilt, Fea began to radiate a light purple glow. KC stood up and looked around.

"You can pick up Fea. I placed her there for you. Trust me, KC. Tell Ish I always will love him and what I do, I do for all of us." It was a voice KC prayed was Princess Derryth's.

She reached and picked up Fea. Holding her sword out in front, a rumbling sound came rippling toward her. Then, a brighter light shown through an opening. She could feel a cool breeze on her face. She walked up to the new doorway that came into view. She held Fea at the ready, and stepping through the opening, she heard a voice she knew was there to save her.

"KC! Stay where you are. I'll be right there."

KC held her hand over her eyes, as the setting twin suns were extra bright. She saw her companion and dear friend soaring above. "I'm so happy to see you and to hear your voice, Mr Scruffy."

CHAPTER 15
SACRIFICIAL LAMB

M r Scruffy landed near the entrance that KC had just passed through. She jumped on his back easily, as it had become customary for her to do. She held Fea out as she said telepathically to Mr Scruffy, "Take off, my friend!"

He flew with the grace of an eagle and the speed of a falcon. She held his wisdom close to her heart. She heard him say 'awesome life experiences will fuel your future in unexpected ways...enjoy each moment.' She rode on his back thinking about the last hours of her captivity in Nukpana's dungeon. It wasn't clear to her what had happened or how it all transpired. Nothing seemed to ring true with what had been revealed about Nukpana and Princess Derryth since her capture. Yet, here she was, flying away from Nukpana and Grave's Mountain—unscathed, at least for now.

Mr Scruffy soared high over Snow Valley. He caught a thermal wind and glided down toward the Wild Woods. KC inhaled the sweet aroma of the forest glen. She took another deep breath, soaking her lungs with the freshness of freedom. She wasn't sure how long this respite might last, but she was relishing in each moment, if for only a few precious ones. Her link with her special friend permitted them to talk with ease while he flew.

"Where are we going?" KC telepathed to Mr Scruffy.

"We will meet with Ish and the rest of King Elder's forces just across the river. They should be near Red Bluffs Divide by now. It is not far, as the owl flies. Hoot! King Elder has set up a makeshift camp just at the ridge. We will meet with him and Ish to plan our next moves. You can share with them at that point what happened. How is Princess Derryth?"

"I'm not sure. She helped me. I'm afraid that act of kindness may have cost her. Our only hope is to reach her in time."

"Did you see anyone else while you were in the dungeon?"

"No. Why?"

"We had someone on the inside working for us. We haven't heard from him in some time. When you were taken, we figured he must have been sacrificed. We're almost at the divide; we can talk more later. Hold on."

Ish, appearing agitated, walked up to Mr Scruffy and KC as they entered King Elder's camp. "Is she safe?"

"Who?" Mr Scruffy asked.

"Princess Derryth! KC, is she safe?"

"I don't know."

"Where is she? Why didn't she come with you?"

"I don't know. She pulled me aside in an alcove. Told me how to escape and said she would not join me. I don't know if she's safe."

"How could you leave her?"

"She wouldn't come with me. She said I had a small window of time to get out. As I left, I could not determine if what she was telling me was true. She had taken Fea from me when I first arrived. She was working with Nukpana. Quite frankly, when she and I first met in the dungeon, I wasn't real fond to learn she had an alliance with Nukpana. I will say, after I made it out of Grave's Mountain and saw Mr Scruffy, I was relieved to know that Princess Derryth had helped me."

"But, you left her!" Ish brought his hands down slamming them into his legs. "You did nothing to help her," he began to cry.

KC moved to him and put her arm around his shoulders. "Ish, I know your pain. I felt it the first time I saw her working with Nukpana. I tried to talk to her then. I tried to get her to come with me earlier. She refused. Please know this was Princess Derryth's choice. I could not change her mind. She told me to tell you that she would always love you and what she chose to do, she chose to do for all of us."

Ish continued to cry. *It was obvious Princess Derryth would be found out for helping me*, KC thought. *It was her choice. A choice I'm not sure I could make. She was stronger willed then I had imagined. If it wasn't for her—.* KC's thoughts trailed off as the enormity of Princess Derryth's decision swept over her.

PRINCESS DERRYTH WALKED BACK into her cold, dark room at the far end of Nukpana's castle in Grave's Mountain. She hadn't really thought much about her situation since she helped KC find her way out of the dungeon. I hope she got away safely, she thought as she sat down on her bed. She rubbed her hands over the fine silk coverings. She knew her love for fine things had been what led her to make the choices she made. Princess Derryth thought about how being in Nukpana's lair had caused her to betray her Father and Mother, and how she would not want to face Ish after what she had done.

"At least, I've made one thing right," she said. She got up and walked over to her dresser, and rubbed her hand over the hairbrush that was made of finely detailed silver encrusted with jewels.

"It is beautiful, as you were," Nukpana said.

Princess Derryth startled turned around and saw Nukpana holding Blazewing. "Am I to die?"

"What is this, My Princess? Are you afraid? Why? Have you done something evil?" Nukpana walked over toward Princess Derryth. "Sit here." Nukpana pointed to a chair off to one side of the dresser. Princess Derryth hesitated. "Sit."

Princess Derryth sat down on the chair and faced the ornate mirror. Nukpana picked up the hairbrush and began to brush Princess Derryth's hair. She continued, "Speak, or do you want Blazewing to find your tongue? What is the meaning of your gloom? You should be happy. We have that human in our dungeon. We have her sword."

"Please, your great Treoraí," said Princess Derryth as she tried to turn around to face Nukpana, but was held steadfast by Nukpana's strong hands. Princess Derryth looked at Nukpana through the mirror and said, "You held them. You did."

"And, where are they now?" Nukpana asked. She continued to brush Princess Derryth's hair. The mirror showed both faces. Princess Derryth's was trying to figure out the best answer and Nukpana's waiting to hear her answers.

"K-K-K-KC managed to—" stammered Princess Derryth.

"To what?" roared Nukpana turning Princess Derryth to face her. Nukpana's face seemed to grow in size as her anger grew. "She is still in the dungeon, isn't she? You didn't let her escape, did you? You wouldn't do that, now would you, My Princess?" Nukpana reached down and pulled Princess Derryth's chin up hard enough to cause Princess Derryth to lean backwards. "How dare you—but no. Say you didn't allow her to escape! You might still be forgiven."

At that moment, Princess Derryth knew her time was almost gone. She would have to warn the others. She noticed a shape standing near the entrance to her room. She wasn't sure, but she thought the figure favored the image of Sam Slavetomé. Could he be the mole that her father and mother spoke about? "She is gone! And, so is her sword!"

Nukpana's anger grew even stronger, Blazewing began to glow a purple haze. Within seconds, Nukpana became the Purple Drakein. A few seconds more, Princess Derryth was enveloped in flames. She screamed out in horror, and then fell into a pile of ash on the ground. The nearby furnishings of the room she had lived in the past few lunations were singed from the flames that had swallowed her. She was no more.

"Let that teach you! You were such the fool." Nukpana had transformed back to herself.

She walked around the area where Princess Derryth once sat. "I hate a mess." Waving her hand to move the charred remains of the chair out of her way, she walked over to the dresser, and picked up the jewel-encrusted hairbrush, looked in the mirror and adjusted her bangs. She turned and walked over to the bed.

Standing back and looking at the headboard, Nukpana studied the details of the woodcarving. Each piece that made up the headboard was a tree specimen from the Wild Woods. She had delighted in harvesting the wood, and its creation by skilled craftsmen she had captured as servants, and then disposed of when they had finished their handiwork. The intricately carved wood depicted a scene of beings frolicking around Stone's River. She smiled as she thought about the horror King Elder would have if he knew his own daughter had rested her head below such a sacrificial piece.

Stepping closer, she rubbed her hand over the carving, and then pushed a flower petal on the right side of the head of a tree spirit that resembled the face of Princess Derryth. The flower petal acted as a lever. A panel opened, and slid away slowly revealing an inner cavity.

Nukpana held Blazewing up to the opening and it cast a light inside. A second panel moved apart when she tapped Blazewing on the inner wall. At the back of the inner most compartment, she could see the Efil Stone—deep dark red amber. Nukpana could see the tree symbol carved into its surface glowing a bright, golden yellow. She reached in, picked it up, and brought the Efil Stone out into the room. It turned a ghostly white. She turned it over in her hands. The ornate carving of the tree symbol, which was its connection to Yggdrasil and Mother Elder, no longer glowed. She placed it back inside the compartment, setting it on a pedestal, and then shut the panel door.

"At least the Efil Stone is where it is safe. Princess Derryth, your death will start the downward spiral of the Eldershire kingdom and all its rulers." She turned, flicking her wrist, sending out purple waves of light that tidied the room as she walked out into her lair.

SAM SLAVETOMÉ WALKED into the same room Nukpana had just left. He couldn't believe what he had witnessed. Princess Derryth had sacrificed herself. She told her KC was gone so that Nukpana would kill her instantly. Princess Derryth was a young and foolish girl, he thought. Yet, she was the Princess. His hatred of Nukpana was reaching new heights. Her sacrifice was needless. He had hoped he'd be able to broker some kind of peace, but it was clear to him now that Nukpana did not care for Eldershire or any of its inhabitants.

At the side of the bed, Sam looked intently at the carving. He confirmed that the face next to the flower was indeed an image of Princess Derryth. He started to push the lever to take the Efil Stone. He stopped. He figured he should wait and take the news to KC and King Elder. Nukpana may have cast a spell on the panel and would know someone opened it, he reasoned.

Back in his own room, he began to gather his stuff. *I must make my move.* He had prepared several pieces of evidence that he thought would help him find the Efil Stone. He no longer needed them, but he didn't need to leave anything incriminating behind. *I've got a small window of time to get to camp and tell KC where she can find the Efil Stone.* His work as a mole in Nukpana's tribe to find the Efil Stone was done. Princess Derryth's sacrifice made it possible. He had no time to waste.

KING ELDER and Queen Esmé came into the thípi where Ish, Mr Scruffy, and KC were resting.

"We must plan our attack to rescue Princess Derryth," King Elder said. He unfolded an old map and laid it on the ground. "Gather around me and I will show you what is known about the interior of Grave's Mountain. KC, you can let us know what you learned and which of the passageways you think you used to escape. You can also point out where you think you were when you last spoke with Princess Derryth."

"I will do my best. Where did this map come from?"

"Many lunations ago, several of Ish's ancestors made a trek into Grave's Mountain. This was when Nukpana first came to power. She was not as strong as she is now and her ability to turn into the Purple Drakein was shaky too. Six went in, two came back. You can see the singe of the map along the edge."

"It was a mournful day mixed with joy that we have this map," Mr Scruffy said. "I lost my great-grandfather. He had gone with them because he had been inside the mountain as an owlet before the days of the evil Nukpana."

KC looked into Mr Scruffy's eyes and saw a pain of loss she knew all too well. She reached out and touched Mr Scruffy's wing. "I'm sorry for your loss."

"We've all lost much because of Nukpana—some, more than most. The magic we have is powerful, but it has its limits. Nukpana has reached into the dark and found evil she can use to build her strength. We, on the other hand, must use what we have and counter her evil moves with all the more cunning acts. Our mole will gather much needed information. We can only hope he is safe." Mr Scruffy patted KC's hand. "Thank you."

After looking at the map, KC pointed out where she thought she had spoken with Princess Derryth. "I'm not sure, but this looks like the alcove. Here is where I walked out." KC pointed to the side of the mountain where Mr Scruffy found her. "This here," she paused. "Yes, right there is where I found Fea." KC held up her sword. "Princess Derryth must have been the one to place it there."

"Are you sure? It could have been our mole who was there looking for you and the Efil Stone. He could have helped, too." King Elder pointed to where the castle inside the mountain housed the living quarters of Nukpana, her servants, and others when she was not in Purple Drakein form and where her lair was when she was there. He also pointed to the location of the dungeons.

"There is more than one dungeon. Maybe Princess Derryth was placed in one of those?" she said with a hopeful tone.

King Elder moved the map around so that they could look at the living quarters area. They looked at each other suddenly grabbing their ears. A sharp, whistling sound pierced the air followed with the horrible sound of someone reacting to excruciating pain.

"The cries you hear are those of Princess Derryth. See the vision of her death projected into your minds," Nukpana said to them all.

Ish screamed in horror, while King Elder and Queen Esmé clutched each other and cried out in a mournful tone of despair. KC knew the feeling of horror. It was a stark reminder of how terrible death could be for any creature. The terror was all the more with images etched in her mind. Despite Princess Derryth's scream, it looked to KC as though she smiled while the flames of the Purple Drakein engulfed her. The stark contrast struck KC. The last thing Princess Derryth said to her was to tell them that what she was doing she was doing for them. Princess Derryth gave her life for all of Eldershire. Was it possible that seeing her smile was Princess Derryth's way of saying she knew those she loved would be safe?

MR SCRUFFY FLEW KC to Mother Elder and Yggdrasil, who had summoned KC to them after hearing about the fate of Princess Derryth. Landing softly at the Land of Promise, they saw Mother Elder and Yggdrasil waiting for them. Seeing Yggdrasil in human form, KC was struck by his appearance. His unmistakable image of a weathered face gave her an impression of many centuries of living and a sense of wisdom.

She watched him walk toward her with Mother Elder at his side. KC judged that he stood about seven feet tall. His clothing was simple, yet elegant in form. His face immortalized the countless souls who lived and had lost their lives through the centuries. A sad, sorrowful expression looked back at her, and then it seemed to change and reflect a different look of grief, as though all of the tree spirits who had lived were being expressed to her. Her mind's eye could see the tree spirits with their drooping branches and moss superimposed upon his body's image. She felt the presence of each tree's soul. They were being revealed to her all at once.

"Greetings, KC," He held out his hand, turned his face at an angle, and then moved his body with quintessence. Standing next to her Yggdrasil said, "I'm honored to see you, again. It is sad that the tragic death of Princess Derryth would bring you here so soon."

KC bowed and said, "Yes, Sir. It is a sad time. King Elder, Queen Esmé, and Ish are grieving."

"Yes. You have a duty to perform now that is critical to your success at completing the prophecy to retrieve the Efil Stone. You must go to Princess Derryth's thípi. There you will find a sapling, a tiny tree spirit, which is a gift to be given to King Elder and Queen Esmé before the second moon disappears behind the night sky. It is critical you do not fail. Will you do this for all of Eldershire?"

"I will."

"Very well. Go, my child. Make haste!" Yggdrasil and Mother Elder gradually moved back to their thrones and out of sight.

"Let's go, Mr Scruffy. Take me to Princess Derryth's thípi as fast as you can."

Landing in front of Princess Derryth's thípi, KC noticed a hue of green that seemed to envelope the structure. She thought back to something her mother told her when she was teaching her about death, trees, and the dogmas of life after death—'One of the beliefs is that souls are eternal. And by extension, with each new season, new life begins from the souls of those departed.' After all of the death and destruction they had recently witnessed, she hoped her mother's teachings would prove true.

KC walked into Princess Derryth's thípi with Mr Scruffy on her heels and looked around for any signs of the sapling that she was told to find. She wasn't sure what she would find or even what she was looking for.

"Do you hear that?" KC said.

"Yes. It sounds like whimpering. Hold on. Be quiet," Mr Scruffy cocked his head to the right and seemed to be in a trance. A moment went by and he continued, "There. By the dresser. Do you see it?"

In the corner of the thípi, KC could make out a small shape. It looked like a tiny tree, yet it had a face with an image that gave her the feeling she was looking at an infant Princess Derryth. "Can it be?" KC said.

"Be gentle. Walk slowly toward it. It will be very frightened. It must have been here since before we left for Grave's Mountain. I'm surprised no one found it before." Mr Scruffy walked up next to the sapling. He stuck out his wing, and said, "There, now. No need to fear us. We are here to help you."

Behind them, KC heard a sound. She turned, only to find the ghostly image of Princess Derryth. "I haven't much time," she said. "You must know by now that Nukpana has destroyed me. But, before I left here, I had placed my twig of a finger that she had cut from my hand in the ground. The twig has now sprouted into a new tree. A portion of my soul will be within this sapling, but you must take it to my parents. It will ease their grief." As Princess Derryth spoke her last words, a portion of her image blended in with the sapling.

"Did you see that?" KC asked Mr Scruffy. "Look, I can see Princess Derryth's smile on the sapling's face."

"It is there. The miracle of the life of a tree. Its roots go far into the ground, twisting and winding, and all are interconnected in ways we cannot begin to explain. Can you pick up the sapling so that we can take it to King Elder? He and Queen Esmé will be so blessed to find this sapling amongst their coterie."

KC reached down and carefully retrieved the sapling. She found a container sitting on Princess Derryth's dresser table and placed the sapling inside with a little bit of earth.

Mr Scruffy tilted his head and said, "Why did you do that?"

"It's how we move seedlings back home. Isn't it how you do it here?"

"I actually do not know. It looks like a fine way to transport this special creature. Come, let's go to King Elder's throne room."

As they walked toward the throne room, many of the other Elderians came up to them and wanted to know what KC was carrying. She tried to speak to them telepathically, but their voices began to overwhelm her. She felt them crowding her and she was concerned about what would happen to the little sapling.

"Stop!" King Elder shouted from the entrance to his throne room. "What is the meaning of all this clamor? I could hear you all the way into my private chambers. Have you no resp—" King Elder stopped suddenly. "KC, what do you hold?"

KC looked at him with tears in her eyes. She held up the sapling and said, "This is from your daughter, Princess Derryth. Mother Elder and Yggdrasil send their blessings of this new life sprung from a twig of your daughter. May you have joy and happiness with your new sapling."

King Elder took his new baby in his arms and held her with care. He looked over each part of his child. Tears began to fall.

KC watched noting her own joy when she held her son, Bill. She remembered Jay-H's face when he first saw Bill.

"KC," The nurse said carrying her son into her hospital room. "When will your husband be here?"

"He should be right out. He stepped into the bathroom."

"Would you like for me to wait? I can take a picture of the three of you."

"Please." KC took Bill from the nurse's arms and positioned him so he could nurse. "I am saddened my first husband, Jack, who was killed serving in the air force will miss meeting his son. But, Jay-H will be a good father."

"Well, look at who has joined us in this world," Jay-H walked over to KC and pulled Bill's blanket back and looked down at his face.

"Would you like for me to take a picture of the three of you?" the nurse asked.

"Yes." KC said.

After the nurse took the picture, she said, "I'll have prints made for you." She left the room.

"Would you like to hold him?"

"He's eating right now. I can wait. He is our little boy." Jay-H got up and walked over to the window.

"He is a healthy eater. I'm so happy you are here to share this with me."

Jay-H turned around, a smile came upon his face, and he walked over to her, then kissed them both on the forehead.

She felt the same joy she saw on Jay-H's face that she now viewed on King Elder's face. The joy they shared knowing there was another being that they would share their lives and world with.

She watched Queen Esmé walk with a slow pace toward King Elder. KC could tell she was deeply moved by seeing the sapling. She placed her hand on her husband's shoulder, bent down, and kissed his head. "She is beautiful."

"Yes. Just like Princess Derryth," he said.

Queen Esmé reached up, wiped her eyes, and then held out her arms to hold their granddaughter. "Words are not coming to me easily right now. The joy in my heart is tempered by the thought our daughter is not here to see our happiness at the birth of her child." Queen Esmé choked back tears. "I know we will be forever honored by our daughter's sacrifice." She placed her hand within her husband's hand, and said, "Life goes on…"

Time seemed to stand still. KC could see the spirit of Princess Derryth shine brightly as it floated up into the mauve skies of the night.

CHAPTER 16
A STRUGGLE AGAINST DEATH

"Life is a struggle, but the greatest desire of life is to avoid death," Mr Scruffy said to KC while walking to see King Elder. "The last moon saw many changes here in Eldershire. Many more will come; I fear not all of them will be to our liking. Nukpana's evil web is growing wider. Death is closer for many."

"Mr Scruffy, how do we move on? The horrific murder of Princess Derryth cannot be ignored. As you've said, many will die if we fight. But, how can we fight Nukpana and win? What magic is available to use? I know so little; yet, I am supposed to help save this world. I am unworthy for this quest."

Mr Scruffy stopped walking. KC picked him up, and placed him on her shoulder. She had gotten used to him sitting there when they talked. At first, his talons would stick her shoulder, but with time, Mr Scruffy had adjusted to sitting on her without digging in. Sometimes, she'd have to move his foot when he got excited, but most of the time, she looked forward to him being close to her. "Okay. Speak your mind."

"I find you falling back into self-doubt. Why?" Mr Scruffy adjusted his seat on her shoulder. "Why can't you believe? You are struggling to avoid dying. Your fear of Nukpana is your fear of death."

"Of course, it is! What do you expect? I can't go home if I die here. I want to return to my time, have my family back with me, and live out my years. Seeing Princess Derryth's death brought home how fragile my own life is while I'm here."

"You do realize you could die anywhere, anytime, right?"

"Sure, I do. If it wasn't for that stupid magic hat—"

"That stupid *magic hat*, as you call it, made it possible for you to turn back time. You are making choices now that may bring your family back to you. Each decision you make, each step you take, determines your future. That magic hat made it possible for you to be here. And, who is to say it won't make other things possible. Where is it now?"

"I don't know. I think Iolair has it. At least, he wore one like it the other day when I saw him. Except…"

"KC?" Mr Scruffy turned his body and placed his face in front of KC's nose. "Are you okay? You trailed off."

"I am. I just thought of something about that hat that Iolair wore. It was different. I pointed it out to him."

"What was different?"

"His hat had a plaid band on it, while mind didn't. I wonder." KC went into deep thought. She stopped walking.

"KC? Hey, KC?" Mr Scruffy used his right claw to nudge her. "KC!"

"Oh, I'm sorry. Did you say something?"

"Yes. Why did you stop walking? We must get to King Elder's throne room. They are waiting on us. Are you okay?"

"I'm fine. I had a thought. Never mind, it can wait." KC increased her step and soon they entered King Elder's throne room.

❧

"Come in, Come in!" King Elder said as KC and Mr Scruffy walked through the door. "We were just wondering where you were. Come over here and sit. We've got much to discuss." King Elder motioned to sit near him. Queen Esmé sat beside him holding their new sapling.

KC looked over and saw Ish sitting off to the side, away from the others. He looked deeply grieved. He no longer moaned, but his face was marred with lines and wrinkles. He looked like he had aged several years since she saw him at mid-day. KC sat down next to Mr Scruffy.

"Did you notice Ish?" KC spoke telepathically to Mr Scruffy.

"Yes. His dark side is shining through."

"I feel his pain. He will always believe he could have saved her."

"Do you feel that way about your family?"

KC looked at Mr Scruffy. "More ways than I can say aloud to the others."

"Ish, we have your plans here before us. Come and explain your idea," King Elder commanded for all to hear. The map with plans laid on a table made of wood. KC wondered about the wood used for the furniture placed around the room. She wanted to ask, but it seemed trivial to be asking such a question now.

Ish stood up. He seemed to wander away to the door for a moment, and then he walked with a slow, direct move toward the group.

She looked at King Elder and Queen Esmé, and then turned toward Ish approaching the table. She could feel his pain, a pain that would not go away, not ever. The night her family was killed, and every night since then, she felt the loss. They were gone. It was what drove her now. She hoped it would sustain her when she must face Nukpana.

"KC, we know you understand. We feel your pain as you expressed it in your thoughts. We are with you," Queen Esmé said. She walked over to KC and held out the sapling for her to hold. "You will feel the power of our thoughts when you hold her. We've given her a name. Would you like to know it?" KC took the sapling into her arms and nodded as she looked up. "We will perform a formal christening after this mission. She is to be given the name of Princess Istar in honor of the Divine Mother."

KC held the sapling with a sense of love and sorrow combined. She looked over at Ish, who was smiling. "Would you like to hold her?"

He walked over and took Princess Istar into his arms. KC observed Ish inspect the newborn much as she imagined Jack would have done had he lived to see his son, Bill.

"She is just as lovely as her mother." He held her up for all to see. "King Elder, I'll keep holding Princess Istar while you explain our plan. I'm ready to find the Efil Stone and make sure Nukpana pays for her evilness."

KC looked into Ish's eyes. He had changed before her. He was renewed.

"It's good to have you back with us, Ish. We will now get down to the business of how we plan to find the Efil Stone. I had expected to hear from our mole by now, but it does not look promising. He may have come to harm." King Elder motioned for everyone to move up to the table.

❧

NUKPANA WALKED around her throne room, surveyed the area, and sat down in a fit. Her anger was growing. She returned to her evil Zu form and left Grave's Mountain after disposing of Princess

Derryth's ashes. Since then, she'd not heard back from the leader of the Grey Menace. Standing up, she walked with long strides to the large, looming window that looked out from her throne room toward the Wild Woods. She tapped her shoe with a rhythmic beat that signaled she was about to explode.

"Where is he?" She bellowed. She turned, bumping into one of her servants. "Get out of my way. Why do you always have to be underfoot? I have a mind to bring out my Dangerous Beauties. How would you like that?" The creature was cowed into silence. "Speak, you fool!"

"Yes'em."

Nukpana laughed at the trembling being. "Get out of my sight. I've got things to do." She walked back to her throne, and flopped into her chair. *He was supposed to be here by now with his armies of support. He swore to me allegiance. He swore his loyalty to see me beat back those insolent and weak Elderians. The human girl thinks she'll beat me. She has no power. None.*

Again, she stood up. Placed her hands on her hips, and tapped her foot. Nukpana walked over to the window and looked out. In the distance, she could make out where the tree line of the Wild Woods began to block her view of Stone's River. It flowed passed King Elder's camp. Earlier that day, she sent her army of Atcenians to the edges of the forest to wait for further orders. It won't be long now. With her armies gaining in number, and her magic building in strength, the final battle with KC will have a fitting climax. *I must beat her. There is no other option.*

Reaching down, Nukpana picked up the goblet. She drank the elixir she had concocted from the dried blood of Princess Derryth. Such a foolish child to think she could overcome my magic. She swirled the goblet to mix its contents and saw the faces of those whose blood was mixed in her sacred drink. The last of the elixir went down hard.

Belching, she said, "Seif's blood was the hardest to dry. You

Snowmen always were a pain in my neck." She wiped her mouth, and then threw the goblet against the wall where it landed in a pile of goblets thrown there over the years. She slowly turned around and said, "So, Sam, were you going to tell me?"

"Tell you what? That my name is in recognition for the servitude of my ancestors? That I would be always true to those who rule with peace and charity? That I'd fight those who were evil and corrupt, who would corrupt others?"

"That you are a mole for the Elderians."

"You can't believe that. I've been loyal to you. Haven't I delivered each and every one you've requested?"

"Yes. I didn't expect you would give up Seif, your own brother. And, when you brought Princess Derryth to me, I was surprised at the depth of your loyalty."

"Then, why do you doubt me now?"

"You gave the Sword of Fea back to KC. I had to send Princess Derryth to the dungeon to retrieve it."

"That is true. I did that for you."

"For me? What do you mean?"

"By giving it back to KC, you sent Princess Derryth to retrieve it, which then would have enabled you to give Ish to Princess Derryth. That was your promise to her. It would have worked, if for one thing."

"Yes. It would have worked if Princess Derryth had not fallen victim to the sword's magic."

"And, that meant I helped you there, too."

"How's that?"

"You saw the sword was more powerful than we had thought."

Nukpana rose up from her chair. She stood before him with

Blazewing glowing beside her. "I watched you when you found the Efil Stone."

"You are going to kill me?"

"Yes."

"Will you give me the chance to die in the Wild Woods? You owe me that for my loyalty."

"You have been loyal. I will miss you. As my father said to me with his last breath, Transform, Transcend, Release." Nukpana laid Blazewing on Sam's chest. She squeezed the handle and blew. A soft cloud enveloped Sam's head. "The great struggle of death is the struggle to avoid it. Go with the pain."

Sam squirmed.

Nukpana's face formed a smile. "I can see the poison flowing through your cold veins. You have a lunation or two before it will be complete. You can't resist the command of Devil's Breath. It takes your free will. You will do as I command."

Nukpana whispered in Sam's ear. Standing transfixed, Sam did not move. "When you join the traitors, you will use this sharpened stylus that I've coated with poison to stab KC. Do you understand?" Sam nodded. "Good. You should go now while you have time."

Sam bowed to her, turned, and left the room.

THE MEETING of the leaders of the Elderian fighting force left King Elder's throne room with plans in hand of how they would attack the Grey Menace. KC wondered how the next days would change the life she'd come to know and love since arriving a little over forty-days ago. She'd kept track of her time by placing hatch marks on the wall of her thípi using a piece of charcoal she found in a fire pit. She counted her time by the rise and fall of the two suns— something she saw each morning that she still found magical. The fact the Elderians used fire had surprised her too, given they were trees. Her time in the Wild Woods taught her all beings needed the basic elements to survive—water, fire, soil, and air.

KC reached for Fea. She carried it in her sheath strapped across her back. Ish showed her the best way to do so. She began to wield it around her room practicing the moves Sam and Seif had shown her. She hadn't seen Sam since Seif's and Princess Derryth's deaths. She wondered where he could be and if she should tell what she knew. Or was what she saw of Sam helping Nukpana a trick played on her mind?

When she saw Mylo, Sam's wife, earlier, she noticed Mylo seemed lost without Sam with her. She and Sam were the last of the Snowquidians still in the Wild Woods. Foursure, a community leader, was called home to Snowboro unexpectedly.

"May I come in?" KC turned and pulled back the flap of her thípi.

"Sure, Mylo. Come on in! I was just thinking about you, Sam, Seif, and Foursure." KC led Mylo over to her cot. "Sit. I'm glad you came by."

"I won't stay long." Mylo sat on the edge of the cot. KC got up and walked over to her basin.

"Would you like some water?" Mylo shook her head no. "Have you heard from Sam?" KC poured herself some water into her pouch, and then walked back to Mylo and sat on the floor.

"Sam's been gone longer than last time. I'm starting to worry. Mr Scruffy said you had a way with your telepathic abilities. I've tried to reach Sam, but these last few days have been difficult. Would you try to reach him?"

KC swallowed her water with a gulp. "Ah, well. I don't know if I can. Mr Scruffy told you that? I had no idea my abilities were any better than anyone else's. Do you know where Sam is now?"

"No. He said his mission was going to be shorter than normal, but it has turned out to be longer. He's been gone since before Princess Derryth was killed."

"Have you mentioned this to King Elder?"

"No. Sam would frown on me for worrying. You being a human girl, I figured you'd understand and could help me. Will you?"

"I'll try, Mylo. I've never done anything like this before. That is, I've never tried to talk with someone far away and not know where they were. I don't know how to begin. Where's Mr Scruffy when you need him?"

"I'm here when you need me," he said, flying through the open flap of the thípi. "Are you ready to begin?"

"I'M TELLING YOU, nothing, not a sound is coming through. I haven't been able to connect with Sam. How about you Mr Scruffy?"

"No. I haven't either. Mylo, did Sam tell you when he'd be returning home?"

"He didn't. He said he was going on a special mission and he didn't know when he'd—"

"Well, there you are!" Sam said walking into the thípi. "I've been looking everywhere for you. I'm home, Mylo. Come kiss me."

KC watched as the two Snowquidians embraced. She turned to speak to Mr Scruffy, but saw him tiptoeing out of the door. KC maneuvered around the couple, and caught up with him.

"Hey! Don't leave me!" KC called while running after Mr Scruffy. "You sure move quick when you need to."

"It wasn't right for us to be there. They are going to need some time alone. Did you know Sam was the mole for King Elder?"

"No. I wondered about it when Mylo said he'd been gone since before Princess Derryth's death. Is that where you're going?"

"King Elder needs to know he's back. Did you think it odd he came to your thípi like that?"

"Not really. I thought he was looking for Mylo."

"I'd buy that if he had responded to our telepathic call. But, he didn't. And then, he shows up while we're trying to reach him. Something isn't right."

"I'm glad you know what to do. I'd still be back there watching two Snowquidians hug and kiss." KC mused.

Mr Scruffy and KC walked into King Elder's room. "May we speak with you?" Mr Scruffy said motioning to KC to stand beside him.

"Sam Slavetomé is back," King Elder said. He stood to greet KC. He reached down and picked Mr Scruffy up, and then placed him on his desk. "What do we know?"

"We just left him. We don't know anything yet. My concern is whether Nukpana found him out. KC tried to raise him with her telepathic powers. He did not respond. The odd thing is he entered her thípi soon after she'd tried to reach him. Something's not right."

"When I tried to reach out to him, it felt strange. It was as if my call was going through but the line went dead. You know?" KC moved her hand up to her ear mocking making a phone call.

"Not exactly. What are you doing with your hand?" King Elder asked.

"I think of my telepathic powers like a phone call," KC said with an anxious laugh. "I forgot where I was."

"Talking about phone calls from your time and world is not what we need to do now. It is important we keep on guard. Nukpana's evil is strengthening. Her reach will harm you if you are caught off guard. It worries me Sam did not respond to your call. We'll have a meeting and see if Sam will give us an explanation." King Elder sat down at his desk.

"Yes, Sire. We will go gather the others," Mr Scruffy said. "Come, KC."

They walked out into the court.

"I can't believe I was so remiss." KC wrung her hands. "He's right. I shouldn't talk about my world when we've got troubles in this one. Not now."

"It will be okay. We must gather Ish, Queen Esmé, Sam, and Mylo, and return to King Elder's room. There is no time to lose."

"COME IN. COME IN," King Elder motioned. The Elderian leaders filed in and sat around King Elder's desk. "The last time we gathered, we celebrated the return of Ish and KC. Today, we have Sam Slavetomé back with us. Welcome home, Sam!"

Sam bowed his head.

Mylo said, "It is good to have him home. And in time to help us."

"Yes. That is indeed why I called this meeting," King Elder smiled at Mylo. "Sam, do you have anything to report?"

"I do, Sire. Nukpana's army is fortified. She added to her armies of the beasts—Dzoavits, Trolls, Buata, Splinter Cats, Woodwose, and other fearsome critters with additional Grey Menace members she created. Her vast armies are spreading out across Eldershire to three of its corners from Emerald Mountain to Grave's Mountain to the edges of Mushroom Alley. They will out match us."

"Balderdash!" King Elder slammed his fist down. The room rattled with the echo of his voice. KC saw Ish flinch. He seemed to have come out of his stupor.

"King Elder?" Ish stood, and walked around the table. "May I ask

Sam a question?"

"Of course."

"Sam, you say Nukpana's armies are fortified. How many would you say?"

"Thousands, if not more. She has them held in and around Emerald and Grave's Mountains. The Grey Menace is stationed at strategic points between the mountains, the Atcenians are at the hills around the Wild Woods, and she has a pack of Goblins, Trolls, Buata, Woodwose, and Splinter Cats along the valley below Atcenian Hills down to Iolair's Bluff at the edge of the Wild Woods." Sam looked over to Mylo. She reached for his hand and smiled. KC noticed that Sam looked tired.

Ish stopped walking, and stood next to KC. He tapped his finger on the table. "Were you at all near Princess Derryth when she died?"

"I was in the room." KC heard an audible gasp. She saw Ish's clenched fists tighten and blood began to trickle onto the table.

"Why didn't you save her?" Ish said each word with distinction.

"Princess Derryth had warned me that she was going to trick Nukpana into killing her. She said it was the only way to break the spell Nukpana had cast on her. She asked me to stay loyal to King Elder, to not give away that I was a mole in her court. Princess Derryth asked me to stay alive long enough to bring back what she had learned being under Nukpana's spell." Sam looked directly at King Elder. "I did as my Princess ordered me to do."

Ish slammed his fists on the table. "You let her die!"

"I did as she commanded me to do. You are a soldier, a warrior, a knight for your land. What would you do if you were commanded to follow an order you knew would result in a loved one's death?"

Hearing Sam's words, KC understood what Sam had done when he helped Nukpana take her. It was part of the plan. He had done his duty.

"She didn't have to die. We could have saved her." Ish clutched his fist.

"Could you? Do you realize the power Nukpana had over her? Princess Derryth did all she could to protect all of you." Sam motioned around the room. "And, she said she was sorry for being jealous of you and KC. It was what Nukpana used to break her."

"Jealous. Of KC?" Ish asked.

"She thought you and KC were becoming closer. After she was totally out from under Nukpana's enchantment, Princess Derryth said she knew that Nukpana had warped her thinking. She came to understand that KC was blameless for any slight she thought you and KC may have done to her."

"This is insane!" Ish stormed around the table and stood next to Sam. Sam rose to meet his eyes. "Are you saying that Princess Derryth died because she was jealous of me and KC? How dare you blame us for her death!"

"I'm not saying that. Calm down Ish. I'm explaining how much power Nukpana's evil magic has grown. She controlled Princess Derryth. Just before she died, she spoke with me. I do not know how, but she did. She warned me that Nukpana's evil was growing and her magic was getting far stronger than any of us could imagine. She died so KC could get away with her sword, Fea, and I could get back here to tell you this. She said she was already lost, but she left a part of herself back here. I was to make sure you found it."

Queen Esmé stepped forward. "Do you mean our new sapling, Princess Istar? We found her. See." Queen Esmé held up her granddaughter. "Isn't she beautiful?"

KC saw joy cross over Sam's face. "I am blessed to be able to see her offspring. This is a good sign. Princess Derryth wasn't sure her quick action had saved the twig when Nukpana cut off her finger. It is a good omen." Sam sat down. Mylo put her arm around her husband. KC noticed a snow tear fall down his cheek.

"King Elder? May Sam and I go back to our thípi? He is tired and needs to rest." Mylo said.

"Yes, by all means. Ish, sit back down. We need to make our final plans. With the news Sam has given us, we need to adjust our tactics." Ish walked back over and took his seat.

"King Elder, Queen Esmé, Ish?" Sam took a deep breath. "My strength is not what it used to be, but I will fight. I will fight to revenge the death of Princess Derryth and to prove to you my loyalty. I ask that I be allowed to fight alongside KC. It is the least I can do to show my support and allegiance to you all."

"Of course. KC, you won't mind having Sam by your side, will you?"

"No, King Elder. Thank you, Sam. I'll be honored to fight alongside you." KC felt Sam's sorrow for what he had had to do. Yet, she wondered why he insisted he should fight beside her. Days ago when they made plans before he left for Nukpana's camp, he had requested to serve as the leader of the pack of Unicorns that would be fighting near Mushroom Alley.

Sam smiled at KC. "I'm honored too." He turned and walked out of the meeting with Mylo seeming to hold him up.

"You don't think he's been compromised, do you?" Ish said with a sneer.

"No. Enough worry. Sam is honorable and has been steadfast the entire time. He will do what is right in the end," King Elder said.

"Let's hope you are right. I'm not sure he did Princess Derryth any favors," Ish picked up his bow and quiver and left the room.

Moving to stop Ish, KC called after him.

"Let him go," King Elder said. "He'll come to his senses. We must make our plans. Mr Scruffy, will you report on the support we have from the other beings of Eldershire?"

"King Elder, our numbers are growing each day. Nukpana has continued to wreak havoc on the other beings that were less than supportive in times past. Their desire to stay out of conflict is being lessened by Nukpana's evil ways. Her armies are robbing their food, killing their children, and causing the other inhabitants of Eldershire to be in constant turmoil."

"It is good to know the Elderians are uniting in the quest to remove Nukpana's power over them. Who are with us now?"

"We have a large contention of beings. Of course, Fergus, a Dryad, will lead all the Moss Folk, Wood Folk, and Dryads from this camp. We have the Sprites, Nymphs, and Elves from Eland; Ish's family is serving as their leaders. They are making their way to Grave's Mountain. At Mushroom Alley, Rakoún, a raccoon, will lead a group of wildlife with the Centaurs, Unicorns, and a few other Elementals. I will lead the sky beings. Besides the contingency of owls, there will be Iolair and his eagles with the hawks led by Gavin of Landéan. They are in position near Emerald Mountain awaiting my arrival and your command."

"Whom will I be with?" KC asked. "I felt funny asking, but I didn't hear my name."

"You will ride with me, as always," Mr Scruffy said. "There will be times we will be on the ground, and during those times, you are to stand with Sam. He and Mylo will be your protectors." Mr Scruffy looked around the room to see if there were any objections. Ish walked in and sat down at the end of the table.

Mr Scruffy continued. "The small creatures of the forest have a group that will stay here in the camp area to protect the females and saplings that will stay behind. In particular, they will protect you and Queen Esmé, and of course, Princess Istar."

"Wait. I plan to fight with you," King Elder stood up. "There will be no arguing or discussion. My mind is made up."

CHAPTER 17
BATTLES OF ELDERSHIRE

The Wild Woods was alive with blood curdling cries echoing the sounds of war. Grave's Mountain, at the east edge of the forest, stood over the scene as though a sentry on duty. A band of Elderians was dying at the hands of the Grey Menace, while other beasts fought for Nukpana at Emerald Mountain and down Mushroom Alley, killing and maiming.

The Elderians and supporting armies were all hand-to-hand fighters; none rode on the backs of four-legged animals. Those who rode in the sky were carried on the backs of birds—owls, eagles, and hawks. More remarkable was the fact that none who flew were protected by spear or shield. All carried bow with arrows and swords. KC wondered about the lack of protection for their bodies, but she trusted King Elder's instincts.

Before KC took flight with Mr Scruffy, she watched the main armies of Eldershire walk into battle on foot. KC noted that as the fighting began, if any of the Elderian army wanted to protect or hide themselves, the warriors had to find the best place they could to save their lives. This often meant hiding behind a stone outcropping, finding a mound, or else jumping out onto a fighting foe. Without shelter, the Elderians struggled in the open, fighting for their survival. Many died.

For a while, KC watched in awe as the battle raged on, while some fought halfheartedly. She saw one poor soul that drew his bowstring only to his breast. The result was the arrow was sent forth weak and harmless. When it hit, it did no harm. He was unceremoniously decapitated by an ogre. Then, there were those bowmen who were up for battle. Their arrows were strategically carried on their right side, while their sword hung on the left, as Ish had shown KC to wear Fea.

Then, she noticed the fighting on foot armies of Eldershire carrying spears attached at their shoulders. She noticed others wore a sort of small shield without a grip that was used to cover the region of the face and neck when wielding a sword. From her perspective, KC felt the ones that showed promise in battle were the warriors riding on the backs of the owls, eagles, and hawks. And, those on foot using shields and spears.

"KC, jump on. I'm ready," Mr Scruffy commanded. "We have work to do." She rode on his back, and was able to see firsthand the prowess and artistry of experienced hunters and bowmen. They were expert riders and were able without difficulty to direct their bows to either side while riding at full speed, and to shoot an opponent whether in pursuit or in retreat. KC watched and tried to repeat what she saw. She pulled back her bowstring near her forehead almost to the side of her right ear. She soon learned this meant she was charging the arrow with such momentum that when she released her arrow, it resulted in a kill.

"Good shot, KC" Mr Scruffy said to her telepathically. "I won't speak much to you, as I know we both need to concentrate. You're a quick learner."

KC smiled, but also knew her skill was improving, not because she was a quick learner, but more because she was scared and didn't want to die before she acquired the Efil Stone. She felt the power of the arrow as it left her bow. She knew it was filled with such force that no one would fail to fall—no shield, no protective clothing, no power could check its force.

The early evening light gave way to late night-light from the multitude of stars. The double moons cast shadows into the valley and traversed the ridge from Grave's to Emerald Mountain. The battle raged on for hours. KC's wrists were beginning to grow weak. She looked around her. Several companions fell from fatal wounds or were knocked from their faithful birds.

"Mr Scruffy. The Atcenians look like they are preparing to make another charge toward King Elder's camp. Let's—" A blow to Mr Scruffy's left flank knocked her sideways. He dove down to the ground. KC hung on, and waited for him to glide to a stop. He landed in a clearing where no fighting was close by.

"Let's duck in that cave over there," Mr Scruffy said reducing to his normal size.

They entered the cave taking care to make sure they would not walk into a trap.

"Are you okay?" KC asked her trusted companion.

"I'm hurt, but nothing I've not encountered before. I'll be fine. You?"

"I'm tiring, but so far I've not been hurt. How was it looking to you out there?"

"We're getting overrun. Nukpana is out to take us all down."

KC turned to her faithful friend. "Tonight, Mr Scruffy, it looks like we may die. What will happen to my life in my own time? Will I ever be able return?" KC looked out beyond the entrance to the cave as the fighting escalated.

Since arriving in Eldershire over fifty moons earlier, KC wondered how her life back home might be different if she knew then what she knew now. She lost count of the number of times she wished to go home—back to her time. She turned and looked at Mr Scruffy. His left wing was mangled; he walked with a limp. She worried he wouldn't survive another battle.

She expressed her worry in the sound of her words, "If I hadn't found that hat, Mr Scruffy, would I be where I am now? Would you be here in this place? Would I be peering through the smoke, looking through these trees, praying we'd make it through the night?" She reached for her sword.

Mr Scruffy raised his battered wing. "The dark forces are all around us. You can hear the Wood Folk dying. The Grey Menace is making their last charge. Whatever happens from here, I'm with you, KC." Mr Scruffy tilted his head toward the exit of the cave.

KC looked at him with compassion. "A wise statesman of my world once said, 'the cost of freedom is high.' The Elderians and we have paid such a price. Tonight, we will choose not to surrender or submit."

"You are the Chosen One. You are the one we are depending on. You must make your move."

"If I do and I fail, my life ends here and now. What then?" She picked Mr Scruffy up, not expecting an answer. She placed him on her shoulder, and they went to take a stand.

The cries of the battle seemed to grow in intensity. The tintinnabulation of the swords, the thuds of those falling, sang out to the night's sky, each bringing home the loss of life on both sides of the battle. Some began to flee as each one could; some were captured; most were slain, while others climbed into the hills. KC climbed upon the back of Mr Scruffy and they took flight. Iolair signaled he and his eagles were holding their own, but Gavin was not seen. KC looked down on the land and could see many Elderians locked in hand-to-hand fighting.

"Mr Scruffy," KC called to him telepathically. "See those Moss Folk down there? They are taking the Dwarves over the ridge, down the cliff with them. It is causing panic and much confusion amongst the Dwarves."

"Good tactic! The Moss Folk do not fear death. For them, it is renewal. You will see them back amongst us in a moon or two."

Mr Scruffy flew toward Grave's Mountain. "We need to see how Sam and Mylo are doing. Look out and see if you can spot them."

KC scanned the landscape as they flew over the lowlands leading to the base of the mountain. She wondered why the Purple Drakein had not appeared. She noticed a large contingency of Goblins, Trolls, and the Grey Menace moving toward Ish's group. It seemed the enemy had no one as commander-in-chief; their movement was erratic. Ish's family led a portion of the Sprites, Nymphs, and other Elves of Eland out to meet them head-on while another group led by Ish were coming from around the rear.

"There's Sam and Mylo on this side of the mountain. Take me down and I'll fight with them while you go find Gavin and his hawks."

"Good plan. I'll be back as soon as I can." Mr Scruffy took flight again while KC got her land legs.

Goblins began to move toward her. She slashed the neck of a Goblin; he fell at her feet. She looked to see where Sam and Mylo had moved. Just as she caught a glimpse of Sam, he suddenly slumped down. KC maneuvered her way to them with Fea slashing and cutting down the beasts she encountered onward. Her weapon connected at different points, first high in the air, and then low, always giving an aggressive edge to each. The fight raged on. KC cleared her way, covered in blood and debris; she reached Sam and Mylo.

"He's not getting up!" Mylo looked up to KC. "Help me!"

They moved Sam under cover of brush away from the fighting. "Is he mortally wounded?" KC asked while moving a pile of leaves.

Mylo sat down and positioned Sam's head in her lap. "No. He went limp. I can't find any wounds. One minute he was talking, and the next he was down. I'm scared. He's not been right since he came back from Nukpana's lair."

"Sam? Can you talk?" KC crouched near them while keeping an eye on any beasts that might come near.

Mylo offered Sam a drink of water from her pouch. He waved it away. "I haven't got much time," Sam said. "Listen."

The sounds from the battle rumbled louder. KC leaned closer to hear Sam's weak voice.

"Nukpana put a spell on me. I'm fighting its urges. She knows I know the secret." Sam gasped.

Two ogres could be heard just pass the area where they were hiding. KC removed Fea from its sheath, and moved to where she could protect Mylo and Sam. Mentally, she called to Ish and Mr Scruffy, "We need your help. Come!"

KC stood and prepared to meet the ogres; their dilated pupils giving an air of madness. Fighting two would be hard, but she would protect her friends at all costs. She did not feel very brave. She wanted to turn and hide, but she had to save them and her. She prepared to rush them and aimed her sword at the ready.

"KC," Mylo whispered. "Sam needs you."

KC turned and heard the ogres clashing their swords, and then two thumps. KC held up her sword and was ready to bring it down. The blow never came.

"It's me and Mr Scruffy," Ish said.

"Oh, what a relief! You stay here. I need to get to Sam." KC turned and moved to Mylo. "Is he —?"

"No. But he's weaker. Sit here so you can hear him. Sam? KC is here now."

Sam tried to raise his head, then laid it back down. "You must get the Efil Stone." He swallowed. "It is in Princess Derryth's bedroom at Emerald Mountain. The headboard. A panel. Press face." Sam retched up with a grimace on his face. "You need to use all of them together as the Chosen One. The Drakein knows."

KC looked to Mylo. She shrugged her shoulders. "Sam, what do you mean the Drakein knows?"

Sam pulled the stylus out of his pocket and stabbed his leg. "I do this for you." Mylo caressed her husband's head as Sam died in her arms.

KC's mind raced. "Why did he have to die?"

Ish and Mr Scruffy walked over to her. "What happened?" Ish asked.

"He stabbed himself with the stylus lying there. I don't dare pick it up."

"No. It was one of Nukpana's. I've seen this used by her before. It's one of her signatures. The poison is strong," Mr Scruffy said.

"The battle, it's too quiet. Is it still raging?" KC looked out to the West.

"The beasts scattered. We're not sure why," Ish said. "Is Mylo going to be okay? She's not wounded, is she?"

"She just watched her husband kill himself. How would you be?"

Ish nodded. "I was a total waste after Princess Derryth's murder."

"Something is strange about all this," Mr Scruffy observed. "We have to get Sam's body back to camp. Can we get him on my back after I grow to flight size? I'll fly him and Mylo home. KC, you can ride, too, to help. Ish, are you rejoining your family?"

"Yes. I must find out the damage from this battle. You are right, Mr Scruffy. Something is not right that the beasts would just leave. I'll rejoin you and the others in King Elder's room. Go in peace."

AFTER RETURNING TO CAMP, helping Mylo to her thípi, and placing Sam's body at the altar of honor, Mr Scruffy and KC joined Ish and the other Elderian leaders in King Elder's war room.

"Tell us what happened, KC. It will help us understand what we are facing," King Elder looked worried to KC.

She stood and shared how Sam died and what he had said. "Does anyone know what he meant when he said the Drakein knows?" She waited for a response. Each face she gazed upon seemed to be lost in thought. She sat down. "That is my report."

"What other Drakein is amongst us but the one Nukpana becomes?" King Elder asked his council. "It seems no one knows. We may need to visit Mother Elder after we finish this meeting before we can be sure what Sam meant. We know there will be other battles. What are our losses?" King Elder asked each leader to report the injuries, deaths, and numbers of those who could still fight.

"It is a grim report you each give me. There is no need for us to dwell on our low numbers. We must begin to focus on what we will do next."

Gavin interrupted, "We began this battle with over one hundred strong hawks. We are down to twenty. Numbers like this means we can't win another battle against such well-organized forces as Nukpana's armies. She knows it. We need to know it, too."

"Aye. You speak truth, Gavin. I fear our numbers are too low. I, like you, do not wish to lose more of our Elderians. But, what are we to do? Our Chosen One is here. We must retrieve the Efil Stone. Our future depends on it. Yet, we have lost so many already. So many." King Elder stood up. He looked into the face of each of his leaders.

"Sire, I agree we must retrieve the Efil Stone, but why use all of us? Why not send in a small contingency with KC at the lead?" Gavin implored.

King Elder walked to one side of the room. "That is a consideration. But, if we are to die, to die because of this quest, should it not be in a way that shores up such a contingency? Should we not do what we can to remove the vast number of enemies away from the Chosen One? We must use patience and time to our advantage. We must think strategically on how we can improve the strength of a small band who go together to retrieve the Efil Stone while fewer Elderians are lost, thus sharing their endeavors and their love of life and peace.

"Yggdrasil's will, I pray not one more Elderian should perish. Damnation to Nukpana and her evil. We all have lost at her hand. Do we allow her to continue or do we stand and fight? I say take a stand. All the signs point to KC as our Chosen One. We are at a turning point in our chance to turn away the evil that has ruled over us these last centuries. Now, we must strike. We must unite!"

King Elder walked back to his seat and stood. He looked up and scanned the room. Then, he continued walking around the room.

"If I'm committing treason by calling for us to fight, then I am the most treasonous amongst us. Gavin, I understand your plight. Your numbers are low. Your clan has suffered. If you believe you should take your hawks and go, so be it! We will fight just as hard for you if you leave as if you were to stay. We are in this together. Today is the day of the Chosen One. So, let it be marked. If we are able to see the two moons of Eldershire set this night and the double suns rise tomorrow, we will be all the more blessed because it will mean we will see victory.

"Ish of Eland, Iolair the Great Eagle, Mr Scruffy of Owl Land, Fergus of the Dryads, the Moss Folk, Wood Spirits, Nymphs, Elves, Fairies, Gnomes, and all other Elementals stand with me! You and we from this day to the ending of Eldershire shall be remembered for what we do. We few. We glorious few. We groves of Elderians. Those who shed their blood with me and those who give up life to cross over to the land of Yggdrasil; we all shall be remembered for our fight, for our gifts of sacrifice on this day of days; the day of the Chosen One!"

"King Elder! Add Gavin, the great white hawk, and his companions to your band. We are with you!"

All around the table stood and cheered. They banged their weapons on the table and rattled their swords. They were rallied by their king. He looked at KC. She smiled back and felt braver than she had at any one moment since arriving in Eldershire. Fear was not reclaiming her soul. At least, not the way it did when she fought the ogre. But, she knew the battle to come would be a hard one. She prayed she would prevail. She prayed they all would be victorious.

THE MEETING BROKE UP. Mr Scruffy said he'd be by to talk with her after he spoke to King Elder. Ish went to visit Princess Istar. For the first time in days, KC was by herself to think, to ponder, and to worry. She walked through her thípi and moved her covers on her bed looking for her hat. She thought about Iolair's words, 'Keep the hat with you. It will be useful in your quest.' She had ignored his suggestion. She wasn't sure why. All she knew was each time she saw or touched the hat she had a strange feeling. One she just as soon ignored. Looking around the room, she tried to remember where she laid the hat the last time she saw it. *I guess I'm afraid it will transport me again. It's how I got here after all.*

Walking over to the small table that held her water basin, she looked inside. She decided she needed to replenish her water. She would want to freshen up before they headed out for another battle. She looked down at her arms; dried blood and dirt were splattered all over. *My body probably reeks of odors that I'd never allow collect on me if I were home.* The two suns would be setting before long. She made sure her sword and sheath were properly slung across her back. She started to pick up her bucket, but there laid the Hat of The Fairy. "How on earth did you get here?" She said aloud.

KC picked it up, and looked at it carefully. The hatband was plaid. *I could have sworn it was solid black before.* She rotated the hat in her hands. A metal ring flopped, hitting her thumb. That's a latch, she thought. *I don't remember seeing it before.* She opened the latch and hooked it onto her belt. *At least this way, it will stay with me.* She reached for her water bucket, closed the flap of her thípi, and walked down to the banks of Stone's River.

CHAPTER 18
A MOMENT AT STONE'S RIVER

L ooking up at the sky, KC scanned for any sight of danger. The evening sky was colored with shades of light pink to purple. The double suns were setting—one in the East, one in the West. The double moons were low in the south sky where they were starting to rise beside each other. She used to love to see the sky in shades of purple before her arrival in Eldershire. Now, purple and all of its shades made her think of the Purple Drakein and Nukpana. Rolling her shoulders back, she walked with determination to the bank of Stone's River to scoop water into her bucket. As she reached down, she felt claws clutch around her abdomen. Fear gripped her. She managed to twist around as she saw the Purple Drakein lift her into the sky.

"Let me go!" she screamed and twisted.

"Be still. A fall from here will kill you," the Purple Drakein said. "Trust me."

"What? Trust you? Are you crazy?"

"We'll land at Grave's Mountain in a few clicks. Then, I'll explain. If I wanted to kill you, I would have crushed you already."

KC looked out over the landscape. She could see the edges of the dark portion of the Wild Woods at the base of the mountain. King Elder had told her the entrance to the Purple Drakein's lair was deep in the forest toward the base of the mountain at Snow Valley. Evil hung in the air and mingled with the forest scents producing foul odors. The Purple Drakein dove down behind a waterfall that flowed into the lake, which provided a submerged entrance.

When they emerged from the cave opening into the dark cavern, KC gagged from the water she inhaled.

"There are easier ways to drown me," KC said.

A glow came from the Drakein's body that lit the room around them. The Purple Drakein released her. KC tumbled away and leaped upon her feet.

Unsheathing her sword, she held it up. "Fight me on equal footing, Nukpana! I'm not afraid to die!"

"Baahaahaa. You pitiful human. Do you think I'm going to stand by and let you stick me with that little pin? I can destroy you with one bolt of fire from my mouth." The Purple Drakein let out a roar.

KC looked around the lair and dove behind a large boulder. She held her sword up in defense. Confusion ran through her veins while fear and uncertainty began to overwhelm her thinking.

"Don't you realize I'm not Nukpana? She's not here right now. I don't have a lot of time. You've got to listen!"

"What?"

"I said I'm not Nukpana. I'm Drakania. Some think because I'm a Drakein, that I'm male. I'm female. Not because Nukpana is female, she can take on male form; it is because I am a female Drakein. Nukpana stole me away when she first acquired her powers, centuries ago. By using her dark magic, she was able to use my form and live within my soul. When she is not in Drakein form, I must dwell in her soul. I see all she does—mayhem, maim, murder, and worse. She is evil. She is *the* Evil."

"Why should I believe you?"

"You are not dead."

"True enough. But, how are you here and Nukpana is not?"

"She is with me. I stilled her power for a little while. I have waited centuries to place a spell on her that I knew I would only be able to use once. Your arrival meant I had my chance to save my soul. I want to live forever. Saving Eldershire, and in the process, Yggdrasil, will save me. It is prophesied that I'll be part of the cycle of life—living my eternity in servitude to the Tree of Life."

KC studied Drakania. The dragon's sharp, intelligent-looking eyes intensified her expression. The hornlets that covered her head accentuated her long neck and legs. KC thought she resembled a dinosaur but with wings that were webbed, her veins bulging. When she spoke about the Tree of Life, tiny flames danced in her nostrils.

"Who told you that?"

Drakania's eyes gleamed with unrestrained greed, "Yggdrasil and the Efil Stone." KC noticed the smell of smoke and sulfur growing stronger. "Our time grows short. I have no abilities to leave Nukpana on my own. When she is morphed into my form, I have no power. You need to listen. There is a way to overcome Nukpana. It is the only way to destroy her and free me. When the time comes, you'll need to have the Efil Stone in your possession while you are wearing the Hat of Iolair and holding the Sword of Fea."

"The 'Hat of Iolair'?"

"The Hat of The Fairy is owned by Iolair. You used it to transport here. The one hanging from your side. The prophecy says a human wearing a hat, carrying a sword, and holding the Efil stone will be able to slay the Drakein, to free her of the evil within."

"Slay the Drakein? But isn't that you?"

"Yes. You will need to kill me." KC recoiled. "It is the only way for my soul to be free. There is no need for you to worry. I've never wanted to kill anyone or anything. I'm weary of Nukpana's control over me. It's always been her evil that has ruled. After watching her poison Sam, I knew one day she would turn on me. It is a matter of time. She has ruled my soul for centuries. I've seen her turn on many other followers."

Drakania breathed a sigh. "It is only because you exist that I have a chance to redeem my soul and join those who've gone before. When I die, she will lose most of her power. I welcome that chance. When I'm slain, I'll be able to reach my destiny of serving as the keeper of the life cycle. And, I'll be able to pay back to those I've watched her murder for her sick enjoyment. She relishes it. I feel it in my blood each time she makes a kill. Nukpana is evil make no mistake. She will overtake you with her magic if you are not prepared. You must not falter when the time comes. You must kill her."

"So that's what Sam meant when he said, 'The Drakein knows.' When did Sam find you out?"

"Nukpana confronted Sam about his serving as a mole for King Elder right after she killed Princess Derryth. Sam was in Princess Derryth's bedroom when she was murdered. While Nukpana was poisoning Sam, I was able to cast my spell, which enabled me to be here now to explain all to you. The elixir Nukpana drank allowed me to come to you. She's still aware of what I'm doing. The sweet part is that she can't change the outcome. Sam taught me the spell when he first arrived from his homeland of Snowboro. He knew about my existence. He said he could see me in Nukpana's eyes. Sam advised me to wait to use the spell at the right moment when I'd be alone with the Chosen One—with you. He said that then, and only then, would be the right time to make my move. Sam wanted to tell you all of this himself. He wanted to explain about where to find the Efil Stone."

"He did manage to tell me where it was located. But, I'm not sure what to do once I get it."

"Sam told me that when we met, I was to make sure you understood everything. You do know that when you wear the Hat of Iolair, you are invisible to all but me, right?"

"No. I had no idea. I learned from Iolair that I should keep it with me, but since I didn't wear hats, it was cumbersome to carry. I've kept the hat in my room. Just this evening, I noticed there was a latch on the inside rim, so I latched it to my belt buckle."

"Good. Sam asked me to take you to where the Efil Stone is hidden in case he did not return. I saw him dying in his wife's arms. He loved her so. As I watched him die, a part of me felt his pain. We were friends. I do this in honor of Sam, and because it is as it was foretold."

"What do you mean?" KC looked up at Drakania and saw kindness in the creature's eyes.

"The prophecy says that a Drakein will rise from evil and give power to the Chosen One. I am that Drakein. You are the Chosen One. My time to be in control of my thoughts grows smaller. Listen, you must get to Princess Derryth's room on your own in case Nukpana takes me back and I must leave you. Princess Derryth's room is the last one in the lower section of Emerald Mountain. It's important that once you get to the bedroom you act quickly. Follow my instructions precisely. Do you understand?"

"Yes, I do."

"When you arrive in her room, there is a huge bed with a wooden headboard that is ornately carved. You will find the Efil Stone hidden in a cavity of the headboard. It opens with a special command."

"A special command? I do not have a good memory. I'm so nervous, I'm not sure I'll remember who I am let alone a special command. Is it written down?"

"No. But, I can imprint it on your mind. Step close. I'll speak the words as I touch your head and you will have the command when you need it." KC moved closer and Drakania placed her paw on KC's head. "You must speak these words slowly as you rub your hand in a circle over the surface of the carved face, and then on the right side of the face, push the flower petal inward."

"I am sworn to my quest.
My heart, though weak at times, knows goodness, honor, and love.
With my sword and hat, I'll defend the defenseless.
With the Efil Stone, I'll defeat the wicked!"

Without warning, what little light was provided from Drakania was gone. KC wasn't sure what happened, but she knew she was alone in the dark. It was quiet.

"Drakania? Where are you?" KC fearing the creature was removed by Nukpana's hand, placed the hat on her head, and drew her sword.

She made her way back to the entrance of the lair. Listening, all she could hear was the sound of water clashing on the stones at the mouth of the river. Not even Drakania breathing. KC stood behind the waterfall and stared into the darkness. She could see the two moons high in the night sky, but nothing more. Their light was that of a single candle. She started to walk through the waterfall.

Stop. Walk through the passageway. Something or someone had whispered to her.

KC looked to her right, and saw the opening. Since arriving in Eldershire, she had learned to listen to the voices in her head. She knew when it was Mr Scruffy or Ish, whose mental voices she had come to recognize. In this case, someone else was giving her guidance.

The passage turned into a tunnel. The moonlight, though dim, cast enough light to show the way. She walked with care, making sure each step she took was sure and true.

After a while, KC walked into a clearing that was riddled with bodies of all kinds of beings—Atcenians, Ogres, Moss Folk, Goblins, Dwarves, Centaurs, and Dryads. Each had died in the arms of another. The hand-to-hand combat must have been fierce. She tried to step with care, but she kept finding large puddles that reached to the tops of her ankles. The liquid the color of bile; the smell was horrific.

Her stomach reacted. KC's resolve to be brave was leaving her. She had seen so much death in the last few days. The weight of the quest was beating her down. She wiped her mouth, took her hat off, latching it to her belt, and turned to sit on a log. She had to regain her strength before she could move on. A horrible taste formed in her mouth; she reached for her pouch.

"You will die creature!" An Atcenian came up behind her wielding a club. KC turned pulling her sword from its sheath. She rushed straight at the Atcenian plunging her sword into his flabby side. She pulled back, removing it and swinging around in a complete turn. The beast had doubled over revealing a clean shot for its neck.

KC brought her sword down upon it with all of her might decapitating him in one blow. All this happened too quickly for her to realize what she had done. She hadn't thought about what she was doing until she saw the beast lying on the ground. Combat had become a reflex to her. She only had time to strike or die. It was dead at her feet. She was covered in blood and bile. She slipped down to the ground and passed out, overcome with fear and exhaustion.

"Did you see her leave?" Mr Scruffy asked Ish.

"No. I thought you were with her." Ish walked around KC's room trying to figure out where she could have gone. "I can't believe she would just walk away from camp. She's strange, but she's not that dumb, is she?"

"No. Something has happened. I'm sure of it."

"That is not a good sign. Should you take flight and see what you can discover from the sky?"

"Perhaps. Can you also call for Iolair? Maybe together we can cover more ground. If she was in dire straits, wouldn't she call for us telepathically?"

"You would think so. That is, of course, if she is conscious or still alive."

"Yes, but maybe she tried and we were blocked from hearing her."

"Maybe." Ish picked up his bow and quiver. "I still have a number of arrows. Let's hope we won't need them. Come, let's go."

"Mr Scruffy? Can you hear me?" a faint voice reached him.

"I've found her!" Ish directed Iolair to dive down to the clearing off from where he could see KC lying against a boulder. Strewn all around her were at least five Atcenians and several other beasts. "Did she fight them all?"

"It doesn't seem possible. She is banged up fairly badly." Iolair walked over to where she lay. "When Mr Scruffy gets here, we'll place her on his back. He can carry her back to camp."

Ish walked around the area surveying the scene. "It appears she fought this one here last. See her sword still drips with his blood."

"She must have called you telepathically, yet she is out cold. It didn't take us that long to reach her from when you heard her. She must have just finished her strike when she collapsed. She will be sore tomorrow if she fought all of these beasts," Iolair said.

Mr Scruffy landed nearby, reduced his size, and then fluttered over to where Ish and Iolair stood. "What happened here?"

"We don't know. We think KC fought them all. She definitely struck down this one here. See her sword?" Ish replied.

"It is amazing she is alive, let alone she got a call off to us," Ish said. "I barely recognized her voice it was so weak. Let's get her back."

"I'll make a poultice to begin working on her wounds. She's suffered a lot here. That is for sure." Mr Scruffy adjusted his size.

Ish and Iolair placed KC onto his back and using vines from nearby trees, strapped her into place to keep her on Mr Scruffy's back.

"Is she awake yet?" Ish asked as he entered KC's thípi.

"No. She has been severely hurt. I still do not know how it was possible she got a telepathic call off to us, but she did. I'm thankful you heard her," Mr Scruffy said placing a poultice on her forehead.

"I will go inform King Elder and will return straight away," Ish left and Mr Scruffy sat on the table near KC's cot.

He watched her slowly breathing and wondered how she had come to be so far from camp. He knows it will be a tale they will tell for years. The Chosen One butchered and slew five Atcenians and many more beasts. He still couldn't believe the scene when they found her leaning against the boulder at the base of Grave's Mountain.

"King Elder said he would be here shortly. Is she still sleeping?" Ish took a seat on the floor. "I don't understand."

"Yes. I was just thinking the same thing. It is a miracle she was not taken by Nukpana. I find it strange Nukpana hasn't been around. I have that feeling again; something is not right."

"Don't do that. Each time you do, you are usually right," Ish said and stretched out his long legs.

"How is Princess Istar doing? It seems like I haven't seen her for a while."

"It's been over fourteen moons," Ish said.

"It couldn't have been that long," Mr Scruffy marveled. "What does she look like now?"

Ish smiled. "She is almost as tall as my waist. Saplings of the Elder clan grow fast. It won't be long, she'll be a teen, and it will be time for me to train and explain the ways of her mother's clan and of mine."

KC moaned. She began to stir. Mr Scruffy got up and moved toward her. "KC? KC? Can you open your eyes?"

"Oh, my head." KC reached up and touched her forehead. "What is that?"

"It is a poultice that Mr Scruffy put on your head wound," Ish said. "Do you need some water?"

KC nodded. She tried to sit up, but laid back down. "I'm dizzy."

"You will be. Can you tell us what happened?" Mr Scruffy asked as he removed the poultice. "I'll freshen this up. Your wound is healing nicely."

"My wound?"

"Yes, you had several places where one or two of the Atcenians must have connected with their clubs. Thankfully, none had a sword or you might not be here to tell us about it."

"But, there was only—"

"Has she passed out again?" King Elder said walking in with Queen Esmé at his side. "Let the Queen use her magic to help her."

"Mr Scruffy, the King didn't mean your healing is not powerful enough." She moved next to KC and pulled a slender bottle from a pocket of her gown.

"I know," Mr Scruffy said. "My power does not equal our Queen's." Mr Scruffy bowed slightly.

"Sometimes it takes a blend of magic from different sources to help healing to begin. KC suffered several bad blows. Are there any other obvious wounds?" Queen Esmé poured some potion into a cup.

"No. We don't think she suffered any internal injuries. She seems to be suffering most from the head wound. One of the Atcenians must have connected a strong blow to her head," Mr Scruffy walked over to the other side of the cot and picked up KC's hand. He held it in his wing, caressing it gently.

"You've come to love her, haven't you?" King Elder asked.

"Haven't we all? She is a ray of hope in our dark world. We can't lose her now," Mr Scruffy laid KC's hand down on the cot. KC stirred.

"Let me see if I can get her to drink this now," Queen Esmé placed her hand behind KC's head and held it up so that she could give her the potion. KC managed to drink it and began to wake at the same time.

"What happened?" KC laid down after swallowing. "How did you find me?"

"You called for us," Ish said. "We were looking for you when your telepathic call came."

"Ish heard you. Iolair and I were there with Ish. You were in a huge battle all by yourself," Mr Scruffy's joy at seeing KC awake made his voice sound giddy with delight. "I'm sorry. I guess I shouldn't sound so joyful."

"It's okay," KC said. "That Atcenian almost got me. I don't know how I was able to defeat him."

"What about the other four?" Ish asked.

"I don't know. I only fought the one."

"If you didn't fight them off, who did?" Mr Scruffy said.

"I don't know. When I walked into the clearing, they were already down with the other beings that had fought them. There was a huge battle before I got there. I sat on a log to get my breath when the Atcenian charged me. I reacted, and then I don't know what happened until I woke up here."

"There is something I don't understand," King Elder said. "How did you get to the base of Grave's Mountain? The last time we saw you, you were on your way here, to this thípi."

"I know I shouldn't have done it, but I needed to get water. So, I gathered up my bucket and went down to Stone's River. Before I could reach for the water, the Purple Drakein grabbed me—"

"What?" All of them said at once.

KC smiled, but her head throbbed. "Yes. It is true. She took me to her lair. I threatened to kill her; she told me about Sam and how Sam had done all he could to save Princess Derryth."

"Wait a minute," Ish stepped up closer to KC's cot. "You are trying to tell us that the Purple Drakein took you to its lair and didn't kill you, but wanted to talk with you about Princess Derryth and Sam?"

"I know it sounds crazy, but yes."

"You must have knocked some stuff loose in your head, because if you think I'm going to believe that, then you are no longer KC, but some possessed creature." Ish pulled out his bow and armed his arrow. "I'll scare you into telling the truth."

Mr Scruffy jumped upon the cot and opened his wings to shield KC. "Ish! Put that away. Let's hear her story. Can't you see she is weak?"

"Let's all calm down," King Elder stepped over to Ish and lowered his bow. "We don't need for someone to get hurt accidentally. Maybe it will be best if we wait and talk with KC after she gets some rest."

"Please. The potion I gave her will be putting her to sleep shortly. It is best she rests. She'll have a clearer head after she sleeps for a while," Queen Esmé said. "Come, let's all go. Mr Scruffy, you will stay with her?"

"Yes, my Queen. It will be my honor."

MR SCRUFFY and the others sat around KC's cot. She was sitting up eating some berries from a variety of local bushes and a slice of special bread that Queen Esmé had made. She took a sip of the healing potion.

"Thank you for all you've done for me. I feel a lot stronger."

"Good. Now, you can tell us what happened with the Purple Drakein," Ish said. KC saw Mr Scruffy give Ish a hard look.

"Come on, Ish. It isn't that mysterious. The Purple Drakein took me to its lair. She said if she wanted to kill me, she would have. When I asked why she brought me to her lair, she said she wanted to share with me that Nukpana is losing her strength over her. She was able to break away for a short time and she saw her chance to tell me that the Chosen One was making an impact on Nukpana."

"Then, why didn't she return you to camp?" King Elder asked.

"She couldn't. I'm not sure exactly why or how, but she disappeared. I was left in the dark of the lair. I walked out and ended up in the clearing where the beasts had fought one another. Besides the Atcenians, there were Ogres, Moss Folk, Goblins, Dwarves, Centaurs, and Dryads. You know the rest."

"KC, I find this remarkable. When we found you, there were only five Atcenians lying around you. No other beasts or Wood Folk," Mr Scruffy said. "Are you sure you saw what you say?"

"Yes. I only fought one Atcenian," KC looked at each of them. She could feel they didn't believe her. "Do you think the Purple Drakein helped me?"

"Why not?" Ish got up and walked out.

KC looked out after him and felt a pain of distrust come over her. She looked to Mr Scruffy, who bowed his head.

"We'll let you rest. Tomorrow, we must face the battle lines again. There was another skirmish today. We lost more ground at the south edge of the Wild Woods near the Atcenian hills. We must retake that ground. We'll talk tomorrow." King Elder patted KC's cot and Queen Esmé smiled at KC as they left.

"KC?"

"Yes, Mr Scruffy?"

"For what it's worth, I believe you. I don't know why, but I do. Try and rest. I will stay with you. You are stronger, but you have had an ordeal. Don't mind Ish. He's still feeling the pain of loss."

"I'm not sure I understand why he is so angry at me."

"I think he's scared that the same thing will happen to you that happened to Princess Derryth."

"What, me get overtaken by Nukpana?"

"Yes."

"That helps me understand. You know you do not need to worry, don't you?"

"I do. You rest. I'll be here sitting and keeping watch."

"Thanks."

KC repositioned herself in her cot and tried to settle down to sleep. She wasn't sure she'd be able to rest. She wasn't sure her story was a good one. She still couldn't believe what actually did happen with Drakania, let alone that the Purple Drakein had not harmed her.

CHAPTER 19
LORNE'S RUSE

The morning two-suns broke through the canopy of trees. KC walked with Mr Scruffy on her shoulder to King Elder's room. She marveled at how accustomed she had become to living in Eldershire.

"Penny for your thoughts," KC said to Mr Scruffy telepathically.

"I was thinking about you and how strong you seem."

"I do feel stronger. I hope I can hold up to the strain of fighting. Walking through all the blood and carcasses after the last battle was horrific."

"War is an evil thing. Only those who survive know its carnage. The dead escape its results."

"True enough. Well, we're here. Let's go see how things will be for this battle."

They walked into the throne room. King Elder was already giving out instructions to his leaders.

"Fergus, you will lead your Dryads up through the Atcenian Hills. Our plan is to get as near to Emerald Mountain as we can. Our scouts report the area is not as well fortified as Grave's Mountain. If we can get into one of the mountains, I feel sure we can gain a stronghold. With our collective forces, we may be able to prevail over a large portion of Nukpana's army. Any questions?"

Mr Scruffy alighted from KC's shoulder and touched down on the table. "I apologize for interrupting like this, but King Elder, I must caution you." Mr Scruffy walked over to the map that lay on the table. He picked up a long-pointed stick and pointed to the Atcenian Hills. "Here, here, and here. These three locations are death traps, you do realize?"

"Yes. We are aware of them. Fergus has fought in that area before," King Elder said.

"Then, why not send some of the armies around to the back side of Emerald Mountain and come in from behind?"

"That is a good idea. We are hoping the Centaurs, Unicorns, and a few other Elementals from Mushroom Alley can make it there by this evening. From our scout reports, Emerald Mountain has been basically left unguarded by Nukpana's armies."

"Does that not surprise you?" Mr Scruffy looked to each of the leaders sitting around the table.

"Yes. But, we must strike now if we expect to overcome Nukpana," King Elder said. "Now, any more questions?" King Elder stood up.

"Will you want the bird armies still at Emerald Mountain?" Mr Scruffy looked to Iolair and Gavin.

"Most definitely. Our aerial attack will be critical to our success," Gavin joined in. "But, I must agree with Mr Scruffy. Fergus must be careful not to get trapped with a hostile enemy surrounding them."

"We will be fine. I've fought in this area before. I know where those traps are and I will avoid them. No worries," Fergus said.

"Good. Then let's do it," King Elder said. The leaders broke away.

KC walked over to Ish who was standing near a window. "May I speak with you?"

"Perchance. I don't know what you can say that will change my opinion of you."

"Point taken. My words are not meant to cause you to change your mind. My words are only to reassure you that I will do what I can to protect you. My quest is to retrieve the Efil Stone. That is my one goal in this world. I am here to accomplish it. If I do something else that does not agree with you, well, then I do. Thank you for finding me and bringing me back. It could be that one day I'll repay you for your act of kindness."

KC walked over to the door where Mr Scruffy waited for her. They walked out into the forest.

FERGUS, leading the Dryads with the Moss Folk and Nymphs accompanied KC and Mr Scruffy. They were marching toward the Atcenian Hills. Gavin had flown to the south side of Emerald Mountain with the rest of the bird armies.

"KC and Mr Scruffy, I'd like to speak with you here a moment, if you would stop?" Fergus said.

"Sure. What do you need?" KC said.

"This may be contrary to what King Elder would like and it might catch the two of you by surprise, but I have a plan that I've already coordinated with Ish. I want to give the Atcenians the idea they are doing better than they are. Up here a bit, there is a place that is shut in on every side by precipitous mountains, and screened in by a forest with wide-spreading trees. I plan to use it to make the Atcenians think we are running away in fear. Are you willing to trust me on this plan?"

"Well, I don't know," KC said. She looked to Mr Scruffy.

"Fergus, do you know what will happen?"

"Yes. Mr Scruffy, I've seen this done before. I know exactly what I'm doing."

"Then, if you feel confident, I trust you."

KC trusted her owl friend. She looked at Fergus. "As do I."

The Atcenians came down over a hill in a full charge. The three leaders broke away and joined the Elderian army. About five minutes into fighting, Fergus called for his beings to make it appear to the Atcenians that they were retreating because they were terrified by their attack. They began to move with speed to the area that Fergus shared was confined on every side by steep mountains, and fully screened in with a thick forest.

The Atcenians followed in pursuit. Fergus kept his army moving back to the point where there was no exit. The Atcenians continued toward them. Ish and his army were concealing themselves in the rough country and waited until the Atcenians passed them by, which put Ish and his army in the rear of the hostile army, yet they kept hidden.

"Keep back until we have them further in the trap," Fergus telepathed to Ish. "When they are further into the mountain, you can come at them."

"The Atcenians are completely ignorant of their own plight," Ish replied.

Without warning, the Atcenians stopped. They began to moan and holler.

"We've got them," Fergus yelled. "They have realized we've trapped them. Charge!"

Ish with his army and Fergus with his army encircled the Atcenians, knocking them down.

KC noticed that Ish was in peril. She tried to call out to him telepathically to warn him of the Grey Menace above him, but Ish was fighting and not noticing them flying toward him.

"Ish! Ish!" KC tried to call out to him, but he didn't hear her. She watched in horror as two Grey Menace grabbed Ish and hauled him off in the direction of Emerald Mountain.

Mr Scruffy landed beside her, KC jumped on his back and they started to fly after Ish, but a large group of Grey Menace flew down to them and engaged them in a fierce battle. Gavin and his army of birds came and joined in the fighting. After several minutes, the remaining Grey Menace turned and left. KC looked down at Fergus. All the Atcenians were either slain or the remaining few were running away.

Back on the ground, KC and Mr Scruffy joined Fergus to plan how they could go after Ish.

"We must wait," Fergus said. "The Atcenians are stronger than this small skirmish indicates. There will be more coming over the mountain in due time. We lost a lot of our force during that last battle. I fear we may have won this battle, but we haven't won the war."

KC stood listening. She thought of the war games her first husband, Jack, would play with his friends. She remembered one time when Jack was on break. They were playing and Jack was sharing about strategic planning. She laughed so hard when Jack had used his jigsaw to cut out an opening in their game board to make a trench.

"A trench!"

"What?" Mr Scruffy said as he looked at KC. "Why a trench?"

"I said that aloud?"

"Yes."

"I think this is what Fergus can do. My idea is based on something my husband, Jack, did when he was showing his friends how to strategically plan a battle that involves committing treachery against an enemy."

"This may prove interesting. Go on, tell us more," Fergus replied.

"It will be better if I share it in steps. Fergus, with all the zeal you can muster, you should go out to meet the Atcenians once they cross over the boundary that you determine is getting too close to your foot hold here within this mountain valley."

"Okay. But, should we not be preparing for their invasion?"

"Yes. You and your forces should busy yourselves by marking off a tract of land that is very long and make a deep trench that is sufficiently wide enough to hold a vast army. But, you must leave in the center a small portion of ground intact, enough for a small army of your forces to cross over safely."

"How small do you think?" Fergus asked and began drawing on the dirt.

"Let's say at least ten or twenty of your Moss Folk. Now, over the trench, place reeds, twigs, branches, and other debris, and then scatter the markings and piles of dirt to conceal that the trench is there. It is important that you tell the Moss Folk when the time comes for them to cause the Atcenians to give chase, that when they reach the trench area, they should draw themselves together into a narrow column and pass rather slowly across this centerpiece of land you have left. They should take care that they should not fall into the trench."

"This is sounding rather clever," Mr Scruffy said. "Your husband, Jack, must have been a fighter."

"He was in the military. He understood the power of treachery."

"The critical thing to remember is that you should not entice the Atcenians to take up the chase. You must be sure they have gotten sufficiently close. That way, they would not just give up and retreat without chasing on into this area."

"How can we be sure they will take up the chase?" Fergus said.

"Let me ride with your scouts. They see me, I'll even wave my sword at them, they should take charge."

"That is a good idea, KC. I can fly above and watch carefully as you proceed," Mr Scruffy said.

Fergus called a few scouts and instructed them to warn him of any changes in the placement of the Atcenians. He then instructed another group of Moss Folk, Dryads, and Nymphs to construct the trench as wide as possible at the entrance to their fortified valley.

"Once the Atcenians begin to charge this way, they will think they have us trapped," Fergus told KC and Mr Scruffy.

Fergus then called forth another small group of Sprites and Moss Folk to make their way to where the Atcenians were holding camp. "KC will accompany you. Allow the Atcenians to see you at a distance. When they have seen you, flee with full speed back here. Keep in mind that when you reach the trench, you draw into a narrow column, and all will pass over and join the rest of us here waiting. Now, go. Yggdrasil speed to each of you."

KC walked out with the Sprites and Moss Folk. They went a good distance before they were in a position to see the Atcenians. At first, KC thought the beasts didn't see them. Then, she could hear a rumbling sound.

"They are on the move toward you," Mr Scruffy telepathed to KC.

"Good," KC held up her sword and waved it in a show of defiance. "Now, let's see what happens."

The small band turned and ran back with full speed to Fergus and the rest of the army. KC motioned to them to draw into a single line and they crossed over the narrow passage. All turned to watch the Atcenians moving toward them.

"Look," KC called out. "The Atcenians are still chasing at full speed. They are possessed with the spirit of fury." She saw them marching forward four abreast. And, four abreast, they tumbled into the trench, every one of them, the first tumbling down and all following behind.

"The fools! They followed in such perilous pursuit. They were so one minded, they failed to notice the catastrophe in front of them. It is a day of victory for us!" Fergus yelled to his army. "Let's give up a cheer for KC!"

KC, Mr Scruffy, Fergus, and his army proceeded to make their way to meet up with Gavin and his army at Emerald Mountain.

"Gavin, it is good to reconnect with you and your army. Are the Hawks and the Owls at the ready?" Mr Scruffy said, greeting his friend.

"Yes, and Iolair sent word that he and his Eagles are not far away. Nukpana's forces are running scared. After their fall at King Elder's Camp, word is reaching the forces about the fall of the Atcenians at Fergus' hand. We've got them on the run!" Gavin said.

KC noted he seemed to be smiling with delight at the upper hand they appeared to have, but inside her heart she worried. Jack had always told her that armies tend to fail after they have had a streak of wins. She hoped this would not be true of the Elderians.

"Gather in. We'll make plans on how we will retrieve Ish," Mr Scruffy said to each motioning them to move toward his makeshift table. He unfolded a map of Emerald Mountain's inner tunnels. "Sam was able to acquire this map before he died and passed it to me the last time he was home." Mr Scruffy began to point out different points of entrance to the mountain.

KC noticed by one of the towers, the mouth of what might be an old underground passage, which she thought she had seen in a dream, but wasn't certain.

※

LATER THAT NIGHT, KC made her way to the entrance she had

noted on the map. She saw it was insecurely concealed with a few small stones. She decided to go in. Taking a step forward she heard a cough. She froze her steps.

"You aren't going in there alone, are you?" the voice said.

KC turned and saw Iolair, Mr Scruffy, and Gavin standing behind her. "I thought about it. Want to come?"

KC picked Mr Scruffy up and placed him on her shoulder. "Do you both want to ride on me, too?" She asked hoping the other two would say no.

"No nccd to worry about us. Fergus is here, too," Gavin said. Fergus stepped out of the trees.

"When were you going to tell me you were here?"

"In due time," Fergus smiled. He placed Iolair and Gavin on his shoulders, one on each side. "Let's go."

"First, let me see where this leads. I'll call back to you telepathically," KC said and walked inside the tunnel. Within a few steps, she was inside what was marked as a circular wall.

"Do we need more light?" KC asked Mr Scruffy.

"I do not think so. We should be able to see by the light of your sword. I'll let Fergus and the others know to come on and join us."

KC looked out through the tunnel. She removed Fea from its sheath and said, "Ancient moons lend your power, give me light this very hour." A dull light lit their path.

The companions made their way through the passage, emerging into the main room of Emerald Mountain. The room opened up into a domed ceiling. Light came down in large swaths from the various skylights high above. KC lowered Fea and the low light from her sword went out.

Carefully, KC and her companions took guarded steps out into the center of the room looking around for any Atcenians or Grey

Menace. They found several guards sleeping and slew them at once. A few guards became aware of intruders and came running toward them, but Fergus and Gavin charged, striking them down. The remainder of their armies came through the tunnel, joining their leaders. By their numbers they gained the upper hand and overcame the few Atcenians and Grey Menace left to fight. Emerald Mountain was captured by storm soon after the beginning of the siege in the valley.

KC turned to Mr Scruffy and said, "It worries me that Nukpana has not been seen since last evening. Something is not right that she has not appeared. Yet, we must find Ish. Where do you think she may have him held captive?"

"It is not known by me or the others. Do you remember what Princess Derryth had said to you at Grave's Mountain about her room?"

"No. And, now I wonder since Nukpana is not here, if this was indeed where she took Ish or if this might be—"

"It's a T R A P!" Iolair screamed an eagle cry.

The fighting that ensued was horrendous and merciless. KC could not keep an eye on any of her companions. She stepped back as a club came down near her crushing the skull of a hawk beside her. She recoiled in horror and stumbled backwards falling down winding stairs. When she came out of her fall, she landed hard and slammed her head against what felt like rock. She started to try to get up, but fell backwards unconscious.

❧

LIFTING HER HEAD UP, KC felt a sharp pain at the back of her head. She moved her hand up, feeling a large lump. She reached for Fea and found it in her sheath. Her hat was still attached to her belt. She felt around where she laid. The dirt was loose in her fingers. She tried to see where she was lying, but the darkness prevented her from seeing anything distinctive. All she could see was a shadow.

"Shhh," a fluting voice said. "Do not say a word. Speak with your mind. I'm Lorne. I saw them bring you in here. You've been out for hours. You must be the Chosen One. I will help you get out, if you trust me. If you don't, I'll kill you."

KC peered through the darkness, but couldn't see clearly. She decided not to say anything to see if the voice would try to speak to her again. She thought she might be able to pinpoint where it was located. She waited.

"Why are you not joining with me? You haven't decided to fight against me, have you?"

Again, KC remained silent. She figured the voice was to her right a little ways. The room might not be too large. She felt as though its voice was moving closer to her somehow. Yet, she didn't hear any movement. Was he moving toward her? The sound of the room was playing with her senses. If the voice was real and would kill her, she figured she'd take her chances. At least, she still had her sword.

The voice spoke again, "I told you that I'm Lorne. By not responding, you're acting as though you don't believe me. Trust me. I'm here to help you. God willed to give me my chance to go back to Earth. I have that chance now, if you will only trust me. I am your best friend, after all. I haven't done anything to you. You should give me a chance."

KC felt uneasy about what she was hearing. Since coming to Eldershire, she'd never heard the name of God mentioned. The Elderians always talked about Yggdrasil and Mother Elder. Her suspicions grew. This can't be right.

"You are wrong. I am who I am. Why do you not believe? You always told me to believe. You said that the last night that I was with you. Don't you remember me?"

A cold chill ran down KC's spine. Who could this be? Why would Nukpana play such a trick on her? This can't be what it seems. She decided to get up and move toward who was speaking. Maybe if she could put on her hat, she could get Fea to shine its light. She moved her right arm forward and felt a tug on her arm. She reached further, but it stopped suddenly. She was chained.

"Hahaha. I knew if I provoked you enough you would try to move. You did. I win. I win. You can't reach me. Hahaha!"

The voice seemed to fade away. KC wondered what kind of being would talk that way, and then laugh at her misery. Whoever it was, it was evil. It enjoyed the pain of others.

She then thought of her friends—Mr Scruffy, Iolair, Gavin, and Fergus. The last time she saw them, they were fighting with everything they could muster to overthrow the Atcenians and Grey Menace that had barged into the domed room. The trap was well played. It was foolish to have thought they could have gotten that far into Emerald Mountain without someone knowing. Why was she so careless?

THE BATTLE RAGED on as Fergus, Mr Scruffy, Iolair, and Gavin fought Nukpana's army from all directions. Mr Scruffy heard the cries of Mylo rushing into the domed room with King Elder, Queen Esmé, and other Elderian forces coming to the rescue. Within minutes the Grey Menace were scattered, and the Elderian army was able to retreat. Many were injured and many more lay dead.

"Where's KC?" Mr Scruffy called out across to Iolair. "Have you seen her?"

"No, I thought she was with you."

"We must go find her," Gavin said as he flew to Mr Scruffy's side.

"No. We must retreat and come back when we're stronger. We've got to be strong to rescue Ish and KC, if she's been captured too."

CHAPTER 20
ESPYING

The images of Eldershire moved across the room like those she had watched on a date at her first drive-in movie. KC continued to study the scenes as they played out in front of her. She soon realized it was a montage of scenes morphed together from the minds of all inhabitants of Eldershire. It appeared to be a record of her experiences since her arrival. From the moment she was grabbed by Ish in the brier patch to the second Ish was dragged away by the Grey Menace, the history of what she had experienced in Eldershire was shown on a large screened three-dimensional theatre wall using the same technologies as her home world.

Mother Elder said, "You thought your technology of moving pictures was so far advanced. It is a digital means to do what we've always done here in Eldershire with our minds. What you refer to as the internet is a web of wires electronically connecting all of your devices. Here, we wire our minds. Our telepathic capabilities far surpass anything your internet can do. The images you see are not on the wall like a movie screen, they are in your mind. This is what we all see."

Mother Elder stood to her side; KC turned her head to the left. She looked back at the images. Her heart had twinges watching Ish's limp body being pulled from her sight.

"No worries, KC. We will retrieve him," Mother Elder said, "I'm breaking the link with your mind by waving my hand to close the view."

Despite Mother Elder's effort, KC saw more images. This time the scenes were different—fuzzy, blurred. As her eyes focused, and what she watched became clearer, KC recognized her family's car sitting beside the road. Her interest intensified. The events of the night her family died unfolded before her. She watched hoping on hope that the outcome might change. And again, she could do nothing to stop the play-by-play—

> KC turns to Jay-H. He is talking on his cell. She gets out of the car, while her family remains in the vehicle. She walks over to the stranded motorist. In the distance, KC notices a tractor-trailer coming up the roadway. And then, she sees long, slithering purple tendrils emerging from a smokey gray fog. The tendrils grabbed hold of the tractor-trailer's cab and steers it toward her family.

KC felt an explosion of pain in her body, her eyes swelled with tears. She screamed, "What was that? I saw it. I saw it kill my family!"

MR. SCRUFFY SAID, "Life marks the passing of time; death erases it from our minds." He plunged to the ground.

KC swung her sword with all her strength. Fea connected blithely on the neck of the Atcenian that was bent toward her laughing at her wee size. "Now, what do you think of that, you creep? You want to laugh anymore!" The Atcenian's head rolled away from its body.

She jumped over the lifeless beast and crouched down beside Mr

Scruffy's body, sprawled lifeless on the ground. She feared he was mortally wounded.

"Mr Scruffy, can you hear me?" she said trying to see him through her tears.

HER HEART STILL BREAKING, KC's tears had stopped.

"They didn't have to die," she said. "They didn't have to die." KC fell over, her arms dangled from where they were cuffed to the wall above her head.

A slither of light crossed her face. She looked up and saw that it shown from a small break in the window high above. She moaned and her sorrow engulfed her. The shock of seeing the tractor-trailer being forced toward her family's car struck KC raw with uncompromising pain. Then, seeing Mr Scruffy dying in her arms brought heartbreak.

She tried to move, but tingling sensations raced through her veins. Her arms felt weak, as though they had dangled for hours and were drained of blood. Her knees, bent up under her, ached with sharp pains when she moved. When she tried to straighten a leg, she could feel the punctured skin where her knees had rested on stones. She barely could drag her foot across the dirt floor. She gave up in despair and hung from the chains in a stupor.

"Is she alive?" a voice asked when a cold slimy hand lifted KC's head up. The light crossed her eyes.

"I believe so, your Treorai." The hand let go of her head. KC allowed her chin to hit her chest to give the appearance she was still out cold.

"Good. We may not need to do anything more to her. She will be in my control from her own stupidity and sorrow. We only need to feed her brain with more images of her family dying again and again." Nukpana let out a harrowing laugh. "I will win! I will win!"

KC came out of darkness, waking from a nightmare. She could see. The light opened up her view of her cell. Across from her were shadows of things, maybe other beings. They appeared skeletal—long dead, like her, hanging from the cell walls, chained in place. She had no sense of time. Her body hurt, yet somehow, she sensed she still had strength within her.

Thinking over the last hours, she didn't believe any of what she had witnessed was real. *I was hallucinating.* She looked at each one of the poor souls. *Is one of you Lorne?* Lorne must be a prisoner, too, she thought, but none of the beings she studied looked like their veins still flowed with life.

"Is it another trick of Nukpana?" KC wondered aloud to herself. Her mouth was dry, her thirst growing as she began to wonder how she could be free.

"It's no trick. I'm here, and I am a friend," Lorne leaned forward. The light cast across her face. "I'm a fox, a female fox, at that. I wasn't always a fox."

"How did you get here?"

"I wasn't always here. I've been here for a while. In my previous world, where I came from, I was a Bulldog. I belonged to a really nice man. He called me Andy. I loved him. He loved me. Then, one day, I came here and now I'm a fox. I have no idea why I'm a fox, but I am. I was living happily here in Eldershire. One day I was out forging for food and got caught in a trap set by the beasts of this place—the Atcenians. I thought they were going to kill me."

"They didn't kill you, but they brought you here. Why?"

"Not exactly. I was a pet to two twin Atcenians. Their names were Gorge and Morge. The Evil One killed them because they didn't bring back a human. They told me once they hated her because she was so evil, but they stayed to fight with her because it gave them something to do."

KC swallowed. "That's sad. Why did you get thrown in here?"

"I was mad and wanted to go after the human that caused my friends to die. Gorge and Morge had treated me well. They could have killed me, but they didn't. They were dumb and sometimes did stupid things. They didn't have to die because they couldn't find the human. It wasn't their fault. The Evil One didn't know they had kept me. When I stepped out of their hut to go find the human, another Atcenian threw me in here to die."

"What do you know about the human?" KC wondered if Lorne realized the truth.

"That Gorge and Morge died because of her. I know she is the Chosen One. I know _you_ are the human."

KC felt a surge of fear flow through her veins. She wasn't sure what to do next, but she knew she had to try to change Lorne's anger toward her. "You realize I didn't know them. I didn't even know where I was when they were after me. It was she who killed your friends, not me."

"I know. I also know you threaten her."

"How? I don't think I look so threatening right now." KC mused at the weirdness of the moment.

"By being alive, you scare her, yet she won't kill you. That puzzles me."

"To be honest, me too."

"Don't you know why?"

"No, not really. Mother Elder and Yggdrasil, as well as Mr Scruffy, tried to explain it to me. All I know is that I've got to find the Efil Stone if I want to go home. I don't want to be here, in this place. I don't want to fight Nukpana. But, until I return the Efil Stone to

Mother Elder, then and only then will I be able to have my family back. Just as you want to revenge your friends, I want to have the life I had before. But, I'm scared. I'm scared I'll die."

"Seems we need each other. I can help you, if you want me to. But, I want you to do something for me in return."

"I'll try. But, if given half the chance, I might run away. Then, again," KC let her head drop in despair. She thought for a moment, saw Jack's smile, and was reminded of his courage. She said, "What is it you want me to do?"

"I want a lock of Nukpana's hair—her real hair. You can't take her hair as long as she is part of the Drakein. You'll know the time is right when the Drakein leaves her body. At that moment, seize a lock of her hair. Plan to give it to me when next we meet."

KC wondered where they'd meet again, but at this point, she didn't have a lot of help coming her way. "I'm not sure I'll succeed. But, if I do, I'll get the hair for you. How will you help me?"

"You'll see soon. You need to know I have no worries about you. And, you should have no worries about succeeding. You will. And, as for us meeting again, just know, we will."

"I must know something. While fighting before I was brought here, I had a sword and a funny looking black hat. I wish I knew where they were now. Have you seen them?"

"They are there with you; both are strapped to your clothes."

"What? How can that be? Why would Nukpana not take them?"

"I do not know, but you have them. Now, hold still, I'm going to release you."

"Aren't you chained?"

"I was, but I have my ways of getting out of things. I am sly like a fox, you know."

A smile came upon KC's face and the blood flowed through her wrists bringing a tingle to her spine. She was starting to get solid feeling back in her fingers. She rolled her shoulders back working out the kinks.

"Thank you, Lorne. You are kind."

"It is curious that Nukpana allowed you to keep your hat and sword."

"I know." KC tried standing. Her feet felt unsteady. She steadied herself bracing against the wall. "You know Lorne. It feels good to stand. What you say about Nukpana letting me keep my sword and hat. It is as if she wants me to fight her."

"I think a beast is coming," Lorne spoke in a whisper. "We've got to get over to the door at the right moment. When you hear the latch spring, you must lunge forward. I'll take care of the beast."

KC wasn't sure if Lorne read her mind, but she said telepathically, "Okay."

Lorne responded, "It's about time you believed in me."

The latch on the cell door echoed a metallic clattering sound. KC jumped in position and waited. The cell door swung open with an echoing rasp and a slither of light shone down on the Atcenian when it lumbered through the opening. KC shoved Fea into his side with all of her might. At the same moment, Lorne jumped on its throat and ripped it open. No sound ever came from the beast before it fell to the ground.

"We make a good team," Lorne telepathed to KC. "We'll stay mentally linked as we make our way through the passages. Do you still want to go to Princess Derryth's room?"

KC started to protest that Lorne had read her mind, but chose not to waste time. "I must. Can you lead me there? I know what I must do."

"I will lead you, but you will be putting yourself in her clutches. She is sure to be waiting for you there."

"It is why I'm here. I must. If you can reach Mr Scruffy and Iolair to let them know where I am, it may save my life."

"You get a lock of her hair, I'll get you the help you need. Let's do it."

❦

Sitting on her ivory throne with gold inlaid atop a raised platform that was surrounded in gilded silver and gold, Nukpana tapped her right forefinger on the upholstered arm. A deep thud emitted from the manchette with each tap of her finger. The room was full with her followers standing in a semi-circle all facing the lone officer of her army, who was charged with giving Nukpana an update on the fighting with the Elderians.

"Is that all you have to tell me?" Nukpana glared down toward him with her left hand moving Blazewing into position. "You do mean to tell me that the Elderians are losing. Correct?" Her voice echoed in the room.

The soldier nodded. He asked if there was anything he should tell his commander. Nukpana looked out over the room and debated whether to strike his head off and send that in reply or send him with actual orders. She was tired of this folly. She wanted to get to KC and put an end to the human's chance at making the prophecy come true. She knew she had to wait.

A ruckus stirred the beasts standing at the back of the room. The followers stepped aside as a Woodwose came lumbering up to Nukpana. He stopped. His gigantic, hairy, club-wielding, green skin-clad body covered with forest debris stood towering over the other beasts.

"Well?" she bellowed.

"Your Treoraí," he bowed with little grace.

"Go on. What is it?"

"Your Treoraí, I bring you information about the human prisoner."

"And?"

"She has escaped."

Calmly, and with a low voice that rose into a crescendo, Nukpana said, "How could this happen now? Who's the fool that let her go? Bring him to me now. I'll have his head!"

Nukpana stormed down the nine steps from her throne and knocked over those followers that knelt as she passed.

She slammed the door to her private chambers. "How can this be? How could she possibly have gotten away?" Her rage was boiling. Blazewing began sending out sparks in many directions, scorching the curtains and fabrics that decorated her room. She noticed she was setting her room on fire when she pulled her rage under control.

There was a slight knock on her door.

"If you don't have information I need, don't come in or it will be the last thing you do."

"Your Treoraí, it is I, your loyal servant," the Troll said as he walked in. "We have learned that the human has not left Emerald Mountain. We believe she is in Princess Derryth's bedroom."

"You believe?"

"Yes, your Treoraí. We are not certain because we have not seen her."

"Then, how do you know she is still here?"

"No one saw her leave. We did see a fox sneak out. He was the one we held in the dungeon."

"Enough. Be gone. I need quiet." The Troll turned and left.

Nukpana paced the floor and tried to remember what she could about the prophecy. It was true that KC should make her way to the Efil Stone, this much she knew. What wasn't certain was whether or not KC would be successful. Nukpana decided she needed to hedge her bets and plan to absorb KC's body in case the Efil Stone was found and KC could use it to kill her.

Moving to her mirror, Nukpana looked into her mind's eye. She was going to speak to herself, but stopped. She walked over to an ornate box, opened it up, and looked at a glass vial that held a light blue elixir, which shown brightly in the muted light. She had prepared it for this special occasion. She took a swig, recapped the vial, and placed it back in its velveteen casing.

Standing before the mirror once again, Nukpana spoke to the Purple Drakein. "You tried to keep me out of your plans when you went to see KC. You thought I wouldn't know everything. I knew what you were doing. You were wrong to double cross me. I will defeat you. You can't win. You never will. Not yet. I have another plan that you never considered."

Dancing around the room, the blue elixir began working its magic. Nukpana felt lovely and free. She looked back at the mirror. "Even though you drugged me, I watched you take KC to Grave's Mountain. At the time, I couldn't harm you or her. But, now, with her on her way to retrieve the Efil Stone, I have my chance. I won't be using Blazewing. I can't harm her body with Blazewing's acid, but I'll do better than that." Nukpana danced around the room, and then sat down in a chair in front of her dressing mirror.

"My plan is perfect. I'll absorb into KC. You know I can only absorb one soul at a time. You planned for years for your revenge on me. It was for nothing. You've lost. I still win."

Nukpana stood up, twirled around and around in delight, laughing out loud with an evil cackle.

❧

KC DECIDED that Nukpana would be waiting for her. The walk to Princess Derryth's bedroom was too easy, she thought. Why can't this fear leave me. *I need courage.*

A voice spoke to her. "Courage comes from conquering your fear." KC responded telepathically, "I don't know who speaks, but I will believe."

She took a deep breath and stepped through the doorway surveying the bedroom. Just as Drakania had said, the bed was across the room and against the back wall. She saw the carved headboard. KC kept Fea close to her side, walked over to the bed taking each step with determination and ready for an evil hand to grab her.

KC remembered Drakania's words. 'You must speak these words slowly as you rub your hand in a circle over the surface of the carved faces.'

KC positioned herself on the bed, reached up, rubbed the faces, and said,

> "I am sworn to my quest.
> My heart, though weak at times, knows goodness, honor, and love.
> With my sword and hat, I'll defend the defenseless.
> With the Efil Stone, I'll defeat the wicked!"

She pushed on the carved flower petal. The panel separated and a deep cavity was revealed.

KC looked into the darkness and saw a glimmer of light deep within. She could tell from the light that the Efil Stone was too far back to reach without her moving inside the cavity. The opening was too tight for her to climb inside while wearing the hat. She looked around the room one last time making sure she was not being watched; removed her hat, and she saw her body reflected in the cheval glass mirror off to the side of the bed. *I forgot I was invisible because I wore the hat and held Fea.*

She then moved into the opening, but was stopped by Fea hitting the edge of the frame. KC retreated. Hesitant about taking off her sword, she reasoned she must. Laying Fea on the bed, KC climbed back through the opening.

Wiggling and pulling herself along, she used her elbows to squirm her way toward the Efil Stone. The stone was within her reach, KC's breathing was labored, and she was getting claustrophobic. Only her feet hung out into the room.

Reaching with her left arm, KC could barely grasp the Efil Stone. One finger clasped around the chain that dangled from the stone. Grabbing the chain, she managed to slip it around her neck, knowing she would need both hands to back out of the tight hole. *I need to get out of here; I'm losing air.*

KC felt something cold and clammy grab her ankle. "Whoa!" she screamed.

Trying to jerk away, the clammy hand held fast and dragged her out of the cavity, dropping her on the bed. Her wits still about her, KC was able to grab ahold of the bedcovers to stop her fall, but she was slammed onto the floor with everything falling down on top of her.

Nukpana grabbed the covers off KC, lifting her up by the throat, wrapping her hands tighter, choking her.

KC flung her arms out and tried to reach back to grab Nukpana. She snagged a section of Nukpana's gown and ripped the material while digging into her arm. Blood gushed out in a spray of purplish black. Nukpana reacted by dropping KC on the floor.

KC took the time she needed to reach for her hat, clicked it on her belt, and reached for Fea. Nukpana came at KC and they were locked in hand-to-hand combat. Hair was pulled out by the roots. KC screamed. Reaching up, KC pulled out several clumps of Nukpana's hair in revenge. Nukpana grabbed KC by the throat; they tumbled to the ground knocking various things to the floor.

Rolling back and forth, Nukpana tried to bite KC's ear. KC grabbed a large metal object that was on the floor. She slammed it against Nukpana's head. KC jumped upon her feet with Fea in her hand. Nukpana jerked the rug KC was standing on out from under her.

KC was lying face down. Nukpana stepped over to KC, reached

down for her, and then knocked KC hard on her back slamming her to the floor. Nukpana then straddled over her. She reached into the side pockets of her gown and pulled out two daggers.

KC saw the room reflected in the cheval glass. Nukpana stood behind her, the two daggers held high above her head.

"I've waited centuries for this fight," Nukpana said as she sneered down at KC. "But, before I absorb you with the stab of these two poison daggers, I want you to know that I've ruled your life on Earth. The images you see are of me bringing you here, to this moment."

KC moved into a crouched position while images flashed before her —her first husband, Jack, dying with purple tendrils holding him under water after his military plane was forced into the sea; the tractor-trailer forced into her family's car, killing all with the purple tendrils slithering away. KC felt her blood warm; her insides twitched; her heart raced.

"I told you I control every aspect of your life. Yes, even your first husband's death. Your family's death. And, now I'll own your life. I own you!" Nukpana's voice roared in KC's mind. "Causing the death of your family while you stopped to help someone couldn't have been more fortunate for me. You were always a sucker for someone needing help. Look where that got you, My Pitiful One."

KC's rage boiled over. She maneuvered her hat onto her head, positioned Fea to where the tip of the blade was aimed at Nukpana's side. Looking down at the Efil Stone hanging from her neck, KC recited Mother Elder's verse —

"Release! Release! Your desires will come forth.
From neither joy nor sorrow be
Like the old man's beard from the Fringe tree—
This blade will release thee!"

At the same time, KC shoved the sword backwards into Nukpana up through her belly. She stood and watched Nukpana's image in the mirror dissolve into millions of particles. Suddenly, a mix of black and purple smoke enveloped them. KC quickly removed her sword, turned to face Nukpana, and severed a lock of her hair.

KC stood back and watched what was left of Nukpana dissolve into a black malodorous mist. Coughing and sneezing in reaction, KC looked around the room for any of Nukpana's army coming through the door. None came to the rescue. Seconds later, KC noticed Nukpana's clothes lying on the dirt floor and Drakania was off to one side breathing with effort. KC moved to her.

"Drakania, what can I do?" She reached down and touched her head.

"It worked. You separated us. I am released from her evil. I am free." Drakania breathed her last breath.

KC watched Drakania slowly transform into a purple cloud in the shape of a dragon. She was larger than before and held her head majestically.

"No fears, now, KC. You see me as I once was, the Queen of my pride." Drakania said, "Nukpana has fled. She is a spirit lost without a home. Go back to the Elderians. You have won."

"Will I—," KC called out but Drakania was gone. The mist slowly faded into the air.

❧

THE IMAGE of Nukpana dissolving into millions of particles caused KC to take in another deep breath. She gagged and coughed again.

The large balcony window off the side of Princess Derryth's bedroom crashed open with Iolair and Gavin flying in.

"KC!" Iolair cried out. KC collapsed to the ground right as Iolair lifted her out of the enveloping vapor.

"Can you hear me?" Iolair asked. KC in a stupor, her body limp, didn't respond. Iolair continued, "Gavin, you take her and protect her. I'll tie her on you with this cord. I will be behind you watching out for the Atcenians."

Gavin replied, "Is she strapped on?"

"Yes, we must save her. She's my princess." Iolair said. "Come on." They lifted off and flew out into the night sky.

CHAPTER 21
THE EFIL STONE

Hours passed and KC slept. When she awoke, she reached for the Efil Stone that still hung around her neck. She looked around the room and realized she was back in her thípi.

"Mr Scruffy?" KC said though her voice was raspy and her throat was dry.

"It is Iolair. I've not left your side."

"Nor, I," Gavin said. "We've been with you the entire time. Would you like some water?" He handed her a pouch.

KC sat up in bed, her head swimming with pain. Her eyes could not focus. "My head hurts. I must have gotten hit."

"We don't think so. But, when we arrived you were standing in the center of a cloud of vapor."

"What color was it?"

"A light purple with a gray mist mixed in," Gavin said. "Was it Nukpana?"

"Maybe. I think it was Drakania."

"Who?" Iolair asked.

"Nukpana had absorbed the Queen of the Drakein, Drakania, over two hundred years ago. Nukpana had enslaved her for evil purposes. The only way to free Drakania was to kill Nukpana and her. I did." KC began to cry. "I killed her."

"Nukpana had to die. We knew that," Gavin said.

"Yes, that is true," KC said rubbing her eyes. "But, Drakania died as a result. She was never evil. Nukpana made her so, yet she had to forfeit her life." KC reached down and held up the Efil Stone for them to see. "I did get it back. When do I take it to King Elder?"

"You don't," Iolair said. "You will need to take it to Mother Elder and Yggdrasil. But first, if you are up to it, Princess, you should attend the Death and Healing Ceremony. It is the ritual we perform for the lost souls during war and to begin the healing and restoration of good."

"I must attend. I've lost several friends. But, Iolair, where are Mr Scruffy and Ish? I thought they would be here."

"I am here," Mr Scruffy said. He was carried into the thípi by an Elderian. "You have not heard about us finding Ish in the mist of the fires of the Wild Woods."

"No, I haven't. I had almost forgot there was a fire. The last I was with you, we were fighting in the Great Hall. Where is Ish?"

Iolair began to explain what he and Gavin did to find Ish. KC was listening to him, but she couldn't help but think about her family— Jack, Bill, Marie, and Boomer and how they died at Nukpana's hand. She wished her life with Jack had been different. She believed it could be, if only he were still alive. She heard Gavin talking.

"So, Ish was retrieved. But, we were too late," Gavin said.

"Too late?" KC sat up, tears began to roll down her eyes. "What do you mean?"

Mr Scruffy stood next to KC, held out a wing, and said, "He didn't make it. His injuries were too severe."

The room was solemn. KC sat there numb. Her tears would not flow; the pain was overwhelming. "Nukpana did this. Nukpana killed our friend."

Iolair motioned for everyone to step out and give KC some time to absorb what she had been told. Mr Scruffy climbed up on KC's cot and sat beside her.

She stroked his back and cried. "He can't be gone!" KC said. "What will we do now? Does Princess Istar know?"

"She does. She is young, resilient. She will mourn, as we all must do, and she will journey on, as will you," Mr Scruffy said. "I think you need to take this in, allow yourself some time to mourn."

Tears streamed down KC's face, "I find myself thinking of all those that died—Ish, Princess Derryth, Seif, Sam, Jack, Bill, Marie, and Boomer. When will the pain end?"

"Death is hard on the soul no matter where you are during your life's journey when it happens."

"Mr Scruffy, I'm not talking about death. Death is something that happens to each of us in time. This was murder. Out and out murder of good souls. Murder. And, Nukpana is at the center of all of that death."

Iolair limped as he walked in carrying a note. KC wondered how many others had suffered at Nukpana's hand during their last battle.

She looked at him quizzically, "Who is this note from?"

"We didn't get to explain that on our way to find you and Ish, we encountered Lorne," Iolair said.

"Lorne? You saw Lorne? Where is she?" KC became excited. She hadn't thought about her since they last talked with each other in the corridor of Emerald Mountain before the fight with Nukpana. "Can I see her?"

"You can see her, KC. She will be at the ceremony," Mr Scruffy said. "But first, should you not read her note?"

KC opened the note and read it aloud, "Love is a fabric that never fades, no matter how often it is washed in the waters of adversity and grief." KC looked up at Mr Scruffy and Iolair. "She is a wise fox."

Mr Scruffy handed KC a towel. "Do you want to clean up before we go?"

She looked down at her clothes covered in bloodstains, mud, debris, and who knew what else. "I guess I should. Could you all give me a few minutes?"

"Sure," Iolair said and he walked over to the bowl on the table. "There is fresh water in here. If you need anything, just let us know. We'll be right outside. We won't leave you alone."

"Thank you." KC shut the flap to her thípi, and looked at herself in the mirror. She hadn't seen her reflection since moments before she stabbed Nukpana. Suddenly, she felt a sharp pain in the side of her head. Her eyes went in and out of focus, and she stopped herself from falling by grabbing the tabletop. She bowed her head and said a prayer.

Then, she rubbed her temple and picked up a pinecone to comb through her hair. It was a tangled mess. She wrapped her hair up into a bun, and then another sharp pain stabbed her temple right above the eye. KC reacted in pain, doubling over.

"Are you okay?" Iolair asked walking into the thípi. "We were beginning to wonder if you fell back asleep."

"I'm fine, but my eyes hurt."

"Do we need to get Queen Esmé? She might give you something to help with your pain. You've had a major shock just now."

"No. I'll be fine." KC turned back to the mirror and dampened the towel, and wiped her face and eyes. "Let me change my clothes. I'll be right out."

Iolair bowed to KC and stepped back out of the room. She changed her clothes, looked at herself again in the mirror, and worried her head would not stop hurting. *I may need to ask Queen Esmé for something later.* She walked out to Iolair and Mr Scruffy.

"You ready to go?"

"Can I ask you something first?" Iolair nodded. "Why did you call me 'Princess' earlier? I'm not a princess."

"You are to me. You saved my world, you saved my life, you made me whole again."

KC looked into Iolair's eyes and noticed that the bald eagle looked directly back into hers. His stare was strong and sure as if he was speaking to her through them. She felt a surge of power in his words. His words were familiar. Jack had said something similar before he left on his last mission. She had all but pushed his words out of her mind. When he was alive, they were so in love. She looked back at Iolair. She knew she was wrong, yet somehow, she felt a strong connection with him.

"I guess I must be acting strange to you," KC said. "It's been a long hard few days."

"Come. This ceremony will help."

SITTING across the makeshift room that was made from two open-sided thípis and placed in a clearing not far from Stone's River, KC looked around the area. On the opposite side of the large room was an opening that gave her a view out into the forest.

Across the room, KC saw Lorne sitting with a group of Elderians. She walked up to them and said, "Lorne?"

The fox got up and immediately hugged KC. "My friend. How are you?"

"I'm well, thanks to you. I see you have made some friends."

"Yes. When I got back into the Wild Woods, I wondered upon their wedding ceremony. They took pity on me when they saw I was hungry. After they fed me, they learned of my plight with the evil one. They asked me to join their family. I'm now a member of their clan."

"Lorne, that is wonderful. It is good to know you made it out of Grave's Mountain to safety. Iolair and Gavin said that you sent them to my rescue. Thank you for all you did for me."

"Did you find the Efil Stone?"

KC nodded. "You made that possible. I'm not sure I'll ever be able to repay you."

"It was my honor to help you and all of Eldershire." Lorne placed her arm around KC.

KC placed the lock of Nukpana's hair in her hand. "It was my pleasure to acquire this for you, my friend."

Lorne squeezed KC's hand and winked at her. "The ceremony is about to start. Go in peace." They hugged and KC made her way back to where Iolair waited.

Fergus stepped forward to the center of the room. He reminded KC of a sketch she had seen once that was of a tree gradually transforming into a bear. Fergus looked around the gathering, picked up an instrument, and began to strum it.

The wafting sound emitted out into the forest was bizarre; it caused the crowd to move in around the fire pit that grew larger with flames. Many more unique musical instruments began to be played.

The sounds mingled hypnotically causing mystical visions to dance in KC's mind.

Then, Fergus started to hum. His voice sounded ethereal, haunting, and cried out for those lost in the final battle. The ritual was magical and mesmerizing. KC looked on in wonder while the music enveloped her soul. She felt free; she was ready to experience the bittersweet celebration of their victory, mixed with the sorrow for those they had lost—especially for her, the lives of Ish and Drakania.

KC's sadness multiplied with the gyrations of the sounds. Many of the Elderians that perished KC had not met personally. Yet, she was able to know each one through the telepathic connection made possible by the minds of all those joined in the ceremony. She could feel and understand the impact of each life force that was lost.

The forest became dark, and then faded to gray. KC looked up into the treetops where she could see the two moons. Their rays sat at ninety-degree angles to each other. The result gave extra luminous power where the rays streamed down on the gathering. It made it look as though strobe lights were caressing each mourner through a halo.

On each side of the openings of the two thípis, torches lit the way. The torches were beacons that led gatherers, helping them find their way to the ceremony from all directions. It looked impossible, but, to KC, the space had grown in size. It appeared all of Eldershire had gathered together in one place.

One torch, near Stone's River, lit a crossing that was carved from rock and mud. Off in the distance, KC saw someone walking across the bridge toward the gathering. The being carried a type of lantern that lit its way. The glow illuminated the legs of others walking with the being. The setting increased the feeling of reverence as the spiritual-looking beings walked down the path with their shadows moving in unison with their steps. Then, KC saw Ish walking into the opening toward the torch by the river. Behind him was her other friends who had perished in the battles to save Eldershire. Mr

Scruffy walked behind closing up the procession. Tears flowed down her cheeks.

Her thoughts went to the last moments of the furious battle that ended up taking Ish's life and almost killing Mr Scruffy. *If I had lost him, too, I could not be here now,* she thought.

> The battle raged around her when she managed to strike down the stinking Grey being that was attacking Mr Scruffy.
>
> She swung Fea to divert the beast's blow right as he swung to knock Mr Scruffy down. Soon, she realized she had not diverted his blow completely. The beast's sword still connected. Mr Scruffy stumbled. His left wing was nearly severed away.
>
> KC's instincts kicked in. "Mr Scruffy," she screamed. She watched him fall. Her anger grew. She stormed to where he lay, crumbled on the ground. She stood her ground protecting him until help could arrive; she would not let the Grey Menace win.

Watching Mr Scruffy bring up the end of the procession, she couldn't help but form a bittersweet smile on her face. She wished that the other friends who gave the ultimate sacrifice, their lives, were as alive as Mr Scruffy was to her now.

"KC, are you all right?" Iolair nudged KC's arm. She didn't respond. "Hello?"

"I'm sorry. I was in deep thought."

"That you were. Are you okay?"

"As okay as someone can be after the battles we've fought, the lives we've seen lost, and the fight with Nukpana I had last night. Seeing my friends who died just now…" KC's voice trailed off. She paused. "I'm still reeling from it all. My mind is filled with the cries, the pain, and the images."

"It is hard to live through something like what you did even when you've lived through something as cruel as Nukpana's anger. Your mind will be troubled with those sounds and images for a while. This ceremony we perform is designed to allow those who survived a chance to release those sounds and visions into the night sky. To bury the pain." Iolair handed KC a slender bundle of a dried plant.

"What's this?"

"White Sage. An herb that is prepared into a wand that we will use as the ceremony continues. And, here is Mr Scruffy's feather. You will use it to help move the smoke we make around you and over your body. This will help you to visualize the smoke taking the evil, negative energy from your life. We will smudge Mr Scruffy, too."

KC took the feather and walked with Iolair at her side to where Mr Scruffy laid on a cot. He looked tired. Gavin walked up holding a wand of white sage and a shell. KC wasn't sure, but it looked like the shell he held was Abalone. It had a pearlized inside surface. Iolair motioned for her to step over near Mr Scruffy.

Iolair said, "We will light the wands, get a good smoke going, and then will use the feathers to spread the smoke up and down our bodies and Mr Scruffy."

"Where did you learn about using sage?" KC asked thinking about the large herb garden she had at home with a bush of sage growing.

"It is an ancient ritual we've always used. It is a Native American practice of your world too. Let us begin."

Iolair lit the wands. He moved it enough to get a good smoke going and KC mimicked him.

"Please say the following chant with me — air, fire, water, earth, cleanse, dismiss, dispel — and wave the smoke up and down Mr Scruffy and over your body and mine. I will do the same. Use the shell to symbolize the pouring away of the pain."

KC followed Iolair's directions. They moved into all corners of the area where they stood. "Together, we will continue to say the incantation telepathically through the circulating smoke." Iolair said. The wands burned down to their hands. "Now, we may quench the smoldering wands in this pouch of water."

After the smudging was complete, KC said, "The ceremony was beautiful. The aroma of the white sage helped in the imaging of the pain leaving and the sorrow subsiding."

"It is a healing that is needed by all." Iolair looked at KC with a solemn face and said, "Mr Scruffy and I believe it is time for you to visit Mother Elder and Yggdrasil. They are expecting you."

KC looked to Mr Scruffy, "Will you be going with me?"

"Iolair and I will take you there. We will not go up to see them with you. It is important that you do this alone. It was your quest and you have succeeded. This will be an awe-inspiring moment for you, Mother Elder, and Yggdrasil."

"After all that I've been through, I feel the most anxious at this moment than I have been in months. It is hard for me to understand that I might actually be going home."

KC LOOKED BACK at Iolair and Mr Scruffy standing at the entrance to the Land of Promise. She wore the Efil Stone around her neck and her fingers rubbed over it. She waved at her friends, and then turned toward the plateau where she saw Mother Elder and Yggdrasil standing off in the distance.

KC took a deep breath, and walked to where they stood waiting for her. She hoped that she would soon learn when she would be returning home. She feared the fact that she had the Efil Stone would not be enough. After all, she reasoned, she failed since she did not defeat Nukpana. At least, she didn't see her dead. All she saw was a purple mist.

Yggdrasil extended his hand to her. "Greetings, KC. We are pleased you came to us and you need not worry."

KC knew they read her mind, but she was apprehensive all the same. "Thank you, Yggdrasil. And, Mother Elder, let me present you with the Efil Stone." She removed the necklace. But, before she let it go, KC held it in her hand. She studied it, looked up, and said, "I found it. I have the Efil Stone and I survived the ordeal."

"You should be happy. You finished your quest."

"I did. I did not die, and in the process, I learned the value of believing and having resilience." KC handed the necklace to Mother Elder.

It glowed brightly. The symbol carved into its surface turned to a deep emcrald green.

"The symbol, it changed?" KC asked.

"Indeed. Walk with us over to the sacred tree."

Yggdrasil and Mother Elder each took one of KC's arms and together they walked up to the majestic elder standing before them. The tree was bathed in a quintessence that gave off a shimmering light that flowed in circles and waves.

"It is beautiful."

"This is where we reside. It is pure. Its essence is filled with the souls that have passed before. They live with us here among the many branches. It is *the* life force; like the air you breathe on Earth. We will enter. Do not be afraid."

Mother Elder took the Efil Stone, held it up to the tree. KC was transported and found herself sitting with Mother Elder and Yggdrasil in throne-like chairs placed in a triangular shape in the center of an opulent space—Yggdrasil to her left and Mother Elder to her right. The room appealed to all of KC's senses. In each direction that she looked, the essence of grandeur was before her; whispered messages came into her mind, odors floated by connecting her to prior life experiences causing memories to appear.

'I exist in everything' was the song her mind sang to her. She was wrapped in beauty and love.

"With the Efil Stone back in its rightful place, we are one again. You share this moment with us. Be at peace." They sat in silence.

Yggdrasil said, "I sense you feel fear. What is it that bothers you, my child?" Mother Elder motioned for KC to speak.

"I did not kill Nukpana. I failed you."

"Your quest was to retrieve the Efil Stone. No one requested you kill Nukpana," Yggdrasil replied. "All beings are part of creation, no matter how evil. It is not for us to judge or exert punishment."

"It is true that Nukpana is still a threat to Eldershire and all of the universe," Mother Elder continued. "But, that is not for you to be concerned with now."

Yggdrasil went on. "You are a part of Eldershire, and always will be."

KC squirmed in her chair. "You don't mean—"

"No. We don't mean you can't return home. You will. Soon. Yggdrasil, explain to her."

"We must warn you to be prepared for anything when you return home. Nukpana is still at large. That we acknowledge. Even so, you must live your life. When you return home, you will be whole again. And, there may come a point when we may need to call upon you again."

"Will you be willing to help us if the need arises?" Mother Elder stood up, walked over to a cabinet that KC had not noticed. Mother Elder turned back and looked at KC. "Will you?"

KC hesitated, but then she said, "What must I do?"

"That will not to be revealed at this time, but we will complete your coronation in celebration of your success at completing this quest. Come stand here, beside me." KC and Yggdrasil walked over to

Mother Elder. She lifted her hand and sprinkled a rain of fairy dust over KC that was scented with lavender.

"Everyone needs a touch of magic. You are free to return home, when you are ready."

"Before you leave us," Yggdrasil took KC's arm. "Walk with me over to this plaque. Join your hands with ours and read these words aloud."

> *"Faith helped me believe that one day I could go back.*
> *It was magic that brought me here.*
> *It was fate that kept me here.*
> *It was the hat that could take me back.*
> *Now—only magic can fix what is broken.*
> *Only magic can give back my life.*
> *Here you leave this world to enter yet another—*
> *Full of magic, mayhem, and fantasy."*

KC looked back and saw Iolair and Mr Scruffy standing at the entrance to the Land of Promise.

"How did I get here? Where are Mother Elder and Yggdrasil?" She turned around to see, but saw them no more.

"KC, you look different somehow," Mr Scruffy said. "I believe you are now part of Eldershire. Always."

"You look content," Iolair said. "Are you ready to go to your home world?"

"Not yet. I want to visit with King Elder, Queen Esmé, and Princess Istar and say my goodbyes. The Land of Promise was so beautiful. How long was I gone?"

"Not long. Time, as you know, does not run by a clock here. Do you know how you will go home?" Mr Scruffy asked as he grew to flying size.

"No. I'm sure it will be magical. Let's go to King Elder's camp."

&

DOWN BY STONE'S RIVER, KC sat with Princess Istar and together they looked out over the water while they talked.

"Since my birth," Princess Istar said. "We've not had a chance to talk about my mother and my father."

"No, we haven't. Your parents were special beings. They each carried strong, good souls that touched many lives."

KC reflected upon her memories before returning her gaze to Princess Istar. "Your Mother's and Father's love transcended the bounds of death. Through your Mother's life, your life came forth. Then, nurtured by the love of your Father, his death gave you his spirit," KC took Princess Istar's hand and placed it in hers. "The life once lived by your mother and father lives on within you, in your spirit. Their branches no longer stretch down and their spirits no longer walk in Eldershire, but they are still here in you. I've found the best way to deal with grief is to share your memories with others. To find joy in the lives our loved ones lived. May the death of your Mother and Father bring memories of peace and joy to comfort you in your sorrow. Through your veins flows their love."

"I don't have any memories of my mother and I had a short time with my father."

"The Elderians will be able to share their memories of your mother, which will aid your heart and spirit to know her. Your spirit is strong because of your parents' love."

"You are wise to speak of our spirits. How do you know this?" Princess Istar had tears in her eyes.

"My words are new to me. I did not feel or think this way before coming to Eldershire. Two great friends—Mr Scruffy and your father, Ish, counseled me. They helped me to see through the many emotions I had to traverse to overcome my grief."

"King Elder said to me that when tree spirits walk, love life, share the joy of peace, and give gratitude of all things, their memories are sustained. Knowing that, gives me some peace." Princess Istar picked up a rock and skipped it across the water's surface.

"My Dad showed me how to do that when I was young." KC said and skipped a rock too.

"That's funny. My father taught me." They smiled at each other.

"Something I learned recently is that though death's touch is difficult, holding on to the memories of those lost, of our time together, close to our hearts will give us peace. It is my hope that one day I, too, will be able to reason this thought into my own heart to ease the pain of the loss of my family. My greatest joy would be to reunite with Bill and Marie and see the springing bounce of Boomer. They would brighten my life. I've not talked of my first husband to many before coming here, but it would be a blessing to be with Jack again."

Princess Istar said, "Finding out that Nukpana killed your family was horrible and I know you know it was the same for me when I learned of my parents murders at her hand."

"It was. Nukpana's defeat has given me some closure." KC felt a pain in her head. She rubbed her temple. "Sometimes it is hard to reconcile that someone you think you love can inflect horrible pain on your soul. It is never worth the anger that results. Jay-H hurt me. I've learned there is a price to pay for hurting those you claim to love. The amount of love between individuals determines the amount of that debt. I have solace knowing that Jay-H's death is the price he paid."

"You do not wish to have him back with you?"

"No. I wish to be home. It would be a glorious thing if I could have Bill and Marie, and to have my first husband, Jack, with me again. It isn't possible. I am learning to seek joy in what has happened here— the lives we've saved. And, the fact that Eldershire is safe and the Efil Stone is back in its rightful place."

"Will I see you again once you go home?" Princess Istar stood up.

"I'm not willing to guess. I didn't think I'd come to a place like this until it happened." KC stood up, too, wiping the dust off her pants.

"Have you said your goodbyes to my grandparents?"

"Yes. They were gracious. I will miss them. Want to walk back now?"

Princess Istar nodded. "The two moons are starting to set in the distance. The suns will rise soon."

"When I go home, I believe that will be the hardest thing for me to adjust to."

"What is that?"

"Only seeing one sun and one moon."

Princess Istar looked down at her hands; she unfolded a slip of paper. "This is for you, it was in my mother's things. I believe she wanted me to give it to you."

KC opened the paper and read—

The Chosen One
Seek the Efil Stone
Freedom will reign
That the one who shall lead
Shall know what to claim
Release! Release!
Your desires will come forth
From neither joy nor sorrow be
Your quest will set you free.

A tear dropped down KC's cheek. "I thank you for sharing this with me." KC and Princess Istar stood up together and they walked back to KC's thípi with their arms interlaced.

After saying good night to Princess Istar, KC walked into her thípi, and looked at the items she had acquired since arriving in Eldershire.

On her cot, she laid down the slip of paper and placed Fea, her trusty sword, and Mr Scruffy's feather, she had used earlier that evening during the smudging ceremony, neatly beside her pillow. *I don't think I've seen myself in this hat.* She walked over to the mirror and placed the Hat of Iolair on her head.

THE LIGHT of the moon cast its rays across the evening sky giving it a color like melted raspberry vanilla ice cream. KC put the car in gear and pulled out of the restaurant parking lot. As she looked over the back of her seat, she saw Bill and Marie cuddling and Boomer sat on the floorboard between their legs. She reached down and patted him on the top of his head. His plaid collar seemed to sparkle.

Putting the car into forward gear, KC looked to her right, "Jack, would you please sit back? I can't see out for any cars coming toward us."

"Oh, sorry. Let me look for you," Jack said looking over his right shoulder. "You can pull on out. All is clear."

"Thanks, Babes." KC pulled out onto the road for home. She moved her hand over to his and caressed it. He squeezed her hand. She looked toward him and smiled. Soon, she maneuvered onto the road to take Bill and Marie to their house. "Look, there is a broken-down vehicle. Jack, would you call 911?"

"What? Aren't you going to stop and help?"

KC said, "No, it is best to leave that to the professionals. We're going home." She looked at Jack, and for a split second she thought see saw Jack's face morph into that of a bald eagle.

"Whoa, what are you doing?" Jack asked when KC jerked the car. "You okay?"

"Oh, I'm sorry. I guess I got distracted."

"Be careful, KC. We want all of us to make it home safe, you know."

"Yes. I know. I'll be extra careful."

After dropping Bill, Marie, and Boomer off at their cabin, KC drove to their home—hers and Jack's. She pulled their Jeep into the garage, they got out of it, and then he shut the garage door.

"It's been a wearying day. Let's get ready for bed. I have a busy day tomorrow," Jack said as he guided his wife toward their bedroom.

KC stopped, turned and kissed Jack on the cheek, and then moved toward the bathroom. "I'll be right there. I seem to have suddenly gotten a horrible headache. I'm going to get some water, and take an aspirin. I'll be in soon."

KC stepped into the bathroom and looked in the mirror. A severe pain caused her to rub her eyes. She looked back in the mirror and thought she saw the image of a different face looking back at her. She was startled and dropped the aspirin bottle.

"Are you okay in there?" Jack called to her.

"Yes. I'm fine." KC looked back in the mirror, the image was gone. *I hope I am.*

TO THE READER

This book is an introduction to Eldershire and its many inhabitants. After this letter, you will find a concordance, *Words of Eldershire*, to help you with pronunciations and meanings of terms, names, and places. As the series grows, words will be added. A complete concordance will be on my website.

This story has been over forty-five years in the making. I put it away right after I graduated from high school, and then worked on it again about the time I found out I was pregnant with our daughter, Julie. Then, around 2005 or so, I became friends with a special writing colleague. In 2009, Rosa and I attended a writing conference where I shared the early chapters of this story. It failed drastically. My writing and creativity came to a halt. Rosa encouraged me to trudge forward. After writing four books (a memoir and a thriller trilogy), I decided I'd think about writing Kay's story once more.

One day, on my way to an audio recording of *The Fire Within*, I saw on the side of the road a lone bowler hat. It had a daisy hanging out of its brim. I thought how strange and considered turning around to take pictures of it, but I was running late for my studio appointment.

Driving on down the interstate, to my left I saw a tall, black witch's hat lying in the median. It was flapping in the wind. It looked like it was waving at me. Nukpana Fraener came into my mind's eye. The witch's hat was in a bad location to get a picture, but I thought I might be able to get a picture of the bowler hat. I called Julie and asked her to try to get a picture; I went onto my recording session. Six hours later, I started for home. Checking with Julie, she said she couldn't find the hat. There was no picture.

The interstate traffic was not crowded driving home, so I was able to look as I drove by where I saw the witch's hat; I thought I would see it. It was gone. My hopes were dashed that I'd find the bowler hat. Driving to where I had seen the bowler hat, I was hesitant to look. There it was lying exactly where it had been earlier that morning.

I pulled over, parked, and got several pictures. The truism, "If I knew then what I know now," came to mind as the shutter clicked. Kay's story began to form in my mind coupled with the magic of a hat and the evil of a witch. The rest came to life in this book and more will be told in the remaining books of the series. If you are interested in Eldershire and KC's future, you will want to follow me to learn a lot more about them in future books.

Thank you, readers, for your support, for reading my words, and for sharing my story with others.

Read on!
Pam

WORDS OF ELDERSHIRE

There is an internal language of the tree spirits that can only be understood by those who are of Elder decent. A common language is used amongst all beings of Eldershire to aid in communicating. This common language is also known as English on Earth. The following listing of words used by me is provided to aid the reader's understanding. As the series grows new words with their meanings will be added to a complete concordance on my website. Due to space limitations, the listing in this book is not extensive. Names are in bold-italics while places and things are bold.

Drakein (syll. drake-in)—origin is Greek. The first type of Greek dragon was the Dracon whose name was derived from the Greek words "drakein" and "derkomai" meaning "to see clearly" or "gaze sharply." The English word, dragon, is derived from drakein.

Elders—clan of Mother Elder and her descendants – King Elder, Queen Esmé, Princess Derryth and others. Derived from the Elder tree.

Eldershire—the world of the Elders and other magical beings. For more details, see *Where is the Land of Eldershire?* in the front of this book.

Fraener (syll. fray-ner)—a variant form of Fafnir (Old Norse). An Old Norse myth name of a dwarf who transformed into a dragon, the symbol of greed. Also called Fáfnir.

Mother Elder—associated closely with Celtic faerie lands, sacred to the goddesses Venus and Holle. The Myth is that of a spirit who inhabits the Elder tree, holds the power to work a variety of magics on Earth and in Eldershire; her skin, bark, and outer wood are strong and hard, offering protection against witches and the sap is the blood of life and the dwelling place of the spirit.

Nukpana (syll. nuk-pa-na)—origin is Native American and means evil one. Nukpana is a mythological hybrid and the offspring of the union between descendants of Anzû and Lilith with Drakein ancestry. Nukpana is a 'Blender'—half witch and half Drakein. She can transform between one or the other at will. When angry, both come out of her.

Snowquids (alt. Snowquidians, Snowquid)—the beings of the Land of Snowboro. Snowquids cherish life but realize everything is subject to change.

Treorai (syll. tre-o-ray)—Irish for leader or navigator.

Yggdrasil (syll. ig-dra-sil)—in Norse mythology, Yaggdrasil is the holy Ash World Tree surrounded by nine worlds. It is said to connect the Underworld to Heaven with its branches and roots. From the symbol of the tree flows human awareness and consciousness.

Visit https://pambnewberry.com for a complete concordance.

ACKNOWLEDGMENTS

The completion of a lifelong dream is wonderful. For you, my devoted readers, who have stuck with me during my writing journey, thank you. You have made it possible. Your steadfast encouragement, your devotion to follow my writing, and your desire to connect with me are key to giving me the courage and aspiration to use my pen to produce this story. There are those people in my world who are critical to the successful completion of any goal.

My husband, Albert, is the best "first" husband any wife would be proud to call her own. Thank you, with all of my heart. You've watched this story ebb and flow for almost all of our forty years of marriage. Your encouragement never ceases to inspire me. I love you, always.

Julie, our daughter, continued to work her magic when she set out to take what I saw in my mind's eye and magically converted it into a cover for this book. Thank you! Daddy and I love you, dearly.

How does one capture in a short sentence or two the value of friends—Rosa Lee Jude, the alpha reader, thank you! If you've not enjoyed Rosa's stories, find her stories through her website: RosaLeeJude.com.

The beta readers—Linda Eisenhauer, Patrick Downes, Glo Frye, Marcella Taylor, Sam Stage, & Amy Stage and the gamma reader and final eyes on my writing, Carole Bybee—all of these readers helped to make this story stellar!

Each offered suggestions, questions, and eagle eyes that propelled me forward and it is hoped, helped me become a better writer, and I am grateful! I salute each of you for being my cheering squad and for reminding me that a dream is only a dream if you let it stay in your mind.

To my friends and friends to be, thank you for being readers of my words. Moreover, thank you for writing to let me know if I've touched your life in some small way. And, for sharing my work with others. There are so many who offer support, please know I thank you very much.

I Write On!

ABOUT THE AUTHOR

Pam B. Newberry lives in the mountains of Southwest Virginia with her husband where she is at work on her next book. She is the author of *The Letter: A Page of My Life*, and The Marine Letsco Trilogy—*The Fire Within*, *The Fire of Revenge*, and *A Time for Fire*. She enjoys fun in the sun—gardening, fishing, and working with her husband on their hobby farm.

Connect with Pam through her website: https://pambnewberry.com

Follow Pam through her Amazon author page: http://amazon.com/author/pambnewberry

ALSO BY PAM B. NEWBERRY

The Chronicles of Eldershire
DarkShadow

The Marine Letsco Trilogy:
The Fire Within

The Revenge of Fire

A Time for Fire

The Letter: A Page of My Life

Connect with Pam through her website: https://pambnewberry.com

On Pinterest: https://www.pinterest.com/pambnewberry/

On FaceBook: https://www.facebook.com/AuthorPamNewberry

On GoodReads: https://www.goodreads.com/pamnewberry

On Amazon: http://amazon.com/author/pambnewberry

To listen to Pam's writing music, visit her YouTube playlist:

YouTube COE Playlist: https://www.youtube.com/playlist?list=
PLrRsvd8Pq34VqkmQghuE1qNypjz-3LfYy